BOOKS BY JAMES PATTERSON

The Private Novels

Private Games (with Mark Sullivan)
Private: #1 Suspect (with Maxine Paetro)
Private (with Maxine Paetro)

A complete list of books by James Patterson is at the back of this book. For previews and information about the author, visit JamesPatterson.com or find him on Facebook or at your app store.

Private Games

James Patterson

AND

Mark Sullivan

LITTLE, BROWN AND COMPANY

LARGE PRINT EDITION

Little, Brown and Company
Hachette Book Group
237 Park Avenue, New York, NY 10017
www.hachettebookgroup.com

First Edition: February 2012

Little, Brown and Company is a division of Hachette Book Group, Inc., and is celebrating its 175th anniversary in 2012. The Little, Brown name and logo are trademarks of Hachette Book Group, Inc.

The publisher is not responsible for websites (or their content) that are not owned by the publisher.

The Hachette Speakers Bureau provides a wide range of authors for speaking events. To find out more, go to www.hachettespeakersbureau.com or call (866) 376-6591.

Library of Congress Cataloging-in-Publication Data
Patterson, James
  Private games : a novel / by James Patterson and Mark Sullivan. — 1st ed.
    p. cm. — (Private)
ISBN 978-0-316-20682-2 (hc) / 978-0-316-20680-8 (large print)
1. Olympic Games (30th : 2012 : London, England) — Fiction. 2. Private security services — Fiction. 3. Private investigators — Fiction. I. Sullivan, Mark T. II. Title.
PS3566.A822P765 2012
813'.54—dc23   2011035738

10 9 8 7 6 5 4 3 2 1

RRD-C

Printed in the United States of America

For Connor and Bridger, chasers of the Olympic dream

—M.S.

It is not possible with mortal mind to search out the purposes of the gods.

—Pindar

For then, in wrath, the Olympian thundered and lightninged, and confounded Greece.

—Aristophanes

PROLOGUE

THERE *ARE* SUPERMEN and superwomen who walk this earth.

I'm quite serious about that, and you can take me literally. Jesus Christ, for example, was a spiritual superman, as were Martin Luther and Gandhi. Julius Caesar was superhuman as well. So were Genghis Khan, Thomas Jefferson, Abraham Lincoln, and Adolf Hitler.

Think about scientists like Aristotle, Galileo, Albert Einstein, and J. Robert Oppenheimer. Consider artists like da Vinci, Michelangelo, and Vincent van Gogh, my favorite, who was so superior it drove him insane. Above all, don't forget athleti-

3

cally superior beings like Jim Thorpe, Babe Didrikson Zaharias, and Jesse Owens; Larisa Latynina and Muhammad Ali; Mark Spitz and Jackie Joyner-Kersee.

Humbly, I include myself on this superhuman spectrum as well—and deservedly so, as you shall soon see.

In short, people like me are born for great things. We seek adversity. We seek to conquer. We seek to break through all limits—spiritually, politically, artistically, scientifically, and physically. We seek to right wrongs in the face of monumental odds. And we're willing to suffer for greatness, willing to engage in dogged effort and endless preparation with the fervor of a martyr—which, to my mind, is an exceptional trait in any human being at any age.

At the moment I have to admit that I'm certainly feeling exceptional, standing here in the garden of Sir Denton Marshall, a sniveling, corrupt old bastard if there ever was one.

Look at him on his knees, with his back to me and my knife at his throat.

Why, he trembles and shakes as if a stone had just clipped his head. Can you smell it? Fear? It surrounds him with an odor as rank as the air after a bomb explodes.

"Why?" he gasps.

"You've angered me, monster," I snarl at him, feeling a deeper-than-primal rage split my mind and seethe through every cell. "You've helped ruin the games, made them a mockery and an abomination."

"What?" he cries, acting bewildered. "What are you talking about?"

I deliver the evidence against him in three damning sentences that turn the skin of his neck livid and his carotid artery a sickening, pulsing purple.

"No!" he sputters. "That's...that's not true. You can't do this. Have you gone utterly mad?"

"Mad? Me?" I say. "Hardly. I'm the sanest person I know."

"Please," he says, tears rolling down his face. "Have mercy. I'm to be married on Christmas Eve."

My laugh is as caustic as battery acid. "In another life, Denton, I ate my own children. You'll get no mercy from me or my sisters."

As his confusion and horror become complete, I look up into the night sky, feeling storms rising in my head, and understanding once again that I *am* superior, superhuman, imbued with forces that go back thousands of years.

"For all true Olympians," I vow, "this act of

sacrifice marks the beginning of the end of the modern games."

Then I wrench the old man's head back so his back arches.

And before he can scream, I furiously rip the blade across his throat with such force that his head comes free of his neck all the way to his spine.

BOOK ONE

THE FURIES

CHAPTER 1

IT WAS MAD-DOG hot for London. Peter Knight's shirt and jacket were drenched with sweat as he sprinted north on Chesham Street past the Diplomat Hotel and skidded around the corner toward Lyall Mews in the heart of Belgravia, home to some of the most expensive real estate in the world.

Don't let it be true, Knight screamed internally as he entered the mews. *Dear God, don't let it be true.*

Then he saw a pack of newspaper reporters gathering at the yellow tape of a London Metropolitan Police barricade that blocked the road in front of a cream-colored Georgian-style townhome. Knight lurched to a stop, feeling like he was going to retch up the eggs and bacon he'd had for breakfast.

What would he ever tell Amanda?

Before Knight could compose his thoughts or still his stomach, his cell phone rang. He snatched it from his pocket without looking at caller ID.

"Knight," he managed to choke out. "That you, Jack?"

"No, Peter, it's Nancy," the voice replied in an Irish brogue. "Isabel has come down sick."

"What?" he groaned. "No . . . I just left the house an hour ago."

"She's running a temperature," the full-time nanny insisted. "I just took it."

"How high?"

"One hundred. She's complaining about her stomach, too."

"Lukey?"

"He seems fine," she said. "But—"

"Give them both a cool bath, and call me back if Isabel's temp hits a hundred and one," Knight said. He snapped the phone shut, swallowed the bile burning at the back of his throat.

A wiry man about six feet tall, with an appealing face and light brown hair, Knight had once been a special investigator assigned to the Old Bailey, home of England's Central Criminal Court. Two years ago, however, he joined the London office of Private International at twice the pay and prestige. Private has been called the Pinkerton Agency of the twenty-first century, with offices in every major city in the world staffed by top-notch forensic scientists, security specialists, and investigators such as Knight.

Compartmentalize, he told himself. *Be professional.* But this felt like the straw that would break the camel's back. Knight had already endured too much grief and loss, both personally and professionally. Just the week before, his boss, Dan Carter, and three of his colleagues had perished in a plane crash over the North Sea that was still under investigation. Could he live with another death?

Pushing that question and his daughter's illness to one side, Knight forced himself to hurry on through the sweltering heat toward the police barrier, giving the Fleet Street crowd a wide berth, and in so doing spotted Billy Casper, a Scotland Yard inspector he'd known for fifteen years.

He went straight to Casper, a blockish man with a pockmarked face who scowled the second he saw Knight. "Private's got no business in this, Peter."

"If that's Sir Denton Marshall dead in there, then Private does have business in this, and I do, too," Knight shot back forcefully. "Personal business, Billy. Is it Sir Denton?"

Casper said nothing.

"Is it?" Knight demanded.

Finally the inspector nodded, but he wasn't happy about it, and asked suspiciously, "How are you and Private involved?"

Knight stood there a moment, feeling lambasted by the news and wondering again how the hell he was going to tell Amanda. Then he shook off the despair and said, "The London Organising Committee for the Olympic Games is Private London's client. Which makes Sir Denton Private's client."

"And you?" Casper demanded. "What's your personal stake in this? You a friend of his or something?"

"Much more than a friend. He was engaged to my mother."

Casper's hard expression softened a bit and he chewed at his lip before saying, "I'll see if I can get you in. Elaine will want to talk to you."

Knight felt suddenly as if invisible forces were conspiring against him.

"Elaine caught this case?" he said, wanting to punch something. "You can't be serious."

"Dead serious, Peter," Casper said. "Lucky, lucky you."

CHAPTER 2

CHIEF INSPECTOR ELAINE Pottersfield was one of the finest detectives working for the Metropolitan Police, a twenty-year veteran of the force with a prickly, know-it-all style that got results. Pottersfield had solved more murders in the past two years than any other inspector at Scotland Yard. She was also the only person Knight knew who openly despised his presence.

An attractive woman in her forties, the inspector always put Knight in mind of a borzoi, with her large round eyes, aquiline face, and silver hair that cascaded about her shoulders. When he entered Sir Denton Marshall's kitchen, Pottersfield eyed him down her sharp nose, looking ready to bite at him if she got the chance.

"Peter," she said coldly.

"Elaine," Knight said.

"Not exactly my idea to let you into the crime scene."

"No, I imagine not," replied Knight, fighting to control his emotions, which were heating up by the second. Pottersfield always seemed to have that effect on him. "But here we are. What can you tell me?"

The Scotland Yard inspector did not reply for several moments. Then she finally said, "The maid found him an hour ago out in the garden, or what's left of him, anyway."

Flashing on memories of Sir Denton, the learned and funny man he'd come to know and admire over the past two years, Knight's legs felt wobbly, and he had to put his vinyl-gloved hand out on the counter to steady himself. "What's left of him?"

Pottersfield grimly gestured at the open French door.

Knight absolutely did not want to go out into the garden. He wanted to remember Sir Denton the last time he'd seen him, two weeks before, with his shock of startling white hair, scrubbed pink skin, and easy, infectious laugh.

"I understand if you'd rather not," Pottersfield

said. "Inspector Casper said your mother was engaged to Sir Denton. When did that happen?"

"New Year's past," Knight said. He swallowed and moved toward the door, adding bitterly, "They were to be married on Christmas Eve. Another tragedy. Just what I need in my life, isn't it?"

Pottersfield's expression twisted in pain and anger, and she looked at the kitchen floor as Knight went by her and out into the garden.

Outside, the temperature was growing hotter. The air in the garden was still and stank of death and gore. On the flagstone terrace, five quarts of blood—the entire reservoir of Sir Denton's life—had run out and congealed around his decapitated corpse.

"The medical examiner thinks the job was done with a long curved blade that has a serrated edge," Pottersfield said.

Knight again fought off the urge to vomit. He tried to take the entire scene in, to burn it into his mind as if it were a series of photographs and not reality. Keeping everything at arm's length was the only way he knew to get through something like this.

Pottersfield said, "And if you look closely, you'll see some of the blood's been sprayed back toward the body with water from the garden hose. I'd expect the killer did it to wash away footprints and such."

Knight nodded, and then, by sheer force of will, moved his attention beyond the body, deeper into the garden, bypassing forensics techs gathering evidence from the flower beds and turning to a crime-scene photographer snapping away near the back wall.

Knight skirted the corpse by several feet and from that new perspective saw what the photographer was focusing on. It was from ancient Greece, and was one of Sir Denton's prized possessions: a headless limestone statue of an Athenian senator cradling a scroll and holding the hilt of a busted sword.

Sir Denton's head had been placed in the empty space between the statue's shoulders. His face was puffy, lax. His mouth was twisted to the left, as if he were spitting. And his eyes were open, dull, and, to Knight, shockingly forlorn.

For an instant, the Private operative wanted to break down. But then he felt himself swell with outrage. What kind of barbarian would do such a thing? And why? What possible reason could there be to behead Denton Marshall? The man was more than good. He was...

"You're not seeing it all, Peter," Pottersfield said behind him. "Go look at the grass in front of the statue."

Knight closed his hands to fists and walked off the terrace onto the grass, which scratched against the paper booties he wore over his shoes, making a sound that was as annoying to him as fingernails on a chalkboard. Then he saw it and stopped cold.

Five interlocking rings, the symbol of the Olympic Games, had been spray-painted on the grass.

Through the symbol, an *X* had been smeared in blood.

CHAPTER 3

WHERE ARE THE eggs of monsters most likely laid? What nest incubates them until they hatch? What are the toxic scraps that nourish them to adulthood?

So often during the headaches that occasionally rip through my mind like gale-driven thunder and lightning, I ponder those kinds of questions, and others.

Indeed, as you read this, you might be asking your own questions, such as "Who are you?"

My real name is irrelevant. For the sake of this story, however, you can call me Cronus. In old Greek myths, Cronus was the most powerful of the Titans, a digester of universes, the Lord God of Time.

Do I think I am a god?

Don't be absurd. Such arrogance tempts fate. Such hubris mocks the gods. And I have never been guilty of that treacherous sin.

I remain, however, one of those rare beings to appear on earth once a generation or two. How else would you explain the fact that long before the storms began in my head, hatred was my oldest memory and wanting to kill was my very first desire?

Indeed, at some point in my second year of life, I became aware of hatred, as if it and I were linked spirits cast into an infant's body from somewhere out there in the void, and for some time that's what I thought of as me: this burning singularity of loathing thrown on the floor in the corner, into a box filled with rags.

Then one day I instinctively began to crawl from the box, and with that movement and freedom I soon understood that I was more than anger, that I was a being unto myself—that I starved and went thirsty for days, that I was cold and naked and left to myself for hours on end, rarely cleaned, rarely held by the monsters that walked all around me, as if I were some kind of alien creature landed among them. That's when my first direct thought occurred: I want to kill them all.

I had that ruthless urge long, long before I understood that my parents were drug addicts, crackheads, unfit to raise a superior being such as me.

When I was four, shortly after I sunk a kitchen knife into my comatose mother's thigh, a woman came to where we lived in squalor and took me away from my parents for good. They put me in a home where I was forced to live with abandoned little monsters, hateful and distrustful of any other beings but themselves.

Soon enough I grasped that I was smarter, stronger, and more visionary than any of them. By the age of nine, I did not know exactly what I was yet, but I sensed that I might be some sort of different species, a supercreature, if you will, who could manipulate, conquer, or slay every monster in his path.

I knew this about myself for certain after the storms started in my head.

They started when I was ten. My foster father, whom we called Minister Bob, was whipping one of the little monsters, and I could not stand to hear it. The crying made me feel weak and I could not abide that sensation. So I left the house and climbed the back fence and wandered through some of the worst streets in London until I found quiet and comfort in the familiar poverty of an abandoned building.

Two monsters were inside already. They were older than me, in their teens, and members of a street gang. They were high on something, I could tell that about them right away, and they said I'd wandered onto their turf.

I tried to use my speed to get away, but one of them threw a rock that clipped my jaw. It dazed me and I fell, and they laughed and got angrier. They threw more stones, which cracked my ribs and broke blood vessels in my thigh.

Then I felt a hard smashing above my left ear followed by a Technicolor explosion that crackled through my brain like the crippled arms of so many lightning bolts ripping a summer sky.

CHAPTER 4

PETER KNIGHT FELT helpless as he glanced back and forth from the Olympic symbol crossed out in blood to the head of his mother's fiancé.

Inspector Pottersfield stepped up beside Knight. In a thin voice, she said, "Tell me about Sir Denton."

Swallowing his grief, Knight said, "Denton was a great, great man, Elaine. Ran a big hedge fund, made loads of money, but gave most of it away. He was also an absolutely critical member of the London Organising Committee. A lot of people think that without Sir Denton's efforts, we never would have beaten out Paris for the games. He was also a nice guy, unimpressed with himself. And he made my mother very happy."

"I didn't think that was possible," the chief inspector remarked.

"Neither did I. Neither did Amanda. But he did," Knight said. "Until just now, I didn't think Denton Marshall had an enemy in the world."

Pottersfield gestured at the bloody Olympic symbol. "Maybe it has more to do with the Olympics than with who he was in the rest of his life."

Knight stared at Sir Denton Marshall's head and returned to the corpse before saying, "Maybe. Or maybe this is just designed to throw us off the track. Cutting off someone's head can easily be construed as an act of rage, which is almost always personal at some level."

"You're saying this could be revenge of some kind?" Pottersfield replied.

Knight shrugged. "Or a political statement. Or the work of a deranged mind. Or a combination of the three. I don't know."

"Can you account for your mother's whereabouts last evening between eleven and twelve thirty?" Pottersfield asked suddenly.

Knight looked at her as though she were an idiot. "Amanda loved Denton."

"Spurned love can be a powerful motive for rage," Pottersfield observed.

"There was no spurning," Knight snapped. "I would have known. Besides, you've seen my mother. She's five foot five and a hundred and ten pounds. Denton was two twenty. There's no way she'd have the physical or emotional strength to cut off his head. And no reason to."

"So you're saying you do know where she was?" Pottersfield asked.

"I'll find out and get back to you. But first I have to tell her."

"I'll do that if you think it might help."

"No, I'll do it," Knight said, studying Sir Denton's head one last time, and then focusing on the way his mouth seemed twisted, as if he wanted to spit something out.

Knight fished in his pocket for a pen-size flashlight, stepped around the Olympic symbol, and shined the beam into the gap between Sir Denton's lips. He saw a glint of something, and reached back into his pocket for a pair of forceps he always kept there in case he wanted to pick something up without touching it.

Refusing to look at his mother's dead fiancé's eyes, he began to probe between the man's lips with the forceps.

"Peter, stop that," Pottersfield ordered. "You're—"

But Knight was already turning to show her a tarnished bronze coin he'd plucked from Sir Denton's mouth.

"New theory," he said. "It's about money."

CHAPTER 5

WHEN I RETURNED to consciousness several
days after the stoning, I was in hospital with a fractured skull and the nauseating feeling that I had
been rewired somehow, made more alien than ever
before.

I remembered everything about the attack and
everything about my attackers. But when the police came to ask me what had happened, I told
them I had no idea. I said I had memories of entering the building, but nothing more; and their
questions soon stopped.

I healed slowly. A crab-like scar formed on my
scalp. My hair grew back, hiding it, and I began to
nurture a dark fantasy that became my first obses-
sion.

Two weeks later, I returned home to the little monsters and Minister Bob. Even they could tell I'd changed. I was no longer a wild child. I smiled and acted happy. I studied and developed my body.

Minister Bob thought I'd found God.

But I admit to you that I did it all by embracing hatred. I stroked that crab-like scar on my head, and focused my hatred, my oldest emotional ally, on things that I wanted to have and to have happen. Armed with a dark heart, I went after them all, trying to show the entire world how different I really was. And though I acted the changed boy—the happy, achieving mate—in public, I never forgot the stoning or the storms it had spawned in my head.

When I was fourteen, I secretly began looking for the monsters that broke my skull. I found them eventually, selling dime bags of methamphetamine on a corner twelve blocks from where I lived with Minister Bob and the little monsters.

I kept tabs on the pair until I turned sixteen, and felt big and strong enough to act.

Minister Bob had been an ironworker before he found Jesus. On the sixth anniversary of my stoning, I took one of his heavy hammers and a pair of his old work coveralls, and I slipped out at night, when I was supposed to be studying.

27

Wearing the coveralls and carrying the hammer in a schoolbag harvested from a trash bin, I found the two monsters that stoned me. Six years of their drug use and six years of my evolution had wiped me from their memory banks.

I lured them to an empty lot with the promise of money, and then I beat their monstrous brains to bloody pulp.

CHAPTER 6

SHORTLY AFTER CHIEF Inspector Pottersfield ordered Sir Denton's remains bagged, Knight left the garden and the mansion consumed by far worse dread than he'd felt when he'd entered.

He ducked the police tape, avoided the reporters, and headed out of Lyall Mews, trying to decide how in God's name he was going to tell his mother about Denton. But Knight knew he had to, and quickly, before Amanda heard it from someone else. He absolutely did not want her to be alone when she learned that the best thing that had ever happened to her was...

"Knight?" a man's voice called to him. "Is that you?"

Knight looked up to see a tall, athletic man in

his midforties, wearing a fine Italian suit, rushing toward him. Below his thick salt-and-pepper hair, anguish twisted his ruddy, blockish face.

Knight had met Michael "Mike" Lancer at Private's London offices twice in the eighteen months since the company was hired to act as a special security force during the Olympic Games. But he knew the man largely by reputation.

A two-time world decathlon champion in the 1980s and '90s, Lancer had served with the Coldstream Regiment and in the Queen's Guard, which had allowed him to train fulltime. At the Barcelona Olympics in 1992, he led the decathlon after the first day of competition, but then cramped in the heat and humidity during the second day, finishing out of the top ten.

Lancer had since become a motivational speaker and security consultant who often worked with Private International on big projects. He was also a member of LOCOG, the London Organising Committee of the Olympic Games, charged with helping to arrange security for the mega-event.

"Is it true?" Lancer asked in a keenly distraught voice. "Denton's dead?"

"Afraid so, Mike," Knight said.

Lancer's eyes welled with tears. "Who would do this? Why?"

"Looks like someone who hates the Olympics," Knight said, and then described the manner of Sir Denton's death, and the bloody *X*.

Rattled, Lancer said, "When do they think this happened?"

"Shortly before midnight," Knight replied.

Lancer shook his head. "That means I saw him only two hours before his death. He was leaving the party at the Tate with..." He stopped and looked at Knight in sad appraisal.

"Probably my mother," Knight said. "There were engaged."

"Yes, I knew that you and she were related," Lancer said. "I'm so, so sorry, Peter. Does Amanda know?"

"I'm on my way to tell her right now."

"You poor bastard," Lancer said, and then looked off toward the police barrier. "Are those reporters there?"

"A whole pack of them, and getting bigger," Knight said.

Lancer shook his head bitterly. "With all due loving respect to Denton, this is all we need with the opening ceremonies tomorrow night. They'll blast the lurid details all over the bloody world."

"Nothing you can do to stop that," Knight said. "But I might think about upping security on all members of the organizing committee."

Lancer made a puffing noise, and then nodded. "You're right. I'd best catch a cab back to the office. Marcus is going to want to hear this in person."

Marcus Morris, a politician who had stood down at the last election, was now chairman of the London Organising Committee.

"My mother as well," Knight said, and together they headed on toward Chesham Street, where they thought taxi traffic would be heavier.

Indeed, they'd just reached Chesham when a black taxi appeared from the south, across from the Diplomat Hotel. At the same time, farther away and from the north, a red taxi came down the near lane. Knight hailed it.

Lancer signaled the black taxi in the northbound lane, saying, "Give my condolences to your mother, and tell Jack I'll be in touch sometime later today."

Jack Morgan was the American owner of Private International. He'd been in town since the plane carrying four members of the London office had gone down in the North Sea with no survivors.

Lancer stepped off the curb and set off in a confident stride, heading diagonally across the street as the red taxi came closer.

But then, to Knight's horror, he heard the growl of an engine and tires squealing.

The black taxi was accelerating, heading right at the LOCOG member.

CHAPTER 7

KNIGHT REACTED ON instinct. He leaped into the street and knocked Lancer from the cab's path.

In the next instant, Knight sensed the black taxi's bumper less than three feet away, and tried to jump in the air to avoid being hit. His feet left the ground, but could not propel him from the cab's trajectory. The fender and grille struck the side of his left knee and lower leg and drove on through.

The action wheeled Knight into the air. His shoulders, chest, and hip smashed on the hood and his face was pressed against the windshield, enabling him to catch a split-second image of the driver. Scarf. Sunglasses. A woman?

Knight was hurled up and over the roof as if he

were no more than a stuffed doll. He hit the pavement hard on his left side, knocking the wind out of him, and for a moment he was aware only of the sight of the black taxi speeding away, the smell of car exhaust, and the blood pounding in his temples.

Then he thought: *A goddamn miracle, but nothing feels broken.*

The red taxi screeched toward Knight and he panicked, thinking he'd be run over after all.

But it skidded into a U-turn before stopping. The driver, an old Rasta wearing a green-and-gold knit cap over his dreads, threw open his door and jumped out.

"Don't move, Knight," Lancer yelled, running at him. "You're hurt!"

"I'm okay," Knight croaked. "Follow that cab, Mike."

Lancer hesitated, but Knight said, "She's getting away!"

Lancer grabbed Knight under the arms and hoisted him into the back of the red cab. "Follow it!" Lancer roared at the driver.

Knight held his ribs, still struggling for air as the Rasta taxi driver took off after the black cab, which was several blocks ahead by now, turning hard onto Pont Street, going west.

"I catch her, mon!" the driver promised. "Dat crazy one tried to kill you!"

Lancer was looking back and forth between the road ahead and Knight. "You sure you're okay?"

"Banged up and bruised," Knight grunted. "And she wasn't trying to run me down, Mike. She was trying to run *you* down."

The driver power-drifted onto Pont Street, heading west. The black taxi was two blocks ahead now, its brake lights flashing red before it lurched in a hard right turn onto Sloane Street.

The Rasta mashed the gas hard, turning the leafy road into a blur. They reached the intersection with Sloane so fast, Knight felt sure they'd actually catch up to the woman who'd just tried to kill him.

But then two more black taxis flashed by them, both heading north on Sloane, and the Rasta was forced to slam on the brakes and wrench the wheel to avoid hitting them. Knight's cab went into a screeching skid, and almost hit another car: a Metropolitan Police vehicle.

The siren went on. So did the flashing lights.

"No!" Lancer yelled.

"Every time, mon!" the driver shouted in frustration, and slowed the taxi to a stop.

Knight nodded in an angry daze, looking through the windshield as the taxi that had almost killed him melted into the traffic heading toward Hyde Park.

CHAPTER 8

BRIGHTLY FLETCHED ARROWS whizzed and cut through the hot midmorning air. They landed on and around the yellow bull's-eyes painted within larger red and blue circles on a long line of targets set up across the lime-green pitch at Lord's Cricket Grounds near Regent's Park in central London.

Archers from six or seven countries were completing their final practice rounds. Archery would be one of the first sports to be decided after the 2012 London Olympic Games opened, with team competition scheduled to start midmorning on Saturday, two days hence, and the medal ceremony to be held that very afternoon.

Which is why Karen Pope was up in the stands,

watching through binoculars, boredom slackening her face.

Pope was a sports reporter for the *Sun,* a British tabloid newspaper that boasts more than seven million readers, thanks to its reputation for aggressive, bare-knuckle journalism and its tradition of publishing photographs of young bare-breasted women on page 3.

Pope was in her early thirties, and attractive in the way Renée Zellweger was in the film *Bridget Jones's Diary,* but too flat-chested to ever be considered for page 3. Pope was also a dogged reporter, and ambitious in the extreme.

Around her neck that morning hung one of only fourteen full-access media passes granted to the *Sun* for the Olympics. Such passes had been severely limited for the British press because more than twenty thousand members of the global media would also be in London to cover the seventeen-day mega-event. The full-access passes had become almost as valuable as Olympic medals, at least to British journalists.

Pope kept thinking she should be happy to have the pass and to be here covering the games at all, but her efforts so far this morning had failed to yield anything truly newsworthy about archery.

She'd been looking for the South Koreans, gold

medal favorites, but had learned that they had already finished their practice session before she arrived.

"Bloody hell," she said in disgust. "Finch is going to kill me."

Pope decided her best hope was to do research for a feature that, with lively writing, might somehow make the paper. But what sort? What was the angle?

Archery: Darts for the Posh?

No, there was absolutely nothing posh about archery.

Indeed, what in God's name did she know about archery? She'd grown up in a footballer family. Earlier that very morning Pope had tried to explain to Finch that she'd be better off assigned to athletics or gymnastics. But her editor had reminded her in no uncertain terms that she'd only just joined the paper six weeks before from Manchester and therefore was the low person on the sports-desk totem pole.

"Get me a big story and you'll get better assignments," Finch had said.

Pope forced her attention back to the archers. It struck her that they seemed so calm. It was almost like they were in a trance up there. Not like a cricket batsman or a tennis player at all. Should she write about that? Find out how the bowmen got themselves into that state?

C'mon, she thought in annoyance. *Who wants to read about Zen in sports when you can look at bare boobs on page 3?*

Pope sighed, set down her binoculars, and shifted her position in one of the Grand Stand seats. She noticed stuffed down into her handbag a bundle of mail she'd grabbed as she left the office. She started going through the stack, finding various press releases and other items of zero interest.

Then she came to a thick manila envelope with her name and title printed oddly in black and blue block letters on the front.

Pope twisted her nose as if she'd sniffed something foul. She hadn't written anything recently to warrant a wack-job letter, most definitely not since she'd arrived in London. Every reporter worth a damn got wack-job letters. You learned to recognize them quickly. They usually came after you'd published something controversial or suggested a diabolical conspiracy.

She slit the envelope anyway and drew out a sheaf of ten pages attached by a paper clip to a folded plain paper greeting card. She flipped the card open. There was no writing inside. But a computer chip in the card was activated and flute music began to play, weird flute music that got under her skin and made her think that someone had died.

She shut the card and then scanned the first page of the sheaf of pages, and saw that it was a letter addressed to her, and typed in a dozen different fonts, which made it hard to read. But then she began to get the gist of it, and Pope read the letter three times, her heart beating faster with every line until it felt like it was throbbing high in her throat.

She scanned the rest of the documents attached to the letter and the greeting card, and almost felt faint. She dug wildly in her bag for her phone and called her editor.

"Finch, it's Pope," she said breathlessly when he answered. "Can you tell me whether Denton Marshall has been murdered?"

In a thick Cockney accent, Finch said, "What? Sir Denton Marshall?"

"Yes, yes, the big hedge fund guy, philanthropist, member of the organizing committee," Pope confirmed, gathering her things and looking for the nearest exit to the stadium. "Please, Finchy, this could be huge."

"Hold on," her editor growled.

Pope had made it outside and was trying to hail a cab across from Regent's Park when her editor finally came back on the line.

"They've got the yellow tape up around Sir Denton's place in Lyall Mews and the coroner's wagon just arrived."

Pope punched the air with her free hand and cried, "Finch, you're going to have to get someone else to cover archery and dressage. The story I just caught is going to hit London like an earthquake."

CHAPTER 9

"LANCER SAYS YOU saved his life," Elaine Pottersfield said.

A paramedic prodded and poked at a wincing Knight, who sat on the bumper of an ambulance on the east side of Sloane Street, a few feet from the Rasta's parked red taxi.

"I just reacted," Knight insisted, aching everywhere and feeling baked by the heat radiating off the pavement.

"You put yourself in harm's way," the chief inspector said coldly.

Knight got annoyed. "You said yourself I saved his life."

"And almost lost your own," she shot back.

"Where would that have left..." She paused. "The children?"

He said, "Let's keep them out of this, Elaine. I'm fine. There should be footage of that taxi on CCTV."

London had ten thousand closed-circuit security cameras spread out across the city, all of which rolled twenty-four hours a day. A lot of them had been there since the 2005 terrorist bombings in the tube—London's subway system—which left fifty-six people dead and more than seven hundred wounded.

"We'll check them," Pottersfield promised. "But looking for a black taxi in London? Since none of you got the license plate, that's going to be near impossible."

"Not if you narrow the search to this road, heading north, and the approximate time she got away. And call all the taxi companies. I had to have done some damage to her hood or grille."

"You're sure it was a woman?" Pottersfield asked skeptically.

"It was a woman," Knight insisted. "Scarf. Sunglasses. Very pissed off."

The Scotland Yard chief inspector glanced over at Lancer, who was being interviewed by another officer, before saying, "He and Sir Denton. Both LOCOG members."

Knight nodded. "I'd start looking for people who have a beef with the organizing committee."

Pottersfield did not reply because Lancer was approaching. He'd torn his tie loose around his neck and was patting at his sweating brow with a handkerchief.

"Thank you," he said to Knight. "I am beyond in your debt."

"Nothing you wouldn't have done for me," Knight replied.

"I'm calling Jack," Lancer said. "I'm telling him what you did."

"It's not necessary," Knight said.

"It is," Lancer insisted. He hesitated. "I'd like to repay you."

Knight shook his head. "LOCOG is Private's client, which means you are Private's client, Mike, and it's all in a day's work."

"No, you…" Lancer said, hesitated, and then completed his thought. "You shall be my guest tomorrow night at the opening ceremonies."

Knight was caught flat-footed by the offer. Tickets to the opening ceremonies were almost as prized as invitations had been to the marriage of Prince William and Kate Middleton the year before.

"If I can get the nanny to cover for me, I'll accept."

Lancer beamed. "I'll have my secretary send you a pass and tickets in the morning." He patted Knight on his good shoulder, smiled at Pottersfield, and then walked off toward the Jamaican taxi driver, who was still getting a hard time from the patrol officers who'd pulled him over.

"I'll need you to make a formal statement," Pottersfield said.

"I'm not doing anything until I've spoken with my mother."

CHAPTER 10

TWENTY MINUTES LATER, a Metropolitan Police patrol car dropped Knight in front of his mother's home on Milner Street in Knightsbridge. He'd been offered painkillers by the paramedics, but had refused them. Getting out of the cop car was brutal, and he kept remembering, in flashes, an image of a beautiful pregnant woman standing on a moor at sunset.

Thankfully, he was able to put her out of his mind by the time he rang the doorbell, suddenly aware of how dirty and torn his clothes were.

Amanda would not approve. Neither would...

The door swung open to reveal Gary Boss, his

mother's longtime personal assistant. Boss was in his thirties, thin, well-groomed, and impeccably attired.

He blinked at Knight from behind round tortoiseshell glasses and sniffed, "I didn't know you had an appointment, Peter."

"Her son and only child doesn't need one," Knight said. "Not today."

"She's very, very busy," Boss insisted. "I suggest…"

"Denton's dead, Gary," Knight said softly.

"What?" Boss said, and then tittered derisively. "That's impossible. She was just with him last—"

"He was murdered," Knight said, stepping inside. "I just came from the crime scene. I need to tell her."

"Murdered?" Boss said, and then his mouth sloughed open. He closed his eyes as if in anticipation of some personal agony. "Dear God. She'll be…"

"I know," Knight said, and moved by him. "Where is she?"

"In the library," Boss said. "Choosing fabric."

Knight winced. His mother despised being interrupted when reviewing samples. "Can't be helped," he said, and walked down the hall toward the doors to the library, getting ready to tell his mother that, in effect, she had just been widowed for the second time.

When Knight was three, his father, Harry, had died in a freak industrial accident, leaving his young widow and son a meager insurance payout. His mother had turned bitter about her loss, but then turned that bitterness into energy. She'd always liked fashion and sewing, so she used the insurance money to start an apparel company she named after herself.

Amanda Designs had started in their kitchen. Knight remembered how she had seemed to look at life and business as one long, protracted brawl. Her pugnacious style succeeded, though. By the time Knight was fifteen, his mother had built Amanda Designs into a robust and respected company by never being happy and by constantly goading everyone around her to do better. Shortly after Knight graduated from Christ Church college at Oxford, she'd sold the concern for tens of millions of pounds and used the cash to fund the launch of four more successful apparel lines.

In all that time, however, Knight's mother never allowed herself to fall in love again. She'd had friends and consorts and, Knight suspected, several short-term lovers. But from the day his father had died, Amanda had erected a solid shield around her heart that no one, except for her son, ever managed to breach.

Until Denton Marshall had come into her life.

They met at a cancer fund-raiser and, as his mother liked to say, "It was everything at first sight." In that one evening, Amanda transformed from a cold, remote bitch into a schoolgirl giddy with her first crush. From that point forward, Sir Denton had been her soul mate, her best friend, and the source of the deepest happiness of her life.

Knight flashed on that image of the pregnant woman again, knocked on the library door, and entered.

An elegant woman by any standard—in her late fifties, she possessed the posture of a dancer, the beauty of an aging movie star, and the bearing of a benevolent monarch—Amanda Knight was standing at her worktable, dozens of fabric swatches arrayed in front of her.

"Gary," she scolded without looking up. "I told you that I was not to be—"

"It's me, Mother," Knight said.

Amanda turned to look at him with her slate-colored eyes and frowned. "Peter, didn't Gary tell you I was choosing..." She stopped, seeing something in his face. Her own face twisted in disapproval. "Don't tell me: your heathen children have driven off another nanny."

"No," Knight said. "I wish it were something as simple as that."

Then he proceeded to shatter his mother's happiness into a thousand jagged pieces.

CHAPTER 11

IF YOU ARE to kill monsters, you must learn to think like a monster.

I did not begin to appreciate that perspective until the night after the explosion that cracked my head a second time, nineteen years after the stoning.

I was long gone from London, my first plan to prove to the world that I was beyond different—that I was infinitely superior to any other human—having been thwarted.

The monsters had won that war against me by subterfuge and sabotage. As a result, when I landed in the Balkans in the late spring of 1995, assigned to a NATO peacekeeping mission, the hatred I felt had no limits. Its depth and dimensions were incalculable.

After what had been done to me, I did not want peace.

I wanted violence. I wanted sacrifice. I wanted blood.

So perhaps you could say that fate intervened on my behalf within five weeks of my deployment to the fractured, shifting, and highly combustible killing fields of Serbia, Croatia, and Bosnia-Herzegovina.

It was July, a late afternoon on a dusty road eighteen miles from the besieged city of Srebrenica, in the Drina Valley. I was riding in the passenger seat of a camouflaged Toyota Land Cruiser, looking out the window, wearing a helmet and flak jacket.

I'd been reading about Greek mythology from a book I'd picked up, and was thinking that the war-torn Balkan landscape through which we traveled could have been the setting of some dark and twisted myth; wild roses were blooming everywhere about the mutilated corpses we'd spotted in the area, victims of one side's atrocity or the other's.

The bomb went off without warning.

I can't recall the sound of the blast that destroyed the driver, the truck, and the two other passengers. But I can still smell the cordite and the burning diesel.

And I can still feel the aftershock of the invisible fist that belted me with full force, hurling me through the windshield and setting off an electrical storm of epic proportions inside my skull.

Dusk had blanketed the land when I regained consciousness, ears ringing, disoriented, nauseated, and thinking at first that I was ten years old and had just been stoned unconscious. But then the tilting and whirling in my mind slowed enough for me to make out the charred skeleton of the Land Cruiser and the bodies of my companions, which were burned beyond recognition. Beside me lay a submachine gun and pistol, a Sterling and a Beretta, which had been thrown from the truck.

It was dark by the time I could stand with the weapons and walk.

I staggered and fell for several miles across fields and forests before I came to a village somewhere southwest of Srebrenica. Walking in, carrying the guns, I heard something above and beyond the ringing in my ears. Men were shouting somewhere in the darkness ahead of me.

Those angry voices drew me, and as I went toward them I felt my old friend hatred building in my head, irrational, urging me to slay somebody.

Anybody.

CHAPTER 12

THE MEN WERE Bosnians. There were seven of them, armed with old single-barrel shotguns and corroded rifles they used to goad three handcuffed teenage girls ahead of them as if they were driving livestock to a pen.

One of them saw me, shouted, and they turned their feeble weapons my way. For reasons I could not explain to myself until much later, I did not open fire and kill them all right there, the men and the girls.

Instead, I told them the truth, that I was part of the NATO mission and that I'd been in an explosion and needed to call back to my base. That seemed to calm them somewhat and they lowered their guns and let me keep mine.

One of them spoke broken English and said I could call from the village's police station, where they were heading.

I asked what the girls were under arrest for, and the one who spoke English said, "They are war criminals. They belong to Serbian kill squad, working for that devil Mladić. People call them the Furies. These girls kill Bosnian boys. Many boys. Each of them does this. Ask oldest one. She speak English."

Furies? I thought with great interest. I'd been reading about the Furies the day before in my book of Greek mythology. I walked more quickly so I could study them, especially the oldest one, a sour-looking girl with a heavy brow, coarse black hair, and dead dark eyes.

Furies? This could not be a coincidence. As much as I believed that hatred had been gifted to me at birth, I instantly came to believe that these girls had been put in front of me for a reason.

Despite the pain that was splitting my head, I fell in beside the oldest one and asked, "You a war criminal?"

She turned her dead dark eyes on me and spat out her reply: "I am no criminal, and neither are my sisters. Last year, Bosnian pigs kill my parents and rape me and my sisters for four days straight.

If I could, I shoot every Bosnian pig. I break their skulls. I kill all of them if I could."

Her sisters must have understood what she was saying, because they, too, turned their dead eyes on me. The shock of the bombing, the brutal throbbing in my head, my jet-fueled anger, the Serbian girls' dead eyes, the myth of Furies—all these things seemed to suddenly gather together into something that felt predestined to me.

The Bosnians handcuffed the girls to heavy wooden chairs bolted to the floor of the police station and shut and locked the doors. The landlines were not working. Neither were the primitive cell-phone towers. I was told, however, that I could wait there until a peacekeeping force could be called to take me and the Serbian girls to a more secure location.

When the Bosnian who spoke English left the room, I cradled my gun, moved close to the girl who'd spoken to me, and said, "Do you believe in fate?"

"Go away."

"Do you believe in fate?" I pressed.

"Why do you ask me this question?"

"As I see it, as a captured war criminal, your fate is to die," I replied. "If you're convicted of killing dozens of unarmed boys, that's genocide. Even if you and your sisters were gang-raped beforehand, they will hang you. That's how it works with genocide."

She lifted her chin haughtily. "I am not afraid to die for what we have done. We killed monsters. It was justice. We put balance back where there was none."

Monsters and Furies, I thought, growing excited before replying, "Perhaps, but you will die, and there your story will end." I paused. "But perhaps you have another fate. Perhaps everything in your life has been in preparation for this exact moment, this place, this night, right now, when your fates collide with mine."

She looked confused. "What does this mean, 'fates collide'?"

"I will get you out of here," I said. "I will get you new identities, hide you, and protect you and your sisters forever. I will give you a chance at life."

She'd gone steely again. "And in return?"

I looked into her eyes. I looked into her soul. "You will be willing to risk death to save me, as I will now risk death to save you."

The oldest sister gave me a sidelong look. Then she turned and clucked to her sisters in Serbian. They argued for several moments in harsh whispers.

Finally, the one who spoke English said, "You can save us?"

The clanging in my head continued, but the fogginess had departed, leaving me in a state of near-electric clarity. I nodded.

She stared at me with those dark dead eyes and said, "Then save us."

The Bosnian who spoke English returned to the room and called out to me, "What lies are these demons from hell telling you?"

"They're thirsty," I answered. "They need water. Any luck with the telephone?"

"Not yet," he said.

"Good," I replied, flipping the safety on the sub-machine gun as I swung the muzzle around at the Furies' captors, opening fire and slaughtering every one of them.

BOOK TWO

LET THE GAMES BEGIN

CHAPTER 13

AS THE TAXI pulled up in front of a sterile sky-scraper deep in the City of London—the city's financial district—Peter Knight could still hear his mother sobbing. The only other time he'd ever seen her cry like that was over his father's body after the accident.

Amanda had collapsed into her son's arms after learning of her fiancé's death. Knight had felt the wracking depths of her despair, and understood them all too well. She'd been stabbed in the soul. Knight didn't wish that sensation on anyone, much less his own mother, and he held her through the worst of the mental and emotional hemorrhaging, reliving his own raw memories of loss.

Gary Boss had come into her office finally, and nearly wept himself when he saw Amanda's abject sorrow. A few minutes later, Knight received a text message from Jack Morgan telling him to come directly to Private London because the *Sun* had hired the firm to analyze a letter from someone who claimed to be Sir Denton's killer. Boss said he would take over Amanda's care.

"I should stay," Knight had replied, feeling horribly guilty about leaving. "Jack would understand. I'll call him."

"No!" Amanda said angrily. "I want you to go to work, Peter. I want you to do what you do best. I want you to find the sick bastard who did this to Denton. I want him put in chains. I want him burned alive."

As Knight rode an elevator to the top floors of the skyscraper, his thoughts were dominated by his mother's charge to him, and despite the steady ache in his side, he felt himself becoming obsessed. It was always like this with Knight when he was on a big case—obsessed, possessed—but given his mother's involvement, this investigation felt more like a crusade: no matter what happened, no matter what the obstacle, no matter how much time was required, Knight vowed to nail Denton Marshall's killer.

The elevator door opened into a reception area, a hypermodern room appointed with art that depicted milestones in the history of espionage, forensics, and cryptography. Though the London office itself was brutally understaffed at the moment, the lobby bustled with Private International agents from all over the world, who had come in to pick up their Olympics security passes and assignments.

Knight circled the mob, recognizing only a few people, before passing a model of the Trojan horse and a bust of Sir Francis Bacon on his way to a tinted bulletproof glass wall. He looked into a retina scan while touching his right index finger to a print reader. A section of the wall hissed open, revealing a scruffy, freckle-faced, carrot-haired man with a scraggly beard. He wore cargo jeans, a West Ham United football jersey, and black slippers.

Knight smiled. "G'day, Hooligan."

"What the fug, Peter?" Jeremy "Hooligan" Crawford said, eyeing Knight's clothes. "Been having sex with an orangutan, have you?"

In the wake of Wendy Lee's death in the plane crash, Hooligan was now the chief science, technology, and forensics officer at Private London. In his early thirties, he was caustic, fiercely independent, and unabashedly foul-mouthed—as well as insanely smart.

Born and raised in Hackney Wick, one of London's tougher neighborhoods, the son of parents who'd never finished secondary school, Hooligan had nevertheless obtained degrees in math and biology from Cambridge by the age of nineteen. By twenty, he had earned a third degree, in forensics and criminal science, from Staffordshire University, and was hired by MI5, where he worked for eight years before coming to work at Private at twice the government salary.

Hooligan was also a rabid football fan and held season tickets to games played by London's West Ham United club. Despite his remarkable smarts, as a youngster he'd been known to get out of control watching big games, at which point his brothers and sisters had given him his current nickname. Although many people would not boast of such a moniker, he wore it proudly.

"I scuffled with the hood and roof of a taxi and lived to tell the tale," Knight told Hooligan. "The letter from the killer here yet?"

The science officer brushed past him. "She's bringing it up."

Knight pivoted to look back through the crowd of agents toward the elevator, which was opening again. *Sun* reporter Karen Pope exited, clutching a large manila envelope to her chest. Hooligan went to her. She seemed taken aback at his scruffy appearance, and shook his hand tentatively. He led her back into the hallway and introduced Knight.

Pope instantly turned guarded and studied the investigator with suspicion, especially his torn and filthy coat. "My editors want this to be done discreetly and quickly, with no more eyes than are necessary. As far as the *Sun* is concerned, that means you and you alone, Mr. Crawford."

"Call me Hooligan, eh?"

Knight had instantly found Pope both abrasive and defensive, but maybe it was because he felt like his entire left side had been beaten with boat oars, and because he had gone through the emotional wringer of his mother's collapse.

He said, "I'm working the Marshall murder on behalf of the firm, and on behalf of my mother."

"Your mother?" Pope said.

Knight explained, but Pope still seemed unsure.

Feeling zero patience, Knight said, "Have you considered that I just might know something about this case that you don't?"

CHAPTER 14

THAT HIT A nerve. Pope's face flushed indignantly.

"I don't recall your byline," Knight continued. "Do you work the city desk? The crime beat?"

"If you must know, I work sports normally," she said, thrusting her chin at Knight. "What of it?"

"It means I know things about this case that you don't," Knight said.

"Is that so?" Pope shot back. "Well, I'm the one holding the letter, aren't I, Mr. Knight? You know, I really would prefer to deal with Mr. . . . uh, Hooligan."

Before Knight could reply, an American male voice said: "It *would* be smart to let Peter in on the examination, Ms. Pope. He's the best we've got."

A lanky man with surfer good looks, the American stuck out his hand and shook hers, saying, "Jack Morgan. Your editor arranged through me for the analysis. I'd like to be there as well, if possible."

"All right," Pope said without enthusiasm. "But the contents of this envelope cannot be revealed to anyone unless you've seen it published in the *Sun*. Agreed?"

"Absolutely," Jack said, and smiled genuinely.

Knight admired the owner and founder of Private. Jack was younger than Knight, and even more in a hurry than Knight. He was also smart and driven, and believed in surrounding himself with smart, driven people and paying them well. He also cared about the people who worked for him. He was devastated at the loss of Carter and the other Private London operators, and had come across the Atlantic immediately to help Knight pick up the slack.

The foursome went to Hooligan's lab, one floor down. Jack fell in beside Knight, who was moving much more slowly than the others. "Good job with Lancer," he said. "Saving his ass, I mean."

"We mean to please," Knight said.

"He was very grateful, and said I should give you a raise," Jack said.

Knight did not reply. They had not talked salary in light of his new responsibilities.

Jack seemed to remember and said, "We'll talk money after the games." Then the American shot him a more critical eye. "Are *you* all right?"

"Feel like I've been playing in the scrum, but I remain chipper," Knight assured him as they entered Private London's science unit, cutting-edge in every respect.

Hooligan led them to a far corner, to an anteroom where he told them all to don disposable white jumpsuits and hoods. Knight groaned, but once in the suit and hood, he followed Hooligan through an air lock and into the clean room. The science officer moved to a workstation that included an electron microscope, and state-of-the-art spectrographic equipment. He took the envelope from Pope, opened it, and looked inside.

He asked, "Did you put these in sleeves, or did they come to you like this?"

Knight heard the question over a headset built into his hood, which made the ensuing conversation sound like transmissions from outer space.

"I did that," Pope replied. "I knew right away they'd need to be protected."

"Smart," Hooligan said, wagging a gloved finger

at her and looking over at Knight and Jack. "Very smart."

Despite his initial dislike of Pope, Knight had to agree. He asked, "Who touched these before you protected them?"

"Just me," Pope said as Hooligan removed the sleeve that contained the letter. "And the killer, I suppose. He has a name. You'll see it there. He calls himself Cronus."

CHAPTER 15

SEVERAL MOMENTS LATER, the weird flute music emanated from the card, irritating Knight and making him feel like the killer was toying with them. He finished scanning the letter and the attached documents, then handed them to Jack.

The music must have gotten to Jack as well, because he slammed the card shut, cutting off the music, and then said, "This guy's off his rocker."

Pope said, "Crazy like a fox, then, especially those bits about Marshall and his former partner, Guilder. The documents back his allegations."

"I don't believe those documents," Knight said. "I knew Denton Marshall. He was a supremely honest man. And even if they were factual, it's hardly justification for cutting the man's head off.

Jack's right. This guy is seriously unbalanced, and supremely arrogant. He's taunting us. He's telling us that we can't stop him. He's saying this is not over, that it could just be the beginning."

Jack nodded, and said, "When you start with a beheading, you're taking a long walk down Savage Street."

"I'll start running tests," Hooligan said. He was looking at the card. "These music-playing chips are in a lot of greeting cards. We should be able to trace the make and model."

Knight nodded, saying, "I want to read through the letter one more time."

While Pope and Jack watched Hooligan slice out the working components of the musical greeting card, Knight returned to the letter and began to read as the flute music died in the lab.

The first sentence was written with symbols and letters that Knight could not read, but he guessed they were ancient Greek. The second and all subsequent sentences in the letter were in English.

The ancient Olympic Games have been corrupted. The modern games are not a celebration of gods and men. They are not even about goodwill among men. The modern games are a mockery, a sideshow that takes place every four years, and were made that way by so many thieves, cheats, murderers, and monsters.

Consider the great and exalted Sir Denton Marshall and his corpulent partner, Richard Guilder. Seven years ago, Sir Denton sold out the Olympic movement as a force for honest competition. From the documents that accompany this letter, you will see that they suggest that in order to assure London would be selected to host the 2012 games, Sir Denton and Mr. Guilder cleverly siphoned funds from their clients and secretly moved the money into overseas bank accounts owned by shell corporations owned by shell corporations owned by members of the International Olympic Committee. Paris, runner-up in the selection process, never had a chance.

And so to cleanse the games, the Furies and I find it just that Sir Denton should die for his offenses, and so that has come to pass. We are unstoppable beings, far superior to you, able to see corruption where you cannot, able to expose monsters and slay them for the good of the games when you cannot.

—Cronus

CHAPTER 16

READING THE LETTER a second time, Knight felt more upset, more anxious than before. In light of what had been done to Sir Denton, Cronus came off as a madman—albeit a rational one—who made Knight's skin crawl.

Making it worse, the creepy flute melody would not leave Knight's mind. What kind of psyche produces that music and that letter? How did Cronus make them work together to achieve such a sense of imminent threat and violation?

Or was Knight too close to the case to feel any other way?

He got a camera and began shooting close-ups of the letter and supporting documents. Jack came over. "What do you think, Peter?"

"There's a good chance that one of the Furies, as he calls them, tried to run Lancer down this afternoon," Knight replied. "A woman was driving that cab."

"What?" Pope protested. "Why didn't you tell me that?"

"I just did," Knight said. "But don't quote me."

Hooligan suddenly brayed, "Big mistake!"

They all turned. He held up something with tweezers.

"What have you got?" Jack asked.

"Hair," Hooligan said in triumph. "It was in the glue on the envelope flap."

"DNA, right?" Pope asked, excited. "You can match it."

"Gonna try, eh?"

"How long will that take?"

"Day or so for a full recombinant analysis."

Pope shook her head. "You can't have it for that long. My editor was specific. We had to turn it all over to Scotland Yard before we publish."

"He'll take a sample and leave them the rest," Jack promised.

Knight headed toward the door.

"Where are you going?" Pope demanded.

Knight paused, not sure of what to tell her. Then he gave her the truth. "I'm guessing that first sentence is written in ancient Greek, so I'm going to pay a call on that bloke James Daring—you know, the bloke who has that show *Secrets of the Past* on the Sky network—see if he can decipher it for me."

"I've seen him," Pope snorted. "Nattering boob thinks he's Indiana Jones."

Hooligan shot back, "That nattering boob, as you call him, holds doctorates in anthropology and archaeology from Oxford and is the bloody curator of Greek antiquities at the museum." The science officer looked to Knight. "Daring *will* know what that says, Peter, and I'll wager he'll have a damn say about Cronus and the Furies, too. Good call."

Through the glass visor of her hood Knight could see the reporter twist her lips, as if tasting something tart. "And then?" Pope asked at last.

"Guilder, I suppose."

"His partner?" Pope cried. "I'm coming with you, then."

"Not likely," Knight said. "I work alone."

"I'm the client," she insisted, looking at Jack. "I can trot along, right?"

Jack hesitated, and in that hesitation Knight saw the weight of concern carried by the owner of Private International. He'd lost five of his top agents in a suspicious plane crash. All of them had been integral players in overseeing Private's role in security at the Olympics. And now Sir Denton and this lunatic Cronus.

Knight knew he was going to regret it, but said, "No need to be on the spot, Jack. I'll change my rules this once. She can *trot* along."

"Thanks, Peter," the American said with a tired smile. "I owe you once again."

CHAPTER 17

IN THE DEAD of night, forty-eight hours after I opened fire and slaughtered seven Bosnians in the summer of 1995, a shifty-eyed and swarthy man who smelled of tobacco and cloves opened the door to a hovel of a workshop in a battle-scarred neighborhood of Sarajevo.

He was the sort of monster who thrives in all times of war and political upheaval, a creature of the shadows, of shifting identity and shifting allegiance.

I'd learned of the forger's existence from a fellow peacekeeper who'd fallen in love with a local girl unable to travel on her own passport.

"Like we agreed yesterday," the forger said when I and the Serbian girls were inside. "Six thousand for three. Plus one thousand for the rush order."

I nodded and handed him an envelope. He counted the money, and then passed me a similar envelope containing three fake passports—one German, one Polish, and one Slovenian.

I studied them, feeling pleased at the new names and identities I'd given the girls. The oldest was now Marta. Teagan was the middle girl, and Petra the youngest. I smiled, thinking that with their new haircuts and hair colors, no one would ever recognize them as the Serbian sisters the Bosnian peasants called the Furies.

"Excellent work," I told the forger, and pocketed the passports. "My gun?"

We'd left my Sterling with him as a good-faith deposit when I ordered the passports. "Of course," he said. "I was thinking just that."

The forger went to a locked safe, opened it, and drew out the weapon. He turned and aimed it at us. "On your knees," he snarled. "I read about a slaughter at a police barracks near Srebrenica, and about three Serbian girls wanted for war crimes. There's a reward out. A large one."

"You stinking weasel," I sneered, keeping his attention on me as I slowly went to my knees. "We give you money, and you turn us in?"

He smiled. "I believe that's called taking it coming and going."

The silenced .9 mm round zipped over my head and caught the forger between the eyes. He crashed backward and sprawled dead over his desk, dropping my rifle. I picked it up and turned to Marta, who had a bullet hole through her right jacket pocket.

For the first time, I saw something other than deadness in Marta's eyes. In its place was a glassy intoxication that I understood and shared. I had killed for her. Now she had killed for me. Our fates were not only completely intertwined, we were drunk on the sort of intoxicating liquor that ferments and distills within members of elite military units after each successive mission, the addictive drink of superior beings who wield power over life and death.

Exiting the forger's building, however, I was acutely aware that more than two days had passed since the bomb had hurled me from the Land Cruiser. People were hunting for the Furies. The forger said so.

And someone had to have found the exploded and burned vehicle I was thrown from. Someone had to have counted and examined the charred bodies and figured out that I was missing.

Which meant people were hunting for me.

Maybe, I decided, they should find me sooner rather than later.

CHAPTER 18

AT THREE TWENTY that Thursday afternoon, Pope and Knight crossed the courtyard and climbed the granite front steps of the venerable British Museum in central London. As they entered the museum, Knight was grinding his teeth. He liked to work alone because it gave him enough silence every once in a while to think things through during the course of an investigation.

Pope, however, had been talking almost nonstop since leaving Private's offices, feeding him all sorts of information he really had no need to know, including her career highlights, the creep Lester she'd dated in Manchester, and the travails of being the only woman currently working on the *Sun*'s sports desk.

"Got to be tough," he said, wondering if he could somehow ditch her without adding to Jack's problems.

Instead, Knight led them to an older woman at the information desk, where he produced his identification and said that someone from Private had called ahead to arrange a brief interview with Dr. James Daring.

She'd sniffed something about the curator being very busy, what with his exhibit about to open that very evening, but then gave them directions.

They climbed to an upper floor and navigated toward the rear of the massive building. At last they came to an archway, above which hung a towering banner that read THE ANCIENT OLYMPIC GAMES: RELICS & RADICAL RETROSPECTIVE.

Two guards stood in front of a purple curtain stretched across the archway. Caterers were setting up tables for food and a bar in the hallway in advance of the opening reception. Knight showed his Private badge and asked for Daring.

The guard replied, "Dr. Daring has gone to take a——"

"Late lunch, but I'm back, Carl," called a harried male voice from back down the hallway. "What's going on? Who are these people? I clearly said no one inside before seven!"

Knight pivoted to see the familiar figure of Dr. Daring—a handsome and ruggedly built man wearing khaki cargo shorts, sandals, and a safari-style shirt—hurrying toward them. His ponytail bounced on his shoulders. He carried an iPad. His eyes jumped everywhere.

Knight had seen James Daring on television several times, of course. For reasons Knight did not quite understand, his almost-three-year-old son, Luke, loved to watch *Secrets of the Past,* though he suspected it was because of the melodramatic music that accompanied virtually every program.

"My kids are big fans," Knight said, extending his hand. "Peter Knight, with Private. My office called."

"And Karen Pope. I'm with the *Sun.*"

Daring glanced at her and said, "I've already invited someone from the *Sun* to view the exhibit along with everyone else—at seven. What can I do for Private, Mr. Knight?"

"Actually, Miss Pope and I are working together," Knight said. "Sir Denton Marshall has been murdered."

The television star's face blanched and he blinked several times before saying, "Murdered? Oh, my God. What a tragedy. He…"

Daring gestured at the purple curtains blocking

the way into his new exhibit. "Without Denton's financial support, this exhibit would not have been possible. He was a generous and kind man."

Tears welled in Daring's eyes. One trickled down his cheek. "I'd planned to thank him publicly at the reception tonight. And…what happened? Who did this? Why?"

"He calls himself Cronus," Pope replied. "He sent me a letter. Some of it is in ancient Greek. We'd hoped you could decipher it for us."

Daring glanced at his watch and then nodded. "I can give you fifteen minutes right now. I'm sorry but—"

"The exhibition," Pope said. "We understand. Fifteen minutes would be wonderful of you."

After a pause, Daring said, "You'll have to walk with me, then."

The museum curator led them behind the curtains into a remarkable exhibition that depicted the ancient Olympic Games and compared them to the modern version. The exhibit began with a giant aerial photograph of the ruins at Olympia, Greece, site of the ancient games.

While Pope showed Daring her copy of Cronus's letter, Knight studied the photograph of Olympia and the diagrams that explained the ruins.

Surrounded by groves of olive trees, the area was

dominated by the Altis, a sanctuary at the center of Olympia that contained several temples, including one devoted to Zeus, the most powerful of the ancient Greek gods. Rituals and sacrifices were performed at the temples during the games. Indeed, according to Daring's exhibit, the entire Olympia site, including the stadium, was a sacred place of worship.

For more than a thousand years, in peace and in war, the Greeks assembled at Olympia to celebrate the festival of Zeus and to compete in the games. There were no bronze, silver, or gold medals given. A crown of wild olive branches was sufficient to immortalize the victor, his family, and his city.

The exhibit went on to contrast the ancient games with the modern.

Knight had been highly impressed with the exhibit. But within minutes of reaching the displays that contrasted the old with the new, he began to feel that the ancient games were heavily favored over the modern Olympics.

He'd no sooner had that thought than Pope called to him from across the hall. "Knight, I think you're going to want to hear this."

CHAPTER 19

STANDING IN THE exhibition hall in front of a display case featuring ancient discuses, javelins, and terra-cotta vases painted with scenes of athletic competitions, Dr. Daring gestured to the first sentence in the text.

"This *is* ancient Greek," he said. "It reads, 'Olympians, you are in the laps of the gods.' That's a phrase from Greek mythology. It means that the fate of specific mortals is in the gods' control. I think the phrase is most often used when some mortal has committed a wrongdoing grave enough to upset the residents of Mount Olympus. But you know who would be better to ask about this sort of thing?"

"Who's that?" Knight asked.

"Selena Farrell," he replied. "Professor of classics at King's College—eccentric, brilliant. In another life she worked for NATO in the Balkans. That's where I—uh, met her. You should go see her. Very iconoclastic thinker."

Writing Farrell's name down, Pope said, "Who is Cronus?"

The museum curator picked up his iPad and began typing, saying, "A Titan, one of the gods who ruled the world before the Olympians. Again, Selena Farrell would be better on this point, but Cronus was the god of time, and the son of Gaia and Uranus, the ancient rulers of earth and sky."

Daring explained that at his mother's urging, Cronus eventually rebelled against his father and ended up castrating him with a scythe.

A long curved blade, Knight thought. *Wasn't that how Elaine had described the murder weapon?*

"According to the myth, Cronus's father's blood fell into the sea and re-formed as the three Furies," Daring continued. "They were Cronus's half sisters—spirits of vengeance, and snake-haired, like Medusa."

The curator went on to explain that Cronus married Rhea and fathered seven of the twelve gods who would become the original Olympians. Then Daring fell silent, seeming troubled.

"What's the matter?" Pope asked.

Daring's nose twisted as if he smelled something foul. "Cronus did something brutal when he was told of a prediction that his own son would turn against him."

"What's that?" Knight asked.

The curator turned the iPad toward them. It showed a dark and disturbing painting of a disheveled, bearded, and half-naked man chewing on the bloody arm of a small human body. The head and opposite arm were already gone.

"This is a painting by the Spanish painter Goya," Daring said. "It depicts Saturn devouring his son. Saturn was the Romans' name for Cronus."

The painting repulsed Knight. Pope said, "I don't understand."

"In the Roman and Greek myths, Cronus ate his children one by one."

CHAPTER 20

"ATE THEM?" POPE said, curling a lip.

Knight glanced at the painting and envisioned his own children in a playground near his home. He felt even more revolted.

"It's a myth; what can I say?" Daring replied.

The curator went on to explain that Rhea hated her husband for devouring their children, and she vowed that no more of her unborn children would suffer the same fate. So she snuck off to have the son she named Zeus, and hid him immediately after birth. Then she got Cronus drunk and gave him a rock wrapped in a blanket to eat instead of her son.

"Much later," Daring continued, "Zeus rose up, conquered Cronus, forced him to vomit up his children, and then hurled his father into the darkest abysmal pits of Tartarus—or something like that. Ask Farrell."

"Okay," Knight said, unsure if any of this helped or not, and wondering if this letter could possibly be a ruse designed to take them in a wrong direction. "You a fan of the modern Olympics, Doctor?"

The television star frowned. "Why?"

"Your exhibit strikes me as a bit slanted in favor of the ancient games."

Daring turned coolly indignant. "I think the work is quite evenhanded. But I grant you that the ancient games were about honor and excelling in celebration of the Greek religion, whereas the modern version, in my personal opinion, has become too influenced by corporations and money. Ironic, I know, since this exhibit was built with the assistance of private benefactors."

"So, in a way, you agree with Cronus?" Pope asked.

The curator's voice chilled. "I may agree that the original ideals of the Olympics may be getting lost in today's games, but I certainly do not agree with killing people to 'cleanse' the games. Now, if you'll excuse me, I must finish up and change before the reception."

CHAPTER 21

SEVERAL HOURS AFTER Marta killed the forger, the four of us were staying in a no-star hotel on the western outskirts of Sarajevo. I handed the sisters envelopes that contained their passports and enough money to travel.

"Take separate taxis or buses to the train station. Then use completely separate routes to the address I put in your passports. In the alley behind that address, you'll find a low brick wall. Under the third brick from the left you'll find a key. Buy food. Go inside and wait there quietly until I arrive. Do not go out if you can avoid it. Do not be conspicuous. Wait."

Marta translated and then asked, "When will you get there?"

"In a few days," I said. "No more than a week, I should imagine."

She nodded. "We wait for you."

I believed her. After all, where else were she and her sisters to go? Their fates were mine now, and mine was theirs. Feeling more in control of my destiny than at any other time in my life, I left the Serbian girls and went out into the streets, where I found dirt and grime to further soil my torn, bloody clothes. Then I wiped down the guns and threw them in a river.

An hour before dawn, I wandered up to the security gate at the NATO garrison, acting as though I were in a daze. I had been missing for two and a half days.

I gave my superiors and doctors vague recollections of the bomb that tore apart the Land Cruiser. I said I'd wandered for hours, and then slept in the woods. In the morning, I'd set off again. It wasn't until the evening before that I'd remembered exactly who I was and where I was supposed to go; and I'd headed for the garrison with the fuzzy navigation of an alcoholic trying to find home.

The doctors examined me and determined that I had a fractured skull for the second time in my life. Two days later, I was on a medical transport— Cronus flying home to his Furies.

CHAPTER 22

AT FIVE MINUTES to four that Thursday afternoon, Knight exited One Aldwych, a five-star boutique hotel in London's West End theater district, and found Pope waiting on the sidewalk, looking intently at her BlackBerry screen.

"His secretary wasn't putting you off. The doorman says he does come for drinks quite often, but he's not in there yet," Knight said, referring to Richard Guilder, Sir Denton's longtime financial partner. "Let's go wait inside."

Pope shook her head, and then gestured across the Strand to a row of Edwardian buildings. "That's King's College, right? That's where Selena Farrell works—the classical Greek expert the Indiana Jones wannabe told us to talk to. I looked her up. She *has* written extensively about the ancient Greek playwright Aeschylus and his play *The Eumenides,* which is another name for the Furies. We could go chat with her and then swing back for Guilder."

Knight screwed up his face. "In all honesty, I don't know if understanding more about the myth of Cronus and the Furies is going to help us get any closer to catching Sir Denton's killer."

"And now I know something you don't," she said, shaking her BlackBerry at him haughtily. "Turns out Farrell fought the London Olympics tooth and nail. She sued to have the whole thing stopped, especially the eminent domain that took all that land in East London for the Olympic Park. The professor evidently lost her house when the park went in."

Feeling his heart begin to race, Knight set off in the direction of the college, saying, "Denton was in charge of the process that took that land. She had to have hated him."

"Maybe enough to cut off his head," Pope said, struggling to keep up.

Then Knight's cell phone buzzed. A text message from Hooligan:

1st DNA test: hair is female.

95

CHAPTER 23

THEY FOUND SELENA Farrell in her office. The professor was in her early forties, a big-bosomed woman who dressed the part of dowdy earth child: a baggy, faded peasant-style dress, oval black glasses, no makeup, and clogs. Her head was wrapped up in a scarf held in place by two wooden pins.

But it was the beauty mark that caught Knight's eye. Set about midway down her right cheek, it put him in mind of a young Elizabeth Taylor, and made him think that given the right circumstances and manner of dress the professor could have been quite attractive.

As Dr. Farrell inspected his identification,

Knight glanced around at various framed pictures: one of the professor climbing in Scotland, another showing her posing on the edge of Greek ruins, and a third in which she was much younger, wearing sunglasses and a khaki shirt and pants, posing with an automatic weapon beside a white truck that said NATO on the side.

"Okay," Farrell said, returning his badge. "What are we here to discuss?"

"Sir Denton Marshall, a member of the Olympic organizing committee," Knight said, watching for her reaction.

Farrell stiffened and then rolled her lips in distaste. "What about him?"

"He's been murdered," Pope said. "Decapitated."

The professor appeared genuinely shocked. "Decapitated? Oh, that's horrible. I didn't like the man, but...it's barbaric."

"Sir Denton took your house and your land," Knight remarked.

Farrell hardened. "He did. I hated him for it. I hated him and everyone in favor of the Olympics for it. But I did not kill him. I don't believe in violence."

Knight glanced at the photo of her with the automatic weapon, but decided not to challenge her, asking instead: "Can you account for your whereabouts around ten forty-five last night?"

The classics professor leaned back in her chair and took off her glasses, revealing amazing sapphire eyes that bore in on Knight. "I *can* account for my whereabouts at that time, but won't unless it's necessary. I enjoy my privacy."

"Tell us about Cronus," Pope said.

The professor's head drew back. "You mean the Titan?"

"That's the one," Pope said.

She shrugged. "He's mentioned in Aeschylus, especially in the third play in his *Oresteia* cycle, *The Eumenides*. The Eumenides are the three Furies of vengeance born from the blood of Cronus's father. Why are you asking about him? All in all, Cronus is a minor figure in Greek mythology."

Pope glanced at Knight, who nodded. She dug into her bag. She came up with her cell phone, which she fiddled with for several seconds as she said to the professor, "I received a package today from someone who calls himself Cronus and who claims to be Sir Denton's killer. There's a letter and this: it's a recording of a recording, but..."

As the reporter returned to her bag, looking for her copy of Cronus's letter, the weird, irritating flute music began to float from her phone.

The classics professor froze after a few notes.

The melody went on and Farrell stared at her desk, becoming agitated. Then she looked wildly about, as if hearing hornets. Her hands shot up to cover her ears, causing the pins to become dislodged and the scarf to loosen.

She panicked and threw her hands up to hold the scarf in place. Then she leaped to her feet and bolted for the door, choking out the words, "For God's sake turn it off! It's giving me migraines! It's making me sick!"

Knight jumped to his feet and went out after Farrell, who clopped at high speed down the hall before barging into the ladies' room.

"That set off something big," Pope said. She'd come up behind him.

"Uh-huh," Knight said, going back into the office and heading straight to the classics professor's desk while plucking a small evidence bag from his pocket.

He turned the bag inside out before picking up one of the hairpins that had fallen before Farrell bolted. He wrapped the bag around the pin and then drew it out before dropping it back on the desk.

"What are you doing?" Pope demanded in a whisper.

Knight sealed the bag, murmured, "Hooligan says the hair sample from the envelope was from a female."

He heard someone approaching the office, slid the bag into his inside jacket pocket, and sat down. Pope stood and was looking toward the door when another woman, much younger than Farrell but with a similar lack of fashion sense, said, "Sorry. I'm Nina Langor, Professor Farrell's research assistant."

"Is she all right?" Pope asked.

"She said she's suffering from a migraine and going home. She said if you'll call her on Monday or Tuesday, she'll explain."

"Explain what?" Knight demanded.

Nina Langor appeared bewildered. "I honestly have no idea. I've never seen her act like that before."

CHAPTER 24

TEN MINUTES LATER, Knight followed Pope up the stairs into One Aldwych, looking to the hotel doorman he'd spoken with earlier and getting a nod. Knight slipped the doorman a ten-pound note and followed Pope toward the muffled sounds of happy voices.

"That music got to Farrell," Pope said. "She'd heard it before."

"I agree," Knight said. "It threw her hard."

"Is it possible she's Cronus?" Pope asked.

"And uses the name to make us think she's a man? Sure. Why not?"

They entered the hotel's dramatic Lobby Bar, which was triangular in shape and had a soaring vaulted ceiling, a pale polished limestone floor,

floor-to-ceiling windows, and intimate clusters of fine furniture.

In the same way that the Beaufort Bar at the Savoy Hotel up the street was about glamour, the Lobby Bar was about money. One Aldwych was close to London's financial district, and exuded enough corporate elegance to make it a magnet for thirsty bankers, flush traders, and celebrating deal-doers.

There were forty or fifty such patrons in the bar, but Knight spotted Richard Guilder, Sir Denton's business partner, almost immediately: he was a corpulent, silver-haired boar of a man in a dark suit, sitting alone at the bar on the far side of the room, shoulders hunched.

"Let me do the talking at first," Knight said.

"Why?" Pope snapped. "Because I am a woman?"

"How many allegedly corrupt tycoons have you chatted up lately on the sports beat?" he asked coolly.

The reporter grudgingly made a show of having him lead the way.

Sir Denton's partner was staring off into the abyss. Two fingers of scotch, neat, swirled in the crystal tumbler he held. To his left, a bar stool stood empty. Knight made as if to slide into it.

Before he could, an ape of a man in a dark suit got in the way.

"Mr. Guilder prefers to be alone," hc said in a distinct Brooklyn accent.

Knight showed him his identification. Guilder's bodyguard shrugged and showed him his own. Joe Mascolo worked for Private New York.

"You in as backup for the games?" Knight asked.

Mascolo nodded. "Jack called me over."

"Then you'll let me talk to him?"

The Private New York agent shook his head. "Man wants to be alone."

Knight said loud enough for Guilder to hear: "Mr. Guilder? I'm sorry for your loss. I'm Peter Knight, also with Private. I'm working on behalf of the London Organising Committee, and my mother, Amanda Knight."

Mascolo turned, furious that Knight was trying to work around him.

But Guilder stiffened, turned in his seat, studied Knight, and then said, "Amanda. My God. It's . . ." He shook his head and wiped away tears. "Please, Knight, listen to Joe. I'm not in any condition to talk about Denton at the moment. I am here to mourn him. Alone. As I imagine your dear mother is doing as well."

"Please, sir," Knight began again. "Scotland Yard—"

"Has agreed to talk with him in the morning,"

Mascolo growled. "Call his office. Make an appointment. And leave the man in peace for the evening."

The Private New York agent glared at Knight. Sir Denton's partner was turning back to his drink and Knight was resigned to leave him until morning when Pope said, "I'm with the *Sun,* Mr. Guilder. We received a letter from Sir Denton's killer. He mentions you and your company and justifies murdering your partner because of certain illegal activities Sir Denton and you were alleged to have been involved in at your place of business."

Guilder swung around, livid. "How dare you! Denton Marshall was as honest as the day is long. He was never, ever involved in anything illegal as long as I knew him. And I've never been, either. Whatever this letter says, it's a lie."

Pope tried to hand the financier photocopies of the documents Cronus had sent her, saying, "Sir Denton's killer alleges that these were taken from Marshall & Guilder's own records—or, to be more precise, your firm's *secret* records."

Guilder glanced at the pages but did not take them, as if he had no time for considering such outrageous allegations. "We have never kept secret records at Marshall & Guilder."

"Really?" Knight said. "Not even in relation to

foreign currency transactions made on behalf of your high-net-worth clients?"

The hedge-fund manager said nothing, but Knight swore some of the color had seeped from his florid cheeks.

Pope said, "According to these documents, you and Sir Denton were pocketing fractions of every British pound or American dollar—and fractions of every other type of currency—that passed across your trading desks. It may not sound like much, but when you're talking hundreds of millions of pounds a year, the fractions add up."

Guilder set the tumbler of scotch on the bar, doing his best to appear composed. But Knight swore he saw a slight tremor in the man's hand as it returned to his thigh. "Is that all the killer of my best friend claims?"

"No," Knight replied. "He says that the money was moved to offshore accounts and funneled ultimately to members of the International Olympic Committee before their decision in 2005. He says that your partner bribed London's way into the games."

The weight of the allegation seemed to throw Guilder, because he looked both befuddled and wary, as if he'd suddenly realized he was far too drunk to be having this conversation.

"No," he said. "No, that's not…Please, Joe, make them go."

Mascolo looked torn, but said, "Leave him be until tomorrow. I'm sure if we call Jack, he's going to tell you the same thing."

Before Knight could reply, there was a noise that sounded like a fine crystal wineglass shattering. The first bullet pierced a window on the west side of the bar. It just missed Guilder and splintered the huge mirror behind the bar.

Knight and Mascolo both realized what had happened. "Get down!" Knight yelled, going for his gun and scanning the windows for the shooter.

They were too late. A second round was fired through the glass. The slug hit Guilder just below the sternum with a sound like a pillow being plumped.

Bright red blood bloomed on the hedge-fund manager's starched white shirt, and he collapsed forward, crashing into a champagne bucket as he fell to the pale limestone floor.

CHAPTER 25

IN THE FRACTURED silence that seized the fabled Lobby Bar, the shooter, an agile figure in black motorcycle leathers and a visored helmet, spun away and jumped off the window ledge to flee.

"Someone call an ambulance," Pope yelled. "He's been shot!"

The bar erupted as Joe Mascolo vaulted over his prone client and barreled his way forward, ignoring the patrons screaming and diving for cover.

Knight was two feet behind the Private New York operator when Mascolo jumped over a glass cocktail table and up onto the back of a plush gray sofa set against the bar's west wall. As Knight tried to climb up beside Mascolo, he saw to his surprise that the American was armed.

Gun laws in the UK were very strict. Knight had had to work his way through two years' worth of red tape in order to get his license to carry.

Before he could think anything more about it, Mascolo shot through the window. The gun sounded like a cannon in that stone-and-glass room. Hysteria swept the bar. Knight spotted the shooter in the middle of the street—he couldn't get a good look at her face, but she was plainly a woman. At the shot, she twisted, dropped, and aimed in one motion, an ultraprofessional.

She shot before Knight could, and before Mascolo could get off another round. The shooter's bullet caught the Private New York agent through the throat, killing him instantly. Mascolo dropped back off the sofa and exploded through the glass cocktail table.

The shooter was aiming at Knight now. He ducked, raised his pistol above the sill, and pulled the trigger. He started to rise when two more rounds shattered the windowpanes above him.

Glass rained down on Knight, who had a momentary vision of his children and hesitated a moment before he got ready to return fire. Then he heard squealing.

Knight rose up to see the shooter on a jet-black motorcycle. The rear tire was smoking and laying down rubber as the driver went into a power drift that shot her around the corner onto the Strand. She headed west and disappeared before Knight could return fire.

He cursed, turned, and in shock looked at Mascolo, for whom there was no hope. But he heard Pope cry, "Guilder's alive, Knight! Where's the ambulance?"

Knight jumped off the couch and ran back through the shouting and the gathering crowd toward the crumpled form of Richard Guilder. Pope was kneeling at his side amid a puddle of champagne, blood, ice, and glass.

The financier was breathing in gasps and holding tightly to his upper stomach while the blood on his shirt turned darker and spread.

For a moment, Knight swooned in déjà vu, seeing blood spreading on a bedsheet. Then he shook off the vision and got down next to Pope.

"They said there's an ambulance on the way," the reporter said, her voice strained. "But I don't know what to do. No one here does."

Knight tore off his jacket, pushed aside Guilder's hands, and pressed the jacket to the man's torso. Sir Denton's partner peered at Knight as if he might be the last person he would ever see alive, and struggled to talk.

"Take it easy, Mr. Guilder," Knight said. "Help's on the way."

"No," Guilder grunted softly. "Please, listen…"

Knight leaned close to the financier's face, and heard him hoarsely whisper a secret before paramedics burst into the Lobby Bar. But when he finished his confession, Sir Denton's partner just seemed to give out.

Blood trickled from his mouth, his eyes glazed over, and he relaxed, the way a sleeping woman's hand might slip off the side of a bed.

CHAPTER 26

A FEW MINUTES later, Knight stood on the sidewalk outside One Aldwych, oblivious to patrons hurrying past him to the restaurants and theaters, utterly transfixed by the sight and sound of the wailing ambulance speeding Guilder and Mascolo to the nearest hospital.

He had a vision of himself standing on a sidewalk late at night almost three years before, watching another ambulance race away from him, the sirens' fading cry bringing back a misery that still had not lifted entirely.

"Knight?" Pope said. She'd come up behind him.

He blinked and noticed the double-decker buses braking and taxis honking and people hurrying home all around him; suddenly he felt disjointed in much the same way he had that long-ago night when he'd watched the other ambulance speed away from him.

London goes on, he thought without judgment. *London always goes on, even in the face of tragedy and death, whether the victim was a corrupt hedge-fund manager or a bodyguard or a young...*

A hand appeared in front of his nose. The fingers snapped and he started. Pope was looking at him in annoyance. "Earth to Knight. Hello?"

"What is it?" he barked.

"I asked you if you think Guilder will make it."

Knight shook his head. "No. I felt his spirit leave him."

The reporter looked at him skeptically. "What do you mean, you felt it?"

Knight ran his tongue along the inside of his lower lip before replying. "That's the second time in my life I've had someone die in my arms, Pope. I felt it the first time, too. That ambulance might as well slow down. Guilder is as dead as Mascolo is."

Pope's shoulders sank a little and there was an awkward quiet before she said, "I'd better be going back to the office. I've got a nine o'clock deadline."

"You should include in your story that Guilder confessed to the currency fraud just before he died," Knight said.

"He did?" Pope said, digging in her pocket for her notebook. "What'd he say exactly?"

"He said that the scam was his, and that the money did not go to any member of the International Olympic Committee. It went to his personal offshore accounts. Sir Denton was innocent. He died a victim of Guilder's scheming."

Pope stopped writing, the skepticism back. "I don't buy that," she said. "He's covering for Marshall."

"Those were his last words," Knight shot back. "I believe him."

"You have a reason to, don't you? It clears your mother's late fiancé."

"It's what he said," Knight insisted. "You have to include that in the story."

"I'll let the facts speak," she allowed. "I'll include what you say Guilder told you." She glanced at her watch. "I've got to get going."

"We're not going anywhere soon," Knight said, feeling suddenly exhausted. "Scotland Yard will want to talk with us, especially because there was gunfire. Meantime, I need to call Jack, fill him in, and then my nanny."

"Nanny?" Pope said, looking surprised. "You have kids?"

"Twins. Boy and girl."

Pope glanced at his left hand and said in a joking manner, "No ring. What are you, divorced? Drove your wife nuts and she left you with the brats?"

Knight gazed at her coldly, marveling at her insensitivity, before saying, "I'm a widower, Pope. My wife died in childbirth. She bled out in my arms two years, eleven months, and two weeks ago. They took her away in an ambulance with the siren wailing just like that."

Pope's jaw sagged and she looked horrified. "Peter, I'm so sorry, I..."

But Knight already had his back turned and was walking up the sidewalk toward Scotland Yard inspector Elaine Pottersfield, who'd only just arrived.

CHAPTER 27

DARKNESS FALLS ON London, and my old friend hatred stirs at the thought that my entire life has all been a prelude to this fateful moment, exactly twenty-four hours before the opening ceremonies of the most hypocritical event on earth.

It heats in my gut as I turn to my sisters. We're in my office. It's the first chance the four of us have had to talk face-to-face in days, and I take the three of them in at a glance.

Blond and cool Teagan is removing the scarf, hat, and sunglasses she wore while driving the taxi earlier in the day. Marta, ebony-haired and calculating, sets her motorcycle helmet on the floor beside her pistol and zips off her leathers. Fair Petra is the youngest, the most attractive, the best actor, and therefore the most impulsive. She looks in the mirror on the closet door, checking the fit of a chic gray cocktail dress and the dramatic styling of her short ginger-colored hair.

Seeing the sisters like this, each of whom is completely familiar to me, I find it hard to imagine that there was ever a time when we weren't all together, maintaining the facades of our own busy public lives, completely unaligned as far as the rest of the world is concerned.

And why wouldn't the sisters still be with me after seventeen years? In absentia, in 1997, a tribunal in The Hague indicted them for executing more than sixty Bosnians. Ever since Ratko Mladić, the general who oversaw the Serbian kill squads in Bosnia, was arrested last year, the hunt has intensified for my Furies.

I know. I keep track of such things. My dreams depend on it.

In any case, the sisters have lived under the threat of discovery for so long that it pervades their DNA, but that constant, cellular-level menace has made them all the more fanatically devoted to me—mentally, physically, spiritually, and emotionally. Indeed, ever so gradually over the years, my dreams of vengeance have become theirs. Their desire to see those dreams realized burns almost as incandescently as my own.

Over the years, in addition to protecting them, I've educated them, paid for minor plastic surgery, and trained them to be expert markswomen, hand-to-hand fighters, con artists, and thieves. These last two skills have repaid my investment tenfold, but that is altogether another story. Suffice it to say that, as far as I know, they are the best in the world at shadow games, superior to anyone save me.

Now, the jaded among you might be wondering whether I am similar to Charles Manson, an insane "prophet" who, back in the '60s, gathered together a group of traumatized women and convinced them that they were apostles sent to earth for homicidal missions designed to trigger Armageddon. But comparing me to Manson and the Furies to the Helter Skelter girls is deeply misguided; it's like comparing a true story to a myth. We are more powerful, transcendent, and deadly than Manson could have ever imagined in his wildest drug-induced nightmares.

Teagan pours a glass of vodka, gulps from it, and says, "I could not have anticipated that man jumping in front of my cab."

"Peter Knight; he works for Private London," I say, and then push across the table a photograph I found on the Internet. In it, Knight stands, drink in hand, with his mother at the debut of her most recent fashion line.

Teagan considers the photograph and then nods. "That's him. I got a good look when his face smashed against my windshield."

Marta frowns, picks up the photograph, studies it, and then trains her dark agate eyes on me. "He was with Guilder, too, just now, in the bar, before I shot. I'm sure of it. He shot at me after I killed the one guarding Guilder."

I raise an eyebrow. Private? Knight? They've almost foiled my plans twice today. Is that fate, coincidence, or a warning?

"He's dangerous," says Marta, always the most perceptive of the three, the one whose strategic thoughts are most likely to mirror my own.

"I agree," I say, before glancing at the clock on the wall and looking to her ginger-haired sister, still primping in front of the mirror. "It's time to leave for the reception, Petra. I'll see you there later. Remember the plan."

"I'm not stupid, Cronus," Petra says, glaring at me with eyes turned emerald green by contact lenses bought just for this occasion.

"Hardly," I reply evenly. "But you have a tendency to be impetuous, to ad-lib, and your task tonight demands disciplined adherence to details."

"I know what I have to do," she says coldly, and leaves.

Marta's gaze has not left me. "What about Knight?" she asks, proving once again that relentlessness is another of her endearing qualities.

I reply, "Your next tasks are not until tomorrow evening. In the meantime, I'd like you both to look into Mr. Knight."

"What are we looking for?" Teagan asks, setting her drink on the table.

"His weaknesses, sister. His vulnerabilities. Anything we can exploit."

CHAPTER 28

IT WAS ALMOST eight by the time Knight reached home, a restored redbrick town house in Chelsea that his mother had bought for him several years before. He was as exhausted and sore as he'd ever been after a day at work—run over, shot at, forced to destroy his mother's dreams, not to mention interrogated three times by the formidable Inspector Elaine Pottersfield.

The Metropolitan Police inspector had not been happy when she arrived at One Aldwych. Not only were there two corpses as a result of the shootout, she'd heard through the grapevine that the *Sun* had received a letter from Sir Denton's killer and was incensed to learn that Private's forensics lab had had the chance to analyze the material before Scotland Yard.

"I should be arresting you for obstruction!" she'd shouted.

Knight held up his hands. "That decision was made by our client, Karen Pope of the *Sun*."

"Who is where?"

Knight looked around. Pope was gone. "She was on deadline. I know they plan on turning over all evidence after they go to press."

"You allowed a material witness to leave the scene of a crime?"

"I work for Private, not the court. And I can't control Pope. She has her own mind."

The Scotland Yard inspector had responded by fixing him with a glare. "Seems as if I've heard that excuse before from you, Peter, with deadly consequences."

Knight flushed and his throat felt heated. "We're not having this conversation again. You should be asking about Guilder and Mascolo."

Pottersfield fumed, and then said, "Spill it. All of it."

Knight spilled all of it: their meetings with Daring and Farrell, as well as a blow-by-blow account of what had happened in the Lobby Bar.

When he finished, the inspector said, "You believe Guilder's confession?"

"Do dying men lie?" Knight had replied.

121

As he climbed the steps to his front door, Knight considered Guilder's confession again. Then he remembered Daring and Farrell. Were they involved in these killings?

Who was to say that Daring wasn't some kind of nut behind the scenes, bent on destroying the modern games? And who was to say that Selena Farrell wasn't the assassin in the black leather and motorcycle helmet? She'd been holding an automatic weapon in that picture in her office.

Maybe Pope's instincts were spot-on. Could the professor be Cronus? Or at least involved with him? What about Daring? Didn't he say he'd known Farrell from somewhere in his past? The Balkans, back in the '90s?

Then another voice inside Knight demanded that he think less about villains and more about victims. How was his mother? He'd not heard from her all day.

He'd go inside. He'd call her. But before he could get his key into his front lock, he heard his daughter, Isabel, let loose a bloodcurdling scream: "No! No!"

CHAPTER 29

KNIGHT THREW OPEN the front door into the hallway as Isabel's cry turned into a cutting screech: "No, Lukey! No!"

Her father heard a high-pitched maniacal laugh and the pattering of little feet before he entered the living area of his home, which looked like a snow tornado had whirled through it. White dust hung in the air, on the furniture, and coated his almost-three-year-old daughter, who saw him and broke into sobs.

"Daddy, Lukey, he...he..."

A dainty little girl, Isabel went into hiccuping hysterics and ran toward her daddy, who tried to bend down to comfort her. He gritted his teeth at the throbbing ache all down his left side but scooped her up anyway, wanting to sneeze at the baby powder. Isabel's tears had left little streams of baby-powder paste on her cheeks and on her eyelashes. Even covered in talc like this, she was as beautiful as her late mother, with curly fawn-colored hair and wide cobalt blue eyes that could cleave his heart even when they weren't spilling tears.

"It's okay, sweetheart," Knight said. "Daddy's here."

Her crying slowed to hiccups. "Lukey, he…he put fanny powder on me."

"I can see that, Bella," Knight said. "Why?"

"Lukey thinks fanny powder is funny."

Knight held on to his daughter with his good arm and moved toward the kitchen and the staircase that led to the upper floors. He could hear his son cackling somewhere above him as he climbed.

At the top of the stairs, Knight turned toward the nursery, only to hear a woman's voice yell, "Ow! You little savage!"

Knight's son came running from the nursery in his diapers, his entire body covered in talc. He carried a giant-size container of baby powder and was laughing with pure joy until he caught sight of his father glaring narrowly at him.

Luke turned, petrified, and began to back up,

waving his hands at Knight as if he were some apparition he could erase. "No, Daddy!"

"Luke!" Knight began.

Nancy, the nanny, appeared in the doorway behind his son, blocking his way, powder all over her, holding tightly to her wrist, her face screwed up in pain before she spotted Knight.

"I quit," she said, spitting out the words as if they were venom. "They're bloody lunatics." She pointed at Luke, her whole arm shaking. "And that one's a pant-shitting, biting little pagan! When I tried to get him on the loo, he bit me. He broke skin. I quit, and you're paying for the doctor bill."

CHAPTER 30

"YOU CAN'T QUIT," Knight protested as the nanny dodged around Luke.

"Watch me," Nancy vowed, and she barged right by him and down the stairs. "They've been fed, but not bathed, and Luke's crapped his nappy for the third time this afternoon. Good luck, Peter."

She grabbed her things and left, slamming the door behind her.

Isabel started to sob again. "Nancy leaves and Lukey did it."

Feeling overwhelmed, Knight looked at his son and cried in anger and frustration: "That's four this year, Luke! Four! And she only lasted three weeks!"

Luke's face screwed up. He cried, "Lukey sorry, Daddy. Lukey sorry."

In seconds his son had been transformed from a force of nature capable of creating a whirlwind into a little boy so pitiful that Knight softened. Wincing against the pain in his side, still holding Isabel, he crouched down, and gestured to Luke with his free arm. The toddler rushed to him and threw his arms so tightly around Knight that he gasped with the ache that shot through him.

"Lukey love you, Daddy," his son said.

Despite the stench that hung around the boy, Knight blew the talc off Luke's cheeks and kissed him. "Daddy loves you, too, son." Then he kissed Isabel so hard on the cheek she laughed.

"A change and a shower is in order for Luke," he said, and put them down. "Isabel, you shower, too."

A few minutes later, after Knight dealt with the soiled diaper, his children were in the big stall shower in his master bathroom, splashing and playing. Knight got out his cell phone just as Luke picked up a cricket bat made of foam and bonked his sister over the head with it.

"Daddy!" she complained.

"Bonk him back," Knight said.

He glanced at the clock. It was past eight. None of the nanny services he'd used in the past would be open. He punched in his mother's number.

She answered on the third ring, sounding wrung out. "Peter, tell me it's just a nightmare and that I'll wake up soon."

"I'm so sorry, Mother."

She broke down in muffled sobs for several moments, and then said, "I'm feeling worse than I did when your father died. I think I'm feeling as you must have with Kate."

Knight felt stinging tears well in his eyes and a dreadful hollowness in his chest. "And still often do."

He heard her blow her nose and then say: "Tell me what you know, what you've found out."

Knight knew his mother would not rest until he'd told her, so he did rapidly and in broad strokes. She'd gasped and protested violently when he'd described Cronus's letter and the accusations regarding Sir Denton, and then wept when he told her of Guilder's confession and exoneration of her late fiancé.

"I knew it couldn't be true," Knight said. "Denton was an honest man, a great man with an even greater heart."

"He was," his mother said, choking.

"Everywhere I went today, people talked about his generosity and spirit."

"Tell me," Amanda said. "Please, Peter, I need to hear these things."

Knight told her about Michael Lancer's despair over Sir Denton's death and how he'd called the financier a mentor, a friend, and one of the guiding visionaries behind the London Olympics.

"Even James Daring, that guy at the British Museum with the television show?" Knight said. "He said without Denton's support, the show and his new exhibit about the ancient Olympics would never have gotten off the ground. He said he was going to publicly thank Denton tonight at the opening reception."

There was a pause on the line. "James Daring said that?"

"He did," Knight said, hoping she'd take comfort from it.

Instead, she snapped, "Then he's a bald-faced liar!"

Knight startled. "What?"

"Denton did give Daring some of the seed money to start his television show," Amanda allowed. "But he most certainly did not support his new exhibit. In fact, they had a big fight over the tenor of the display, which Denton told me was slanted heavily against the modern Olympics."

"It's true," Knight said. "I saw the same thing."

"Denton was furious," his mother informed him.

"He refused to give Daring any more money, and they parted badly."

Definitely not what Daring told me, Knight thought, and then he asked, "When was this?"

"Two, maybe three months ago," Amanda replied. "We'd just gotten back from Crete and…"

She began to choke again. "We didn't know it, but Crete was our honeymoon, Peter. I'll always think of it that way," she said, and broke down.

Knight listened for several agonizing moments, and then said, "Mother, is there anyone with you?"

"No," she said in a very small voice. "Can you come, Peter?"

Knight felt horrible. "I desperately want to, but I've lost another nanny and—"

She snorted in disbelief. "Another one?"

"She just up and quit on me a half hour ago," Knight complained. "I've got to work every day of the Olympics, and I don't know what to do. I've used every nanny agency in the city, and fear none will send any over."

There was a long silence on the phone that prompted Knight to say, "Mother?"

"I'm here," Amanda said, sounding as level as she'd been since learning of Sir Denton's death. "Let me look into it."

"No," he protested. "You're not—"

"It will give me something to do besides work," she insisted. "I need something to do that's outside myself and the company, Peter, or I think I'll turn mad, or to drink, or to sleeping pills, and I can't stand the thought of any of those options."

CHAPTER 31

AT THAT SAME moment, inside the British Museum, upstairs at the reception in the hallway outside his new exhibit about the ancient Olympics, Dr. James Daring felt like dancing to his good fortune as he roamed triumphantly among the crowd of London's high and mighty, who had gathered for the exhibit's premiere.

It had been a good night. No, a great night!

Indeed, the museum curator had been widely praised by the critics who'd come to see the installation. They'd called it audacious and convincing, a reinterpretation of the ancient Olympics that managed to comment in a completely relevant way about the state of the modern games.

Even better, several impressed patrons told him

they wanted to sponsor and buy advertising on *Secrets of the Past.*

What did that dead asshole Sir Denton know? Daring thought caustically. *Absolutely nothing.*

Feeling vindicated, basking in the glow of a job well done, a job that had gone more than according to plan, Daring went to the bar and ordered another vodka martini to celebrate his exhibit—and more.

Much more.

Indeed, after receiving the cocktail, and fretting sympathetically yet again with one of the museum's big benefactors about Sir Denton's shocking and horrible passing, Daring eagerly cast his attention about the reception.

Where was she?

The television star looked until he spotted a delightfully feline woman. Her hair was ginger-colored and swept above her pale shoulders, which were bared in a stunning gray cocktail dress that highlighted her crazy emerald eyes. Daring had a thing for redheads with sparkling green eyes.

She does look rather like my sister in several respects, the curator thought. The way she tilted her head when she was amused, as she did now, holding a long-stemmed champagne flute and flirting with a man much older than she. He looked familiar. Who was he?

No matter, Daring thought, looking again to Petra. She was saucy, audacious, a freak. The curator felt a thrill go through him. Look at her handling that man, making what were obviously scripted moves seem effortless in their spontaneity. Saucy. Audacious. Freak.

Petra seemed to hear his thoughts.

She turned from her conversation, found Daring across the crowd, and flashed him an expression so filled with hunger and promise that he shuddered as if in anticipation of great pleasure. After lingering on him a moment longer, Petra batted her eyes and returned her attention to the other man. She put her hand on his chest, laughed again, and then excused herself.

Petra angled toward Daring, never once looking his way. She got another drink and moved back to the dessert table, where Daring joined her, trying to seem interested in the crème brûlée.

"He's drunk and taking a taxi home," Petra murmured in a soft Eastern European accent as she used tongs to dig through a pile of kiwifruit. "I think it's time we left, too, don't you? Lover?"

He glanced at her. A freak with green eyes! The television star flushed with excitement and whispered, "Absolutely. Let's say our good-byes and go."

"Not together, silly goose," Petra cautioned as she plucked two fruit slices from the pile and slid them onto her plate. "We don't want to draw attention, now, do we?"

"No, no, of course not," Daring whispered, feeling wonderfully illicit and deceitful. "I'll wait for you down the street, near Bloomsbury Square."

CHAPTER 32

SHORTLY AFTER NINE that evening, shortly after Karen Pope's article appeared on the *Sun*'s website, London radio stations began to pick up the story, fixating on the Cronus angle and rebroadcasting the flute music.

By ten, shortly after Knight had read a story to the twins, changed Luke's diapers, and tucked them both into bed, the BBC was whipped into a frenzy, reporting the allegations about Sir Denton and the Olympic site selection process as well as Guilder's dying confession that the swindle was all his doing.

Knight cleaned and vacuumed baby powder until eleven. Then he poured himself a beer and a whiskey, ate some pain medication, and crawled into bed. Jack called, distraught over Joe Mascolo's death, and insisted that Knight describe in detail the gunfight that had unfolded at One Aldwych.

"He was fearless," Knight said. "Went right after the shooter."

"That was Joe Mascolo all the way," Jack said sadly. "One of Brooklyn's finest before I hired him away to run protection for us in New York. He only got here a couple of days ago."

"That's brutal," Knight replied.

"It is, and about to get worse," Jack said. "I have to call his wife."

Jack hung up. Knight realized that he had not told Private's owner that he'd lost his nanny. Better that way, he decided after several moments of worry. The American already had too much on his plate.

He turned on the television to find the Marshall and Guilder slayings splashed all over the nightly network news and cable news outlets, which were luridly portraying the broader narrative as a scandalous murder mystery, a shocking glimpse into the byzantine world behind the Olympics site selection process as well as a slap in the face for London—and, indeed, the entire UK—on the eve of the games.

Despite Guilder's dying words, the French were said to be particularly unhappy about Cronus's allegation of Olympic corruption.

Knight switched off the television and sat there in the silence. He picked up the whiskey glass and drank deeply from it before looking at the framed photograph on his dresser.

Very pregnant and sublimely beautiful, his late wife, Kate, stood in profile on a Scottish moor lit by a June sunset. She was looking across her left shoulder, seeming to peer out from the photograph at him, radiating the joy and love that had been so cruelly taken from him almost three years before.

"Tough day, Katie-girl," Knight whispered. "I'm beat up bad, and someone's trying to wreck the Olympics. My mother is destroyed. And the kids have driven another nanny from the house and . . . I miss you. More than ever."

He felt a familiar leadenness return to his heart and mind, which triggered a sinking sensation in his chest. He wallowed in that sensation—indeed, drowned in it for a minute or two—and then did what he always did when he was openly grieving for Kate late at night like this.

He took his blankets and pillows and padded into the nursery. He lay on the daybed looking at the cribs, smelling the smells of his children, and was at last comforted into sleep by the gentle rhythm of their breathing.

CHAPTER 33

THE PAINKILLERS STARTED to wear off and Knight felt the throbbing return to his right side around seven the next morning. Then he heard a squeaking noise and stirred where he lay on the daybed in the twins' nursery. He looked over and saw Isabel on her belly, eyes closed and still. But Luke's crib was gently swaying.

His son was on his knees, chest and head on the mattress, sucking his thumb, rocking from side to side, and still asleep. Knight sat up to watch. For much of the last two years, Luke had been doing this before waking up in the morning.

After several moments, Knight snuck out of the

nursery, wondering if his son's rocking had something to do with REM sleep. Was it disturbed? Did he have apnea? Was that why Luke was so wild and Bella so calm? Is it what made his son's language delayed, and kept him from being toilet trained when his sister was months ahead of the norm? Is that why Luke was a biter?

Knight came to no solid conclusions as he showered and shaved while listening to the radio, which was reporting that Sir Denton's murder and the threats from Cronus had resulted in Michael Lancer and representatives of Scotland Yard and MI5 jointly announcing a dramatic tightening of security at the opening ceremonies. Those lucky enough to have tickets were being told to try to arrive at Olympic Park during the afternoon in order to avoid an expected crush at the security checkpoints in the evening.

After hearing that Private would be given a role in the increased security, Knight tried to call Jack. No answer, but the American was probably going to need him soon.

He knew his mother had promised to help, but he needed a nanny now. He got a painfully familiar file from a drawer and opened it. Inside was a list of every nanny agency in London, and he began calling them in order. The woman who'd found

Nancy and the nanny before her laughed at him when he explained his plight.

"A new nanny?" she said. "Now? Not likely."

"Why not?" he demanded.

"Because your kids have a terrible reputation and the Olympics are starting tonight. Everyone I've got is working for at least the next two weeks."

Knight heard the same story at the next three agencies, and his frustration began to mount. He loved his kids, but he'd vowed to find Sir Denton's killer, and Private was being called upon for additional security at the Olympics. He was needed. Now.

Rather than get angry, he decided to hope that his mother would have better luck at finding someone to care for the twins, and started doing what he could from home. Remembering the DNA material he'd taken off Selena Farrell's hairpin, he called a messenger to come and take the evidence to Hooligan at Private London.

Then he thought about Daring and Farrell, and decided he needed to know more about them—where their paths had crossed, at least. Didn't Daring say something about the Balkans? Was that where the photo of her holding the gun was taken? It had to be.

But when Knight went online and started searching for Farrell, he came up only with references to her academic publishing, and, seven years back, her opposition to Olympic Park.

"This decision is flat-out wrong," Farrell stated in one piece published in the *Times*. "The Olympics have become a vehicle to destroy neighborhoods and uproot families and businesses. I pray that someday, the people behind this decision are made to pay for what they've done to me and to my neighbors at the public's expense."

Made to pay, Professor? Knight thought grimly. *Made to pay?*

CHAPTER 34

ALMOST TWENTY-FOUR hours after the flute music had triggered a brutal migraine and a violent bout of nausea, the melody still played in her head, a cruel sound track to Selena Farrell's thoughts as she lay in bed, curtains drawn.

How was it possible? And what did Knight and Pope think of her? The professor had all but given them a reason to suspect her of something when she'd fled the scene like that. What if they started digging?

For what seemed like the thousandth time since bolting from her office and fleeing home to her tidy little flat in Wapping, Farrell swallowed hard to relieve a burning in her throat that would not leave. She'd drunk water all afternoon and taken a handful of antacids. They had helped only a bit.

She'd been dealing with migraines since she was a child, however, and a prescription medicine had extinguished the electric halo, leaving a burned, dull ache at the back of her skull.

Farrell tried to fight the urge to ease that feeling with alcohol. Not only was it a bad idea given the medicine she was on, but when the professor drank she tended to become another personality almost entirely.

I'm not going there tonight, she thought before remembering the image of an exotic woman sitting deep in the corner of a pink tufted couch. At that, the decision was made for her. Farrell got out of bed, padded to the kitchen, opened the freezer, and took out a bottle of Grey Goose vodka.

Soon the classics professor was on her second martini, the ache at the back of her head was gone, and she believed she'd erased the memory of the flute melody. It was a syrinx melody, actually. The syrinx, or panpipe, consisted of seven reeds bound side by side. Along with the lyre, the panpipe was one of the oldest musical instruments in the world. But its eerie, breathy tonality had been banned from the ancient Olympics because it sounded too funereal.

"Who cares?" Farrell grumbled, and then gulped at her drink. "To hell with the Olympics. To hell with Sir Denton. To hell with the lot of them."

Buzzing on the vodka now, becoming another person, Farrell vowed that with the migraine behind her she wasn't going to dwell on loss, injustice, or oppression. It was Friday night in London. She had places to go. People to see.

The professor felt a thrill go through her that deepened into hunger when she swayed down the hall, went into her bedroom closet, and unzipped a garment bag hanging there.

Inside was a dramatic, hip-hugging, A-line black skirt slit provocatively up its right side, and a sexy, sleeveless, satin maroon blouse designed to show plenty of abundant cleavage.

CHAPTER 35

AT FIVE O'CLOCK that Friday afternoon, Knight was in his kitchen, making the twins dinner and resigned to the fact he would not witness the opening ceremonies live and in person.

Knight felt spent anyway. All day long, from the moment Luke had awakened crying, he had been consumed by the needs of his children, his frustration with the nanny issue, and his inability to push the Cronus investigation forward.

Around noon, while the twins played, he had called his mother and asked her how she was holding up.

"I slept two hours," she replied. "I'd nod off and all I could see in my dreams was Denton, and every time I'd feel the joy of that I'd wake up and face heartbreak all over again."

"God, how horrible, Mother," said Knight, remembering the insomnia and anguish he'd suffered in the immediate weeks after the birth of the twins and Kate's death. Many nights he'd thought he was going crazy.

He changed the subject. "I forgot to tell you: Mike Lancer invited me as his guest to sit in the organizing committee's box for the opening ceremonies. If you find me a nanny, we can go together."

"I don't know if I'm ready for that volume of pity quite yet. Besides, no memorial service has been planned. It's unseemly for me to appear as if I'm celebrating."

"The Olympics are part of Denton's legacy," Knight reminded her. "You'd be honoring him. Besides, it would do you good to get out of the house and help me defend Denton's reputation to one and all."

"I'll consider it."

"And by the way, no nanny, no work on Denton's murder investigation."

"I'm not a nincompoop, Peter!" she snapped. Then Amanda Knight hung up on her son.

Around three, when the children were napping,

Knight reached Jack. Private's owner was usually laid-back and very cool, but Knight could hear the pressure Jack was under over the phone.

"We're doing everything to find a nanny," Knight had said.

"Good," Jack said. "Because we need you."

"Bollocks," Knight fumed after he'd hung up.

His doorbell rang around five thirty. Knight looked out the security peephole and saw his mother, wearing a stylish black blouse and slacks, black pumps, and a gray pearl necklace and earrings. Dark sunglasses covered her eyes. He opened the door.

"I arranged a nanny for the evening," Amanda said, and then stepped aside to reveal a very unhappy Gary Boss, resplendent in khaki pedal pushers, argyle socks, penny loafers, and a bow tie with barber's-pole stripes.

His mother's personal assistant sniffed at Knight as if he were the purveyor of all things distasteful, and said: "Do you know that I personally spoke with Nannies Incorporated, Fulham Nannies, the Sweet and Angelic Agency, and every other agency in the city? Quite the reputation, I'd say, Peter. So where are they? The little brutes? I'll need to know their schedules, I suppose."

"They're in the living room, watching the telly,"

Knight said, and then looked at his mother as Boss disappeared inside. "Is he up for this?"

"At triple his exorbitant hourly wage, I'm sure he'll figure out a way," Amanda said, taking off her sunglasses to reveal puffy red eyes.

Knight ran up the stairs to his bedroom and changed quickly. When he came down he found the twins hiding behind the couch, eyeing Boss warily. His mother was nowhere to be seen.

"Her highness is in the car," Boss said. "Waiting."

"I make, Daddy," Luke said, patting the back of his diapers.

Why couldn't he just use the toilet?

"Well, then," Knight said to Boss. "Their food is in the fridge in plastic containers. Just a bit of heating up to do. Luke can have a taste of ice cream. Bella's allergic, so graham crackers for her. Bath. Book. Bed by nine, and we'll see you by midnight, I'd think."

Knight went to his children and kissed them. "Mind Mr. Boss, now. He's your nanny for tonight."

"I make, Daddy," Luke complained.

"Right," Knight said to Boss. "And Luke's had a BM. You'll need to change it straightaway or you'll be bathing him sooner rather than later."

Boss turned even more distressed. "Change a shitty nappy? Me?"

"You're the nanny now," Knight said, stifling a laugh as he left.

CHAPTER 36

AS KNIGHT AND his mother made their way to the St. Pancras train station and the high-speed rail line that would take them to Stratford and Olympic Park, Professor Selena Farrell was feeling damn sexy, thank you very much.

Dusk was coming on in Soho. The air was sultry, she had vodka in her, and she was dressed to kill. Indeed, as she walked from Tottenham Court Road west toward Carlisle Street, the classics professor kept catching glimpses of herself in the store windows she passed, and in the eyes of men and women who could not help but notice every sway of her hips and every bounce of her chest in the skirt and sleeveless blouse that clung to her like second skins.

She wore alluring makeup, startling blue contact lenses, and the scarf was gone, revealing dyed-dark hair cut in swoops that framed her face and drew the eye to that little dark mole on her right jawline. But for the mole, no one—not even her research assistant—would ever have recognized her.

Farrell loved feeling like this. Anonymous. Sexual. On the prowl.

She was far from who she was in her day-to-day life, truly someone else. The illicitness of it all excited the professor yet again, empowered her, and made her feel magnetic, hypnotic, and, well, downright irresistible.

When she reached Carlisle Street, she found number 4 and entered. The Candy Bar was one of the oldest and largest lesbian nightclubs in London, and it was Farrell's favorite place to go when she needed to let off steam.

The professor headed toward the long bar on the ground floor and the many beautiful women milling about it. A petite woman, quite exquisite in her loveliness, caught sight of Farrell, spun in her seat, mojito in hand, and threw her a knowing smile. "Syren St. James!"

"Nell," Farrell said, and kissed her on the cheek.

Nell put her hand on Farrell's forearm and studied her outfit. "My, my, Syren. Look at you: more brilliant and delicious than ever. Where have you been lately? I haven't seen you in almost a month."

"I was here the other night," Farrell said. "Before that I was in Paris. Working. A new project."

"Lucky you," Nell said, then turned conspiratorial and added, "You know, we could always leave and—"

"Not tonight, lover," Farrell said gently. "I've already made plans."

"Pity," Nell sniffed. "Your plan here yet?"

"Haven't looked," Farrell replied.

"Name?"

"That's a secret."

"Well," Nell said, miffed. "If your secret is a no-show, come back."

Farrell blew Nell a kiss before setting off, feeling anticipation make her heart beat along with the dance music thudding up from the basement. She peered into the nooks and crannies of the ground floor before heading upstairs, where she scanned the crowd gathered around the pink pool table. No luck.

Farrell was beginning to think she'd been stood up until she went to the basement, where a femme kink performer was pole dancing to the riffs and dubs of a disc jockey named V. J. Wicked. Pink sofas lined the walls facing the stripper.

The professor spotted her quarry on one of those sofas in the far corner of the room, nursing a flute of champagne. With jet-black hair pulled back severely, she was elegantly attired in a black cocktail frock and a pillbox hat covered by a black lace veil that obscured all the features of her face save her dusky skin and ruby lips.

"Hello, Marta," Farrell said, sliding into a chair beside her.

Marta took her attention off the dancer, smiled, and replied in a soft Eastern European accent. "I had faith I'd see you here, my sister."

The professor smelled Marta's perfume and was enthralled. "I couldn't stay away."

Marta ran her ruby fingernails over the back of Farrell's hand. "Of course you couldn't. Shall we let the games begin?"

CHAPTER 37

BY SEVEN THAT evening the world's eye had turned to the six-hundred-plus acres of decaying East London docklands that had been transformed into the city's new Olympic Park, which featured a stadium packed with eighty thousand lucky fans, a teeming athletes' village, and sleek, modern venues for cycling, basketball, handball, swimming, and diving.

These venues were all beautiful structures, but the media had chosen British sculptor Anish Kapoor's *ArcelorMittal Orbit* as the park's—and indeed, the games'—signature design achievement. At three hundred and seventy-seven feet, the *Orbit,* which soared just outside the east side of the stadium, was taller than Big Ben and taller than the Statue of Liberty. The tower was rust-red and featured massive hollow-steel arms that curved, twisted, and wove together in a way that put Knight in mind of DNA helices gone mad. Near the top, the structure supported a circular observation deck and restaurant. Above the deck, another of those DNA helices was curved into a giant arch.

From his position high on the west side of the stadium, at the window of a lavish hospitality suite set aside for LOCOG members, Knight trained his binoculars on the massive Olympic cauldron, which was set on a raised platform on the roof of the *Orbit's* observation deck. He wondered how they were going to light it, and then found himself distracted by a BBC broadcaster on a nearby television screen saying that nearly four billion people were expected to tune in to coverage of the opening ceremonies.

"Peter?" Jack Morgan said behind him. "There's someone here who would like to talk to you."

Knight lowered his binoculars and turned to find the owner of Private standing next to Marcus Morris, the chairman of LOCOG. Morris had been a popular minister for sport in a previous Labour government.

"Morris," Morris said, and the two men shook hands.

"An honor," Knight said.

Morris said, "I need to hear from you exactly what Richard Guilder said before he died regarding Denton Marshall."

Knight told him, finishing with, "The currency scam had nothing to do with the Olympics. It was greed on Guilder's part. I'll testify to that."

Morris shook Knight's hand again. "Thank you," he said. "I didn't want there to be any hint of impropriety hanging over these games. But it does nothing to make any of us feel any better about the loss of Denton. It's a tragedy."

"In too many ways to count."

"Your mother seems to be holding up."

Indeed, upon their arrival, Amanda had been showered in sympathy and was now somewhere in the crowd behind them.

"She's a strong person, and when this Cronus maniac tried to say Denton was crooked, she got angry—very angry. Not a good thing."

"No, I suppose not," Morris said, and smiled. "And now, I've got a speech to give."

"And an Olympics to open," Jack said.

"That, too," Morris said, and walked away.

Jack looked out the window at the packed stadium, his eyes scanning the roofline.

Knight noticed and said, "Security seems bril-

157

liant, Jack. It took more than an hour for Amanda and me to get through screening at Stratford. And the blokes with the weapons were all Gurkhas."

"World's most fearsome warriors," Jack said, nodding.

"Do you need me somewhere?"

"We're good," Jack said. "Enjoy the show. You earned it."

Knight looked around. "By the way, where's Lancer? Poor form to miss his own party."

Jack winked. "That's a secret. Mike said to thank you again. In the meantime, I think you should introduce me to your mother so I can offer my condolences."

Knight's cell phone buzzed in his pocket. "Of course. One second, Jack."

He dug out the phone, saw that Hooligan was calling, and answered just as the lights in the stadium dimmed and the audience began to cheer.

"I'm at the stadium," Knight said. "The opening ceremony's starting."

"Sorry to bother you, but some of us have to work," Hooligan snapped. "I got results on that hair sample you sent over this morning. They're..."

A trumpet fanfare erupted from every speaker in

the stadium, drowning out what Hooligan had just said.

"Repeat that," Knight said, sticking his finger in his ear.

"The hair in Cronus's envelope and Selena Farrell's hair," Hooligan yelled. "They fuggin' match!"

CHAPTER 38

"WE'VE GOT CRONUS!" Knight said in a hoarse whisper as he hung up and a powerful spotlight broke the darkness, fixing on a lone figure crouched in the middle of the stadium floor.

"What?" Jack said, surprised.

"Or one of his Furies, anyway," Knight said, and then described the match. "Farrell's house was razed to make way for this stadium. She said publicly that the people who did it to her were going to pay, and she completely flipped when we played the flute music for her."

"Call Pottersfield," Jack advised. "Have her go to Farrell's house. Put her under surveillance until they can get a warrant."

Out in the stadium, a solo clarinet played, and

out of the corner of his eye Knight saw the figure on the stadium floor rise. He wore green and carried a bow. A quiver of arrows was slung across his back. Robin Hood?

"Unless Farrell's in the stadium," Knight said, anxiety rising in his chest.

"They've got names attached to every ticket somewhere," Jack said, and started moving away from the window toward the exit with Knight trailing him.

Behind them, the crowd roared as a spectacle designed by British filmmaker Danny Boyle moved into high gear, depicting through song and dance the rich history of London. Knight could hear drums booming and music echoing in the long hallway outside the heavily guarded hospitality suite. He speed-dialed Elaine Pottersfield, got her on the third ring, and explained the DNA evidence linking Selena Farrell to Cronus's letter.

Beside him, he heard Jack explaining the same information over the phone to whoever the watch commander was inside Olympic Park at the moment.

"How did you come by Farrell's DNA?" Pottersfield demanded.

"Long story," Knight said. "We're looking for her inside the Olympic stadium at the moment. I suggest you start doing the same at her home."

He and Jack both hung up at the same time. Knight glanced at the four armed Private operatives guarding the entrance to LOCOG's hospitality suite.

Reading his thoughts, Jack said: "No one's getting in there."

Knight almost nodded, but then thought of Guilder and Mascolo, and said, "We can't consider LOCOG members as the only targets. Guilder proved that."

Jack nodded. "We have to think that way."

The pair entered the stadium in time to see Mary Poppins launch off the *Orbit,* umbrella held high as she floated over the roof and the delirious crowd toward a replica of the Tower of London that had been moved onto the stadium floor. She landed near the tower, but disappeared in smoke when lights began flashing red and white and kettledrums boomed to suggest the Blitz during World War II.

The smoke cleared and hundreds of people dressed in myriad costume styles danced about the replica of the tower, and Knight thought he heard someone say that they were depicting modern London and the diverse citizenry of the most cosmopolitan city in the world.

But Knight was not interested in the spectacle; he was looking everywhere about the stadium, trying to anticipate what a madwoman might do in a situation like this. He spotted an entryway on the west side of the venue.

"Where does that go?" he asked Jack.

"The practice track," Jack replied. "That's where the teams are getting ready for the Parade of Nations."

For reasons Knight could not explain, he felt drawn to that part of the stadium. "I want to take a look," he said.

"I'll walk with you," Jack said, and they traversed the stadium as the lights dimmed again—all except a spotlight that keyed on the Robin Hood figure, who was now perched high above the stage at the venue's south end.

The actor was pointing up at the top of the *Orbit,* above the observation deck, where spotlights revealed two armed members of the Queen's Guard marching stiffly toward the cauldron from opposite sides of the roof. They pivoted and stood at rigid attention, flanking the cauldron in their red tunics and black bearskin hats.

Two more guardsmen appeared in the stadium at either side of the main stage. The music faded and an announcer said, "Ladies and gentlemen, *mesdames et messieurs:* Queen Elizabeth the Second and the royal family."

CHAPTER 39

THE LIGHTS ON the stage came up to reveal the queen in a blue suit. She was smiling and waving as she moved to a microphone, while Charles, William, Kate, and various other members of the House of Windsor followed her.

Knight and Jack slowed to gawk for several moments while the queen gave a short speech welcoming the youth of the world to London, but then they moved on toward that entryway.

As more dignitaries gave speeches, Knight and Jack reached the grandstands above the tunnel entry and had to show their Private badges and ID's to get to the railing. Teams of armed Gurkhas flanked both sides of the tunnel below them. Several of the Nepalese guards immediately began studying Knight and Jack, gauging their level of threat.

"I absolutely would not want one of those guys pissed at me," Jack said as athletes from Afghanistan started to appear in the entryway.

"Toughest soldiers in the world," Knight said, studying the traditional long curved knives that several of the Gurkhas wore sheathed at their belts.

A long curved knife cut off Sir Denton's head, right?

He was about to mention this fact to Jack when Marcus Morris cried in conclusion to his speech, "We welcome the youth of the world to the greatest city on earth!"

On the stage at the south end of the stadium, the rock band the Who appeared, and broke into "The Kids Are Alright" as the parade of athletes began with the contingent from Afghanistan entering the stadium.

The crowd went wild, and wilder still when the Who finished and Mick Jagger and the Rolling Stones appeared, as Keith Richards launched his guitar into the opening riff of "Can't You Hear Me Knocking."

Thousands of flashbulbs went off, and London went into full Olympic frenzy.

Below Jack and Knight, the Cameroon team filed into the stadium.

"Which one's Mundaho?" Jack asked. "He's from Cameroon, right?"

"Yes, indeed," Knight said, searching among the contingent dressed in green and bright yellow until he spotted a tall, muscular, and laughing man with his hair done up in beads and shells. "There he is."

"Does he honestly believe he can beat Shaw?"

"He certainly thinks so," Knight said.

Filatri Mundaho had appeared out of nowhere on the international track scene at a race in Berlin only seven months before the Olympics. Mundaho was a big, rangy man built similarly to the transcendent Jamaican sprinter Zeke Shaw.

Shaw had not been in Berlin, but many of the world's other fastest men had. Mundaho ran in three events at that meet: the one-hundred-meter, two-hundred-meter, and four-hundred-meter sprints. The Cameroonian won every heat and every race convincingly, which had never been done before at a meet that big.

The achievement set off a frenzy of speculation as to what Mundaho might be able to accomplish at the London games. At the 1996 Atlanta games, American Henry Ivey won a gold medal and set world records in both the four-hundred-meter and two-hundred-meter races. At Beijing in 2008, Shaw won the one-hundred- and two-hundred-meter sprints, also setting world records in both events. But no man—or woman, for that matter—had ever won all three sprinting events at a single games.

Filatri Mundaho was going to try.

His coaches claimed that Mundaho was discovered running in a regional race in the eastern part of their country after he'd escaped from rebel forces that had kidnapped him as a child and turned him into a boy soldier.

"Did you read that article the other day where he attributed his speed and stamina to bullets flying at his back?" Jack asked.

"No," Knight said. "But I can see that being a hell of a motivator."

CHAPTER 40

TWENTY MINUTES LATER, with the Who and the Stones still counterpunching songs from their greatest hits collections, the contingent from the United States entered the stadium, led by their flag bearer, Paul Teeter, a massive bearded man whom Jack knew from Los Angeles.

"Paul went to UCLA," Jack said. "Throws the shot and discus, insanely strong. A really good guy, too. He does a lot of work with inner-city youth. He's expected to go big here."

Knight took his eyes off Teeter and caught sight of a woman he recognized walking behind the flag bearer. He'd seen a picture of her in a bikini in the London *Times*, of all places, the week before. She was in her late thirties and easily one of the fittest women he'd ever seen. And she was even better-looking in person.

"That's Hunter Pierce, isn't it?" Knight said.

Jack nodded in admiration. "What a great story she is."

Pierce had lost her husband in an auto accident two years before, leaving her with three children under the age of ten. Now an emergency room doctor in San Diego, she'd once been a twenty-one-year-old diver who'd almost made the 1996 Olympic team, but then quit the sport to pursue medicine and a family.

Fifteen years later, as a way to deal with her husband's death, she began diving again. At her children's insistence, Pierce started competing again at age thirty-six. Eighteen months later, with her children watching, she'd stunned the American diving community by winning the ten-meter platform competition at the US Olympic qualifying meet.

"Absolutely brilliant," Knight said, watching her waving and smiling as the team from Zimbabwe entered the stadium behind her.

Last to enter was the team from the UK—the host country. Twenty-three-year-old swimmer Audrey Williamson, a two-time gold medalist at Beijing, carried the Union Jack.

Knight pointed out to Jack the various athletes

from the British contingent who were said to have a chance to win medals, including marathoner Mary Duckworth, eighteen-year-old sprinting sensation Mimi Marshall, boxer Oliver Price, and the nation's heavyweight crew team.

Soon after, "God Save the Queen" was sung. So was the Olympic Hymn. The athletes recited the Olympic Creed, and a keen anticipation descended over the crowd, many of whom were looking toward the entry below Knight and Jack.

"I wonder who the cauldron lighter will be," Jack said.

"You and everyone else in England," Knight replied.

Indeed, speculation about who would receive the honor of lighting the Olympic cauldron had only intensified since the flame had come to Britain from Greece earlier in the year, and had been taken to Much Wenlock in Shropshire, where Pierre de Coubertin, considered the father of the modern Olympics, first publicly suggested a resurrection of the games in 1892.

Since then, the torch had wound its way through England, Wales, and Scotland. At every stop, curiosity and rumor had grown.

"Oddsmakers like Sir Cedric Dudley, the UK's five-time gold medalist in rowing," Knight told

Jack. "But others are saying that the one to light the cauldron should be Sir Seymour Peterson-Allen, the first man to run a mile in under four minutes."

But then a roar went up from the crowd as the theme from the movie *Chariots of Fire* was played, and two men ran into the stadium directly below Knight and Jack, carrying the torch between them.

It *was* Sir Cedric Dudley, running beside...

"My God, that's Lancer!" Knight cried.

It was Mike Lancer, smiling and waving joyously to the crowd as he and Sir Cedric ran along the track toward a spiral staircase alongside the replica of the Tower of London and a figure in white, who awaited them there.

CHAPTER 41

AT THAT VERY moment, Karen Pope was in the *Sun*'s newsroom on the eighth floor of a modern office building on Thomas More Square near St. Katharine Docks on the Thames's north bank. She wanted to go home to get some sleep, but could not break away from the coverage of the opening ceremonies.

Up on the screen, Lancer and Dudley ran toward that figure in white standing at the bottom of a steep staircase that led up onto the tower. Seeing the joy on the faces all over the stadium, Pope's normal cynicism faded and she started to choke up.

What an amazing, amazing moment for London, for all of Britain.

Pope looked over at Finch, her editor. The crusty

sports veteran's eyes were glassy with emotion. He glanced at her and said, "You know who that is, don't you? The final torchbearer?"

"No idea, boss," Pope replied.

"That's goddamn—"

"You Karen Pope?" a male voice behind her said, cutting Finch off.

Pope turned to see—and smell—a scruffy bicycle messenger, who looked at her with a bored expression.

"Yes," she said. "I'm Pope."

The messenger held out an envelope with her name spelled out in odd-looking block letters of many different fonts and colors. Pope felt her stomach yawn open into an abysmal pit.

CHAPTER 42

AS THE FINAL torchbearer climbed the staircase adjacent to the Tower of London replica, the entire crowd was cheering and whistling and stomping their feet.

Knight frowned and glanced up at the top of the *Orbit* and the guardsmen flanking the cauldron. How the hell were they going to get the flame from the top of the Tower of London replica to the top of the *Orbit*?

The final torchbearer raised the flame high overhead as the applause turned thunderous and then cut to a collective gasp.

Holding his bow, an arrow strung, Robin Hood leaped into the air off the scaffolding above the south stage and flew out over the stadium on guy wires, heading for the raised Olympic torch.

As the archer whizzed past, he dipped the tip of his arrow into the flame, igniting it. Then he soared on, higher and higher, drawing his bow as he went.

When he was almost level with the top of the *Orbit*, Robin Hood twisted and released the fiery arrow, which arced over the roof of the stadium, split the night sky, and passed between the queen's guardsmen, inches over the cauldron.

A great billowing flame exploded inside the cauldron, turning the stadium crowd thunderous once more. The voice of Jacques Rogge, the president of the International Olympic Committee, rang out over the public-address system:

"I declare the 2012 London Olympic Games open!"

Fireworks erupted off the top of the *Orbit* and exploded high over East London, while church bells all over the city began to ring. Down on the stadium floor, the athletes were all hugging each other, trading lapel pins, and taking pictures and videos of this magical moment, when each and every dream of Olympic gold seemed possible.

Looking at the athletes, and then up at the Olympic flame as chrysanthemum rockets burst in the sky, Knight got teary-eyed. He had not expected to feel such overwhelming pride for his city and for his country.

Then his cell phone rang.

Karen Pope was near hysterical: "Cronus just sent me another letter. He takes credit for the death of Paul Teeter, the American shot-putter!"

Knight grimaced in confusion. "No, I just saw him, he's..."

Then Knight understood. "Where's Teeter?" he shouted at Jack, and started running. "Cronus is trying to kill him!"

CHAPTER 43

KNIGHT AND JACK fought their way down through the crowd. Jack was barking into his cell phone, apprising the stadium's security commander of the situation. They both showed their Private badges to get onto the stadium floor.

Knight spotted Teeter holding the US flag and talking to Filatri Mundaho, the Cameroonian sprinter. He took off across the infield just as the American flag he was holding began to topple. The flag bearer went with it and collapsed to the ground, convulsing, bloody foam at his lips.

By the time Knight reached the US contingent, people were screaming for a doctor. Dr. Hunter Pierce broke through the crowd and went to the shot-putter's side while Mundaho watched in horror.

"He just falls," the former boy soldier said to Knight.

Jack looked as stunned as Knight did. It had all happened so fast. Three minutes' warning. That's all they'd been given. What more could they have done to save the American?

Suddenly, the public-address system crackled and Cronus's weird flute music began playing.

Panic surged through Knight. He remembered Selena Farrell turning crazed in her office, and then realized that many of the athletes around him were pointing up at the huge video screens around the Olympic venue, all displaying the same three red words:

OLYMPIC SHAME EXPOSED!

BOOK THREE

THE FASTEST MAN ON EARTH

CHAPTER 44

KNIGHT WAS INFURIATED. Cronus was acting with impunity, not only managing to poison Teeter but somehow hacking into the Olympic Park computer system and taking over the scoreboard as well.

Could Professor Farrell do such a thing? Was she capable?

Mike Lancer ran up to Knight and Jack, looking like he had aged ten years in the past few moments. He pointed at the screens. "What the hell does that mean? What's that infernal music?"

"It's Cronus, Mike," Knight said. "He's taking credit for the attack."

"What?" Lancer cried, looking distraught. Then

he spotted Dr. Pierce and a couple of paramedics gathered around the US shot-putter. "Is he dead?"

"I saw him before Dr. Pierce got to him," Knight said. "He had bloody foam around his mouth. He was convulsing and choking."

Shaken, bewildered, Lancer said, "Poison?"

"We'll have to wait for a blood test."

"Or an autopsy," Jack said as the paramedics put an unconscious Teeter on a gurney and rushed toward the ambulance with Dr. Pierce in tow.

Some in the remaining crowd at the Olympic stadium were softly clapping for the stricken American. But more were heading for the exits, holding their hands to their ears to block the baleful flute music and taking worried glances at Cronus's message, still glowing up there on the screens.

OLYMPIC SHAME EXPOSED!

Jack's voice shook as the ambulance pulled away. "I don't care what claim Cronus might have. Paul Teeter was one of the good guys, a gentle giant. I went to see one of his clinics in LA. The kids adored him. Absolutely adored him. What kind of sick bastard would do such a thing on a night like this to such a good person?"

Knight thought of Professor Farrell fleeing her office the day before. Where was she? Did Pottersfield have her in custody? Was she Cronus? Was she one of the Furies? And how did they poison Teeter?

Knight went over to Mundaho, introduced himself, and asked him what had happened. The Cameroonian sprinter said in broken English that Teeter was sweating hard and appeared flushed in the minutes before he collapsed.

Then Knight approached other American athletes and asked whether they'd seen Teeter drink anything before the start of the opening ceremony. A high jumper said he had seen the shot-putter drinking from one of the thousands of plastic water bottles that London Olympic volunteers, or "Games Masters," were handing out to athletes as they lined up for the Parade of Nations.

Knight told Jack and Lancer, who went ballistic and barked into his radio, ordering all Games Masters held inside Olympic Park until further notice.

The security commander, who had arrived on the scene a few minutes earlier, glared up at the glowing screens and bellowed into his radio, "Shut down the PA system and end that goddamn flute music! Get that message off the scoreboards, too. And I want to know how in the bloody hell someone cracked our network. Now!"

CHAPTER 45

PAUL TEETER, PREMIER track-and-field athlete and tireless advocate for disadvantaged youth, died en route to the hospital shortly after midnight. He was twenty-six.

Hours later, Knight suffered a nightmare that featured the flute music, the severed head of Denton Marshall, the blood blooming on Richard Guilder's chest, Joe Mascolo crashing through the cocktail table at the Lobby Bar, and the bloody foam on the shot-putter's lips.

He awoke with a start, and for several heart-racing moments the Private agent had no idea where he was.

Then he heard Luke sucking his thumb in the darkness and knew. He began to calm down, and pulled the sheets up around his shoulders, thinking of Gary Boss's face when Knight had arrived home at three in the morning.

The place had been a shambles, and his mother's personal assistant vowed to never, ever babysit Knight's insane children again. Even if Amanda quintupled his salary he would not do it.

His mother was upset with Knight as well. Not only had he cut out on her at the opening ceremonies, he'd not responded to her calls after Teeter's death was announced. But he'd been swamped.

Knight tried to doze again, but his mind lurched between worry about finding a new nanny for his kids, his mother, and the contents of Cronus's second letter. He, Jack, and Hooligan had examined the letter in the clean room at Private London shortly after Pope brought them the package, around one a.m.

"What honor can there be in a victory that is not earned?" Cronus had written to start the letter. "What glory in defeating your opponent through deceit?"

Cronus claimed that Teeter was a fraud "emblematic of the legions of corrupt Olympic athletes willing to use any illegal drug at their disposal to enhance their performance."

The letter had gone on to claim that Teeter and other unnamed athletes at the London games were using an extract of deer- and elk-antler velvet to increase their strength, speed, and workout recovery time. Antlers are the fastest-growing substance in the world, because the nutrient-rich sheathing, or velvet, that surrounds them during development is saturated with IGF-1, or insulin-like growth factor 1, a superpotent growth hormone banned under Olympic rules. Administered carefully, however, and delivered by mouth spray rather than direct injection, the presence of antler velvet was almost impossible to detect.

"The benefits of IGF-1 are enormous," Cronus wrote. "Especially to a strength athlete like Teeter, because it gives him the ability to build muscle faster and recover faster from workouts."

The letter had gone on to accuse two herbalists—one in Los Angeles and another in London—of being involved in Teeter's elaborate deception.

Documents accompanying the letter seemed to shore up Cronus's claims. Four were receipts from the herbalists showing sales and delivery of red-deer velvet from New Zealand to the post office box of an LA construction company that belonged to Teeter's brother-in-law, Philip. Other documents purported to show the results of independent, cutting-edge tests on blood taken from Teeter.

"They clearly note the presence of IGF-1 in Teeter's system within the last four months," Cronus wrote before concluding. "And so this willful cheat, Paul Teeter, had to be sacrificed to cleanse the games and make them pure again."

In the daybed in the twins' nursery, several hours after reading those words, Knight stared at the dim forms of his children, thinking, *Is this how you make the Olympics pure again? By murdering people? What kind of insane person thinks that way? And why?*

CHAPTER 46

I ROAM THE city for hours after Teeter's collapse on the global stage, secretly gloating over the vengeance we've taken, reveling in the proof of our superiority over the feeble efforts of Scotland Yard, MI5, and Private. They'll never come close to finding my sisters or me.

Everywhere I go, even at this late hour, I see Londoners in shock and newspapers featuring a photo of the jumbotrons in the stadium and our message on them: OLYMPIC SHAME EXPOSED!

And the headline: DEATH STALKS THE GAMES!

Well, what did they think? That we'd simply let them continue to make a mockery of the ancient rites of sport? That we'd simply let them defile the principles of fair competition, earned superiority, and immortal greatness?

Hardly.

And now Cronus and the Furies are on the lips of billions upon billions of people around the globe, uncatchable, able to kill at will, bent on exposing and eliminating the dark side of the world's greatest sporting event.

Some fools are comparing us to the Palestinians who kidnapped and murdered Israelis during the 1972 summer games in Munich. They keep describing us as terrorists with unknown political motives.

Those idiots aside, I feel like the world is beginning to understand me and my sisters now. A thrill goes through me when I realize that people everywhere are sensing our greatness. They are questioning how it could be that such beings walk among them, wielding the power of death in the face of deceit and corruption and making sacrifices in the name of all that is good and honorable.

In my mind I see the monsters that stoned me, the dead eyes of the Furies the night I slaughtered the Bosnians, and the shock on the faces of the broadcasters explaining Teeter's death.

At last, I think, *I'm making the monsters pay for what they did to me.*

I'm thinking the same thing as dawn breaks and bathes the narrow thin clouds over London in a deep red hue that makes them look like raised welts.

I knock on the side entrance of the house where the Furies live, and enter. Marta is the only one of the sisters still awake. Her dark agate eyes are shiny with tears and she hugs me joyfully, her happiness as incandescent as my own.

"Like clockwork," she says, closing the door behind me. "Everything went off perfectly. Teagan got the bottle to the American, and then changed and slipped out before the chaos began, as if it were all fated."

"Didn't you say the same thing when London got the Olympics?" I ask. "Didn't you say that when we found out about the corruption and the cheating, just as I said we would?"

"It's all true," Marta replies, her face as fanatical as any martyr's. "We are fated. We are superior."

"Yes, but make no mistake: they will hunt us now," I reply, sobering. "You said we were good on all counts?"

"All counts," Marta says, all business now.

"The factory?"

"Teagan made sure it's sealed tight. No possibility of discovery."

"Your part?" I ask.

"Went off flawlessly."

I nod. "Then it's time we stay in the shadows. Let Scotland Yard, MI5, and Private operate on high alert long enough for them to tire, to imagine that we're done, and allow themselves to let their guard down."

"According to plan," Marta says. Then she hesitates. "This Peter Knight, is he still a threat to us?"

I consider the question, and then say, "If there is one, it's him."

"We found something, then. Knight has a weakness. A large one."

CHAPTER 47

KNIGHT BOLTED AWAKE in the twins' nursery. His cell phone was ringing. Sun flooded the room and blinded him. He groped for the phone and answered.

"Farrell's gone," Scotland Yard chief inspector Elaine Pottersfield said. "Not at her office. Not at her home."

Knight sat up, still squinting, and said, "Did you search them?"

"I can't get a warrant until my lab corroborates the match Hooligan got."

"Hooligan found something more last night in Cronus's second letter."

"What?" Pottersfield shouted. "What second letter?"

"It's already at your lab," Knight said. "But Hooligan picked up some skin cells in the envelope. He gave you half the sample."

"Goddamn it, Peter," Pottersfield cried. "Private is not to analyze anything to do with this case without—"

"That's not my call, Elaine," Knight shot back. "It's the *Sun*'s call. The paper is Private's client!"

"I don't care who the—"

"What about holding up your end?" Peter demanded. "I always seem to be giving you information."

There was a pause before she said, "The big focus is on how Cronus managed to hack into the..."

Knight noticed the twins weren't in their cribs and stopped listening. His attention shot to the clock. Ten a.m.! He hadn't slept this late since before the twins were born.

"Gotta go, Elaine! Kids," he said, and hung up.

Every bad thought a parent could have sliced through him as he lurched through the nursery door and out onto the landing above the staircase. What if they've fallen? What if they've mucked around with...?

He heard the television spewing coverage of the swimming competition's four-hundred-meter freestyle relay heats and felt as if every muscle in his body had gone to rubber. He had to hold tightly to the railings to get down to the first floor.

Luke and Isabel had pulled the cushions off the sofa and piled them on the floor. They were sitting on them, Buddha-like, beside empty cereal and juice boxes. Knight thought he'd never seen anything so beautiful in his life.

He fed and dressed them while tracking the broadcast coverage surrounding Teeter's murder. Scotland Yard and MI5 weren't talking. Neither was F7, the company hired by LOCOG to run security at the games.

But Mike Lancer was all over the news, assuring reporters that the Olympics were safe, defending his actions but taking full responsibility for the breaches in security. Shaken and yet resolved, Lancer vowed that Cronus would be stopped, captured, and brought to justice.

Knight, meanwhile, continued to struggle with the fact that he had no nanny and would not be actively working the Cronus case until he could find one. He'd called his mother several times, but she hadn't answered. Then he called another of the agencies, explained his situation, and begged for a temporary. The manager told him she might be able to recruit someone by Tuesday.

"Tuesday?" he shouted.

"It's the best I can do; the games have taken everyone available," the woman said, then hung up.

The twins wanted to go to the playground around noon. Figuring it would help get them to nap, he agreed. He put them in their stroller, bought a copy of the *Sun,* and walked to a playground on the grounds of the Royal Hospital Chelsea, about ten minutes from his house. The heat had dropped off and there wasn't a cloud in the sky. London at its finest.

But as Knight sat on a bench and watched Luke playing on the big-boy slide and Isabel digging in the sandbox, his thoughts weren't on his children or on the exceptional weather for the first full day of Olympic competition. He kept thinking about Cronus and wondering if and when he'd strike again.

A text message came in from Hooligan:

Skin cells in 2nd letter are male, no match yet. Off to Coventry for England-Algeria football match.

Male? Knight thought. *Cronus? So Farrell is one of the Furies?*

In frustration, Knight picked up the newspaper.

Pope's story dominated the front page under the headline DEATH STALKS THE OLYMPICS.

The sports reporter led with Teeter's collapse and death in a terse, factual account of the events as they had unfolded at the opening ceremony. Near the end of the piece, she'd included a rebuttal of Cronus's charges from Teeter's brother-in-law, who was in London for the games. He claimed that the lab results Cronus provided were phony, and that he, in fact, was the person who bought the deer-antler velvet. He said that because he worked in construction all day long, he needed it for relief from chronic back spasms.

"Hello? Sir?" a woman said.

The sun was so brilliant at first that Knight could only see a figure standing in front of him holding out a flyer. He was about to say he wasn't interested, but then he threw his hand up to his brow to block the sun. She had a rather plain face, short, dark hair, dark eyes, and a stocky, athletic build.

"Yes?" he said, taking the flyer.

"I am so sorry," she said with a humble smile, and he heard the soft Eastern European accent for the first time. "Please; I see you have children and I was wondering...do you know someone who needs, or do you need, a babysitter?"

Knight blinked several times in astonishment

and then looked down at her flyer, which read: "Experienced babysitter/nanny with excellent references available. Undergraduate degree in early childhood development. Accepted into graduate program in speech and language therapy."

It went on, but Knight looked up at her. "What's your name?"

She sat down beside him with an eager smile.

"Marta," she said. "Marta Brezenova."

CHAPTER 48

"YOU'RE AN UNEXPECTED answer to my prayers, Marta Brezenova, and your timing could not have been better," Knight announced, feeling pleased at his good fortune. "My name is Peter Knight, and I am actually in desperate need of a nanny at the moment."

Marta's face blossomed with incredulity and then happiness. Her fingers went to her lips, as she said, "But you are the first person I've handed my flyer to! It's like fate!"

"Maybe," Knight said, enjoying her infectious enthusiasm.

"No, it is!" she protested. "Can I apply?"

He looked again at her flyer. "Do you have a résumé? References?"

"Both," she said without hesitation, then dug in her bag and produced a professional-looking résumé and an Estonian passport. "Now you know who I am."

Knight glanced at the résumé and the passport before saying, "Tell you what. Those are my kids over there. Luke's on the slide and Isabel is in the sandbox. Go introduce yourself. I'll look this over and give your references a call."

Knight wanted to see how his kids interacted with Marta, a total stranger. He'd had them revolt against so many nannies that he did not want to bother calling references if she and the twins did not click. No matter how badly he needed a nanny, it wasn't worth the effort if they did not get along.

But to his surprise, Marta went to Isabel, the more cynical of his children, and won her over almost immediately, helping her build a sand castle with such enthusiasm that Luke soon left the slide to help. In three minutes, she had Lukey Knight, the big, bad, biting terror of Chelsea, laughing and filling buckets.

Seeing his children fall so easily under Marta's sway, Knight read the résumé closely. She was an Estonian citizen, in her midthirties, but had done her undergraduate studies at the American University of Paris.

During her last two years at the university, and for six years after graduating, she had worked as a nanny for two different families in Paris. The mothers' names and phone numbers were included on the résumé.

Marta's résumé also indicated that she spoke English, French, Estonian, and German, and had been accepted into the graduate program in speech and language therapy at City University London, class of 2014. In several ways, she typified the many educated women streaming into London these days: willing to take jobs beneath their qualifications in order to live and survive in the greatest city in the world.

My luck, Knight thought. He got out his cell phone and started calling the references, thinking: *Please let this be real. Please let someone answer the...*

Petra DeMaurier came on the line almost immediately, speaking French. Knight identified himself and asked if she spoke English. In a guarded tone, she said she did. When he told her he was thinking of hiring Marta Brezenova as nanny to his young twins, she turned effusive, praising Marta as the best nanny her four children had ever had—patient, loving, yet strong-willed if need be.

"Why did she leave your employ?" Knight asked.

"My husband was transferred to Vietnam for two years," she said. "Marta did not wish to accompany us, but we parted on very good terms. You are a lucky man to have her."

The second reference, Teagan Lesa, was no less positive, saying, "When Marta was accepted to graduate studies in London, I almost cried. My three children did cry, even Stephan, who is normally my brave little man. If I were you, I'd hire her before someone else does. Better yet, tell her to come back to Paris. We wait for her with open arms."

Knight thought for several moments after hanging up, knowing he should check with the universities here and in Paris, something he couldn't do until Monday at the earliest. Then he had an idea. He hesitated, but then called Pottersfield back.

"You hung up on me," she snapped.

"I had to," Knight said. "I need you to run an Estonian passport for me."

"I most certainly will not," Pottersfield shot back.

"It's for the twins, Elaine," Knight said in a pleading tone. "I've got an opportunity to hire a new nanny who looks great on paper. I just want to make sure, and it's the weekend and I have no other way to do it."

There was a long silence before Pottersfield said, "Give me the name and passport number if you've got it."

Knight heard the Scotland Yard inspector typing after he read her the number. He watched Marta get onto the slide holding Isabel. His daughter on the slide? That was a first. They slid to the bottom with only a bit of terror surfacing on Isabel's face before she started clapping.

"Marta Brezenova," said Pottersfield. "Kind of a plain Jane, isn't she?"

"You were expecting a supermodel moonlighting as a nanny?"

"I suppose not," Pottersfield allowed. "She arrived in the UK on a flight from Paris ten days ago. She's here on an educational visa to City University."

"Graduate program in speech and language therapy," Knight said. "Thanks, Elaine. I owe you."

Hearing Luke shriek with laughter, he hung up and spotted his son and daughter running through the jungle gym with Marta in hot pursuit, playing the happy monster, laughing maniacally.

You're not much to look at, Knight thought. *But thank God. You're hired.*

CHAPTER 49

EARLY THAT AFTERNOON, Metropolitan Police inspector Billy Casper eyed Knight suspiciously and said, "Can't say I think it's proper for you to have access. But Pottersfield wanted you to see for yourself. So go on up. Second floor. Flat on the right."

Knight mounted the stairs, fully focused on the investigation now that Marta Brezenova had come into the picture. The woman was a marvel. In less than two days she'd put his children under a spell. They were cleaner, better behaved, and happier. He'd even checked with City University. No doubt: Marta Brezenova had been accepted into their speech and language therapy program. He hadn't bothered to call the American University of Paris. That aspect of his life felt settled at last. He'd even called up the agency that had offered him part-time help and canceled his request.

Now Chief Inspector Elaine Pottersfield was waiting for Knight at the door to Selena Farrell's apartment.

"Anything?" he asked.

"A lot, actually," she said, and after he'd put on gloves and booties, she led him inside. A full crime scene unit from Scotland Yard and specialists from MI5 were tearing the place apart.

They went into the professor's bedroom, which was dominated by an oversize vanity that featured three mirrors and several drawers open to reveal all manner of beauty items—about twenty different kinds of lipstick, an equal number of nail polish bottles, and jars of makeup.

Dr. Farrell? It didn't fit with the professor he and Pope had met at the college. Then he looked around and spotted the open closets, which were stuffed with what looked like high-end, expensive women's clothing.

She was a secret fashionista or something?

Before he could voice his confusion, Pottersfield gestured past a crime tech examining a laptop sitting on the vanity toward a file cabinet in the corner. "We found all sorts of written diatribes against the destruction the games caused in the East End and the Docklands, including several poisonous letters to Denton —"

"Inspector?" the crime tech interrupted excitedly. "I think I've got it!"

Pottersfield frowned. "What?"

The tech struck the keyboard and flute music began to play from the computer, the same haunting melody that had echoed inside the Olympic stadium the night Paul Teeter was poisoned, the same brutal tune that had accompanied Cronus's first letter.

"That's on the computer?" Knight asked.

"Part of a simple EXE file designed to play the music and to display this."

The tech turned the laptop around to show three words centered on the screen:

OLYMPIC SHAME EXPOSED!

CHAPTER 50

WEARING A SURGICAL cap and mask, a long rubber apron, and the sort of elbow-length rubber gloves that butchers use to disembowel cattle, I carefully load the third letter into an envelope addressed to Karen Pope.

More than seventy-two hours have passed since we slew the monster Teeter, and the initial frenzy we caused in the global media has subsided by many degrees because the London games have gone on, and gold medals have been won.

On Saturday we dominated virtually every broadcast and every written account of the opening ceremonies. On Sunday, the stories about the threat we posed were shorter and focused on law enforcement efforts to figure out how the Olympic computer system was hacked, as well as insignificant coverage of the impromptu memorial service the US athletes held for the corrupt swine Teeter.

Yesterday we were mentioned in news features that trumpeted the fact that, other than Teeter's murder, the 2012 summer Olympics were going off flawlessly. This morning we didn't even make page 1, which was dominated by the search of Serena Farrell's home and office, where conclusive evidence had been found linking her to the Cronus murders, and by word that Scotland Yard and MI5 had launched a nationwide manhunt for the classics professor.

This is troubling news at some level, but not unexpected. Nor is the fact that it will take more than a death or two to destroy the modern Olympic movement. I've known that since the night London won the right to host the games. My sisters and I have had seven years since to work out our intricate plan for vengeance; seven years to penetrate the system and use it to our advantage; and seven years to create enough false leads to keep the police scattered and foggy, unable to anticipate our final purpose until it's much too late.

Still wearing the apron and gloves, I slip the envelope into a Ziploc bag and hand it to Petra, who stands with Teagan, both sisters clad in disguises that render them fat and unrecognizable to anyone but me or their older sister.

"Remember the tides," I say.

Petra says nothing and looks away from me, as if having an internal argument of some sort. The movement raises unease in me.

"We will, Cronus," Teagan says, sliding on dark sunglasses below the official Olympic volunteer's cap she wears.

I go over to Petra and say, "Are you all right, sister?"

Her eyes are conflicted, but she nods.

I kiss her on the cheeks, and then turn to Teagan, my cold warrior.

"The factory?" I ask.

"This morning," she replies. "Food and medicine enough for four days."

I embrace her and whisper in her ear, "Watch your sister. She's impulsive."

When we part, Teagan's face is expressionless. My cold warrior.

Removing the apron and gloves, I watch the sisters leave, and my hand travels to that crab-like scar on the back of my head. As I scratch it, the hatred ignites almost instantly, and I deeply wish that I could be one of those two women tonight. But in consolation, I remind myself that the ultimate revenge will be mine and mine alone. The disposable cell phone in my pocket rings. It's Marta.

"I managed to put a bug in Knight's cell phone before he left for work," she informs me. "I'll tap the home computer when the children sleep."

"Did he give you the evening off?"

"I didn't ask for it," Marta says.

If the stupid bitch were in front of me right now, I swear I'd wring her pretty little neck. "What do you mean, you didn't ask?" I demand in a tight voice.

"Relax," she says. "I'll be right where I'm needed when I'm needed. The children will be asleep. They'll never even know I was gone. And neither will Knight. He told me not to expect him until almost midnight."

"How can you be sure the brats will be sleeping?"

"How else would I do it? I'm going to drug them."

CHAPTER 51

SEVERAL HOURS LATER, inside the aquatics center on the grounds of Olympic Park, US diver Hunter Pierce flipped backward off the ten-meter platform. She spun through the chlorine-scented air, corkscrewing twice before cutting the water with a slitting sound that left a shallow whirlpool on the surface and little else.

Knight joined the packed house, cheering, clapping, and whistling. But no one in the crowd celebrated more than the American diver's three children—one boy and two girls—who sat in the front row stomping their feet and pumping their fists at their mommy as she surfaced, grinning wildly.

That was Pierce's fourth attempt—and her best,

in Knight's estimation. After three dives, she had been in third place behind athletes from South Korea and Panama. The Chinese were a surprisingly distant fourth and fifth.

She's in the zone, Knight thought. *She feels it.*

As he'd been for much of the past two hours, Knight was standing in the entryway opposite the ten-meter platform, watching the crowd and the competition. Nearly four days had passed since Teeter's death—four days without subsequent attack—and one day since the discovery of the software program in Selena Farrell's computer that had been designed to breach and take over the Olympic stadium's electronic scoreboard.

Everyone was saying it was over now. Capturing the mad professor was only a matter of time. The investigation was just a manhunt.

But Knight was nevertheless fearful that another killing might be coming. He'd taken to studying the Olympic schedule at all hours of the night, trying to anticipate where Cronus might strike again. It would be somewhere high-profile, he figured, with intense media coverage, as there was here in the aquatics center, where Pierce was trying to become the oldest woman ever to win the platform competition.

The American diver hoisted herself from the

pool, grabbed a towel, and ran over to slap the outstretched hands of her children before heading toward the Jacuzzi to keep her muscles supple. Before she got there, a roar went up at the scores that flashed on the board: all high eights and nines. Pierce had just moved herself into the silver medal position.

Knight clapped again, with more enthusiasm. The London games needed a feel-good story to counteract the pall Cronus had cast over them, and this was it. Pierce was defying her age, the odds, and the murders. Indeed, she'd become something of a spokesman for the US team, decrying Cronus in the wake of Teeter's death. And now here she was, within striking distance of gold.

I am damn lucky to be here, Knight thought. *Despite everything, I'm lucky in many ways, especially to have found that Marta.*

The woman felt like a gift from on high. His kids were different creatures around her, as if she were the Pied Piper or something. Luke was even talking about using the "big-boy loo." And she was incredibly professional. His house had never looked so organized and clean. All in all, it was as if a great weight had been lifted from his shoulders, freeing him to hunt for the madman stalking the Olympics.

At the same time, however, his mother had begun to retreat into her old, pre–Denton Marshall ways. She'd opted to hold a memorial for Denton after the Olympics, and then disappeared into her work. And there was a bitterness creeping into her voice every time Knight talked to her.

"Do you ever answer your cell, Knight?" Karen Pope complained.

Knight started and looked over, surprised to see the reporter standing next to him in the entryway. "I've been having problems with it, actually," he said.

That was true. For the past day, there'd been an odd static in the connection during Knight's calls, but he had not had time to have the phone looked at.

"Get a new phone, then," Pope snapped. "I'm under a lot of pressure to produce and I need your help."

"Looks to me like you're doing just fine on your own," Knight said.

Indeed, in addition to the story about the things found on Farrell's home computer, she'd published an article that detailed the results of Teeter's autopsy: he'd been given a cocktail not of poison but of drugs designed to radically raise the shot-putter's blood pressure and heart rate, which had resulted in a hemorrhage of his pulmonary artery, hence the bloody foam Knight had seen at his lips.

In the same story, Pope had gotten the inside scoop from Mike Lancer, who explained how Farrell must have isolated a flaw in the Olympic IT system, which allowed her a gateway into the games' server and the scoreboard.

Lancer said the flaw had been isolated and fixed and all volunteers were being doubly scrutinized. Lancer also revealed that security cameras caught a woman wearing a Games Masters uniform handing Teeter a bottle of water shortly before the Parade of Nations, but she'd been wearing one of the hats given to volunteers, which had hidden her face.

"Please, Knight," Pope pleaded. "I need something here."

"You know more than I do," he replied, watching as the Panamanian in third place made an over-rotation on her last dive, costing her critical points.

Then the South Korean athlete in first place faltered. Her jump lacked snap and it affected the entire trajectory of her dive, resulting in a mediocre score.

The door was wide open for Pierce now. Knight could not take his binoculars off the American doctor as she began to climb to the top of the diving tower for her fifth and final dive.

Pope poked him in the arm and said, "Someone told me that Inspector Pottersfield is your sister-in-law. You have to know things that I don't."

"Elaine does not talk to me unless she absolutely has to," Knight said, lowering his binoculars.

"Why's that?" Pope asked, skeptically.

"Because she thinks I'm responsible for my wife's death."

CHAPTER 52

KNIGHT WATCHED PIERCE reach the three-story-high platform, and then glanced over at Pope to find the reporter shocked.

"Were you? Responsible?" she asked.

Knight sighed. "Kate had problems during the pregnancy, but wanted to deliver naturally and at home. I knew the risks—we both knew the risks—but I deferred to her. If she'd been in the hospital, she would have lived. I'll wrestle with that the rest of my life, because Elaine Pottersfield won't let me forget it."

Knight's admission confused and saddened Pope. "Anyone ever tell you you're a complicated guy?"

He did not reply. He was transfixed by Pierce,

praying that she'd pull it off. He'd never been a huge sports fan, but this felt...well, monumental for some reason. Here she was, thirty-eight, a widow and a mother of three, about to make her fifth and final dive, the most difficult in her repertoire.

At stake: Olympic gold.

But Pierce looked cool as she settled and then took two quick strides to the edge of the platform. She leaped out and up into the pike position. She flipped back toward the platform in a gainer, twisted, and then somersaulted twice more before knifing into the water.

The crowd exploded. Pierce's son and daughters began dancing and hugging each other.

"She did it!" Knight cried, and felt tears in his eyes. He also felt confusion: why was he getting so emotional about this?

He couldn't answer the question, but he had goose bumps as he watched Pierce run to her children amid applause that turned deafening when the scores went up, confirming her gold medal win.

"Okay, so she won," Pope said snippily. "Please, Knight. Help a girl out."

Knight got a foul look about him as he yanked out his phone. "I've got a copy of the complete inventory of items they found at Farrell's flat and her office."

Pope's eyes got wide. Then she said, "Thanks, Knight. I owe you."

"Don't mention it."

"It is over, then, really," Pope said, with more than a little sadness in her voice. "Just a manhunt from here on out. With all the beefed-up security, it would be impossible for Farrell to strike again. I mean, right?"

Knight nodded as he watched Pierce holding her children, smiling through her tears, and felt thoroughly satisfied. Some kind of balance had been achieved with the American diver's performance.

Of course, other athletes had already shown remarkable fortitude in the last four days of competition. A swimmer from Australia came back from a shattered right leg last year to win gold in the men's four-hundred-meter freestyle race. A flyweight boxer from Niger, raised in abject poverty and subjected to long periods of malnourishment, had somehow developed a lion's heart that had allowed him to win his first two matches with first-round knockouts.

But Pierce's story and her vocal defiance of Cronus seemed to echo and magnify what continued to be right with the modern Olympic Games.

The doctor had shown grace under incredible pressure. She'd shaken off Teeter's death and won. As a result, the games no longer felt as tainted. At least to Knight.

Then his cell phone rang. It was Hooligan.

"What do you know that I don't, mate?" Knight asked in an upbeat voice, provoking a sneer from Pope.

"Those skin cells we found in the second letter?" Hooligan said, sounding shaken. "For three days, I get no match. But then, through an old friend from MI5, I access a NATO database in Brussels, and I get a hit, a mind-boggling hit."

Knight's happiness over Pierce's win subsided, and he turned away from Pope, saying, "Tell me."

"The DNA matches a hair sample taken in the mid-1990s as part of a drug screening test given to people applying as consultants to the NATO peacekeeping contingent that went to the Balkans to enforce the cease-fire."

Knight was confused. Farrell had been in the Balkans at some point in the 1990s. But Hooligan had said his initial examination indicated the skin cells in the second letter from Cronus belonged to a male.

"Whose DNA is it?" Knight demanded.

"Indiana Jones," Hooligan said, sounding very disappointed. "Indiana fuggin' Jones."

CHAPTER 53

FIVE MILES AWAY, in Greenwich, Petra and Teagan walked under leaden skies toward the security gate of the O2 arena, an ultramodern white-domed structure several hundred yards south of the Thames. The dome was perforated by and trussed to yellow support beams that held the roof in place. The O2 sits at the north end of a peninsula and normally plays host to concerts and large theatrical productions. But for the Olympics, it had been transformed into the gymnastics venue and re-named the North Greenwich Arena.

Petra and Teagan were dressed in official Games Masters uniforms, and carried official credentials that identified them as recruited and vetted volunteers for that evening's most anticipated event: the women's team gymnastics final.

Teagan looked grim, focused, and determined as they walked toward the line of volunteers and concessionaires waiting to clear security. But Petra appeared uncertain, and she was walking with a hesitant gait.

"I said I was sorry," Petra said.

Teagan said icily, "Hardly the actions of a superior being."

"My mind was elsewhere," her sister replied.

"Where else could you possibly be? This is the moment we've waited for!"

Petra hesitated before complaining in a whisper, "This isn't like the other tasks Cronus has given us. It feels like a suicide mission. The end of two Furies."

Teagan halted and glared at her sister. "First the letter and now doubts?"

Petra hardened. "What if we get caught?"

"We won't."

"But—"

Teagan cut her off, asking archly, "Do you honestly want me to call Cronus and say that now, at the last minute, you are leaving this to me? Do you really want to provoke him like that?"

Petra blinked and then her face twisted in alarm.

"No, no. I never said anything like that. Please. I'll…I'll do it." She straightened and brushed her jacket with her fingers. "A moment of doubt," Petra added. "That's all. Nothing more than that. Even superior beings entertain doubt, sister."

"No, they don't," said Teagan. "Impetuous"—wasn't that how Cronus had described her younger sister?

Some of that was definitely true. Petra had only just proved it, hadn't she?

As they'd waited on a sidewalk near King's College, their only stop on the way to the gymnastics venue, the youngest of the Furies had forgotten to keep her gloves on when getting out the latest letter to Pope. Teagan had gone over the package with a disposable wipe, and then held it with the wipe until she could give the envelope over to a stoned bicycle messenger, who barely noticed them in their fat-women disguises.

As if in reaction to the same memory, Petra raised her chin toward Teagan. "I know who I am, sister. I know what fate holds for me. I'm clear about that now."

Teagan hesitated, but then gestured to Petra to lead. Despite her sister's doubts, Teagan felt nothing but waves of certainty and pleasure. Drugging a man to death was one thing, but there was no substitute for looking the person you were about to kill in the eye, showing that person your power.

It had been years since that had happened—since Bosnia, in fact. What she had done back then should have been fuel for nightmares, but it wasn't that way for Teagan.

She often dreamed of the men and boys she'd executed in the wake of her parents' death and the gang rape. Those bloody dreams were Teagan's favorites, true fantasies that she enjoyed reliving again and again.

Teagan smiled, thinking that the acts she would commit tonight would ensure that she'd have a new dream for years to come, something to celebrate in the dark, something to cling to when times got rough.

At last they reached the X-ray screeners. Stone-faced Gurkhas armed with automatic weapons flanked the checkpoint, and for a moment Teagan feared Petra might balk and retreat at the show of force.

But her sister acted like a pro and handed her identification to the guard, who ran her badge through a reader and checked her face against computer records that identified her as Caroline Thorson. Those same records indicated that she was a diabetic and therefore cleared to bring an insulin kit into the venue.

The guard pointed to a gray plastic tub. "Insulin kit and anything metal in there. Jewelry, too," he said, gesturing to the pitted silver ring she wore.

Petra smiled, tugged the ring off, and set it beside the insulin kit in the tray. She walked through the metal detectors without incident.

Teagan took off a ring identical to her sister's and put it in the tray after her credentials checked out. "Same ring?" the guard said.

Teagan smiled and gestured toward Petra. "We're cousins. The rings were presents from our grandmum, who loved the Olympics. The poor dear passed on last year. We're wearing them in her honor to every event we work."

"That's nice," he said, and waved her through.

CHAPTER 54

THE *ORBIT'S* OBSERVATION deck revolved slowly clockwise, offering a panoramic view of the interior of the Olympic stadium, where several athletes and coaches were inspecting the track, and of the aquatics center, which Knight had only just left.

Standing at the deck's railing in a cooling east wind, which scudded clouds across a leaden sky, Mike Lancer squinted at Knight and said, "You mean the television guy?"

"And Greek antiquities curator at the British Museum."

Jack said, "Does Scotland Yard know about this yet?"

Knight had rushed over to join them after he had called Jack and been told that he and Lancer were up in the *Orbit*, inspecting security on the Olympic flame. Knight nodded to Jack's question and said, "I just spoke with Elaine Pottersfield. She has squads en route to the museum and to his house."

For several moments there was silence, and all Knight was really aware of was the odor of carbon in the air, given off by the Olympic cauldron, which was burning on the roof above them.

"How do we know for sure Daring has gone missing?" Jack asked.

Knight replied, "I called his secretary before I called Elaine, and she told me that the last time anyone saw Daring was last Thursday night around ten o'clock, as he was leaving his exhibit's opening reception. That was probably six hours after Selena Farrell was last seen as well."

Lancer shook his head. "Did you see that coming, Peter? That they could have been in on it together?"

"I didn't even consider the possibility," Knight admitted. "But they both served with NATO in the Balkans during the nineties, they both had issues with the modern Olympic Games, and there's no denying DNA results."

Lancer said, "Now that we know who they are, it's only a matter of time until they're caught."

"Unless they manage to strike again before they're caught," Jack said.

The LOCOG security adviser blanched, puffed out his lips, and exhaled in worry. "Where? That's the question I keep asking myself."

"Somewhere big," Knight said. "They killed during the opening ceremonies because it gave them a world audience."

Jack said, "Okay, so what's the biggest event left?"

Lancer shrugged. "The sprints have drawn the most interest. Millions of people applied for seats in the stadium this coming Sunday evening, the finals of the men's hundred-meter sprint, because of the possibility of a showdown between Zeke Shaw and Filatri Mundaho."

"What about today or tomorrow? What's the ticket everyone wants?" Knight asked.

"Has to be women's gymnastics, I'd think," Jack said. "Carries the biggest television audience in the States, anyway."

Lancer glanced at his watch and reacted as though his stomach had just soured. "The women's team final starts in less than an hour."

Anxiety coiled through Knight as he said, "If I

were Cronus, and wanted to make a big statement, women's gymnastics *is* where I'd attack next."

Lancer grimaced and started heading for the elevator, saying, "I hate to say it, but I think you may be right, Peter."

"What's the fastest way to the gymnastics venue?" Jack demanded, hustling after the LOCOG member.

"Blackwall Tunnel," Knight said.

"No," Lancer said. "Scotland Yard's got them closed during the competitions to prevent a possible car bombing. We'll go by river bus."

CHAPTER 55

AFTER CHECKING IN with Petra's immediate supervisors, the sisters scouted out the seats for which she would act as usher. They were low and at the north end of the arena, just off the floor in the area where the vaulting competition would take place. Teagan left her sister at that point and found the hospitality suite she'd been assigned to as a waitress. She told her team leader there that she would return after a quick trip to the loo.

Petra was waiting. They took stalls next to each other.

Teagan opened the seat-cover dispenser in her stall and retrieved two slender green CO_2 canisters and two plastic tweezers that had been taped there.

She kept one canister and one pair of tweezers

and handed the others under the partition that separated the stalls. In return, Petra handed Teagan two tiny darts, not even the length of a bee's stinger, the miniature plastic vanes of which were glued to tiny insulin needles and stuck to a small strip of duct tape.

Next came a six-inch length of thin clear plastic tubing with miniature pipe-fitting hardware at either end. Teagan took off her ring, then screwed the male fitting into one of the silver pits on the back of the ring.

Satisfied with the connection, she unscrewed it and coiled the line back to where she'd attached the CO_2 cartridge. She taped the cartridge and coiled gas line to her forearm, and then slid on the ring.

She'd no sooner finished than Petra pushed the vial from the insulin kit under the partition. Teagan used the tweezers to grab one of the darts. She stuck the tip through the rubber gasket into the vial and the liquid, drew it out, and inserted it, vane first, into a tiny hole on her ring opposite the gas connection.

After dipping the second tiny dart, she blew on it until the liquid dried, and then stuck it ever so carefully into the lapel of her uniform in case she needed a second shot. With utmost care, she drew down her blouse sleeve before flushing and leaving the stall.

Petra appeared as Teagan washed her hands. She smiled uncertainly at her older sister, but then whispered, "Aim twice."

"Shoot once," Teagan said, thinking that this felt like part of a dream already. "Do you have your bees?"

"I do."

CHAPTER 56

UNDER A SPITTING rain, an unseasonable fog crept west up the Thames to meet the river bus as it sped past the Isle of Dogs, heading toward the Greenwich Peninsula and the Queen Elizabeth II Pier. The boat was packed with latecomers holding tickets to the team gymnastics finals, which were just a few minutes from starting.

Knight's attention, however, was not on the other passengers; it roved off the bow of the ferry, looking toward the brilliantly lit O_2 dome coming closer, feeling strongly that it could be the scene of Farrell and Daring's next strike.

Beside him, Lancer was talking insistently on his phone, explaining that he was on the way with reinforcements to the security detail, which he ordered on highest alert. He had already called Scotland Yard's Marine Policing Unit and been told a patrol boat was anchored off the back of the arena.

"There it is," Jack said, pointing through the mist at a large, rigid, inflatable craft with dual outboard engines bobbing in the water south of them as they rounded the head of the peninsula.

Five officers in black slickers, carrying automatic weapons, stood in the boat, watching them. A single officer, a woman in a dry suit, rode an ultraquiet black Jet Ski that trailed the river bus into the dock.

"Those are primo counterterror vessels, especially that Jet Ski," Jack said in admiration. "No chance of entry or escape by water with those suckers around."

Security around the arena itself was just as tight. There were ten-foot-high fences around the venue, at which armed Gurkhas were stationed every fifty yards. The screening process was brutal. There was still a long line waiting to get in. Without Lancer it would have taken them at least a half hour to clear the scanners. But he'd gotten them inside in less than five minutes.

"What are we looking for?" Knight asked as they heard applause from the entryway in front of them and a woman's voice on the public-address system announcing the first rotation of the women's team finals.

"Anything out of the ordinary," Lancer said. "Absolutely anything."

"When was the last time dogs swept the building?" Jack asked.

"Three hours ago," Lancer said.

"I'd bring them back," Jack said as they emerged into the arena itself. "Are you monitoring cell service?"

"We jammed it," Lancer said. "We figured it was easier."

While LOCOG's security chief gave orders over his radio to recall the canine bomb squad, Knight and Jack scanned the arena floor, seeing teams lining up near individual pieces of gymnastics apparatus.

The Chinese were at the south end of the venue, preparing to compete on the uneven parallel bars. Beyond, the Russians stretched by the balance beam. The UK contingent, which had performed remarkably well in the qualifying rounds, thanks to gutsy performances by star gymnast Nessa Kemp, was arranging gear near the floor-exercise mat. At the far end of the arena, the Americans prepared to vault. Guards, many of them Gurkhas as well, stood at posts about the floor, facing away from the competitors so they could scan the crowd with zero distraction.

Knight concluded that an attack on one of the athletes down on the floor was virtually impossible.

But what about their safety back in the locker rooms? Or on the way to and from the athletes' village?

Would the next target even be an athlete?

CHAPTER 57

AT SIX FIFTEEN that Tuesday evening, the last of the Chinese gymnasts stuck her dismount off the balance beam, landing on her feet with nary a bobble.

The crowd inside the Chinese Gymnastics Association's luxury box high in the arena roared with delight. With one round to go, their team was winning handsomely. The Brits were a surprising second, and the Americans sat solidly in third. The Russians had unexpectedly imploded and were a distant fourth.

Amid the celebration, Teagan set her drinks tray on the bar and then dropped a pen on purpose. She squatted and in seconds had the thin gas line running along her wrist, up across her palm, past her pinkie finger, and attached to the back of the ring.

She stood to smile at the bartender. "I'm going to bus glasses a bit."

He nodded and returned to pouring wine. As the Chinese team moved to the vaulting area, Teagan's senses were on fire. She moved through the crowded luxury box toward a stocky woman in a gray suit watching at the window.

Her name was Win Bo Lee. She was chairwoman of the national committee of the Chinese Gymnastics Association, or CGA. She was also, in her own way, as corrupt as Paul Teeter and Sir Denton Marshall had been. *Cronus was right,* Teagan thought. *People like Win Bo Lee deserved exposure and death.*

As she neared the woman, Teagan held her right arm low and by her waist while her left hand slipped into the pocket of her uniform and felt something small and bristly there. When the distance between her and Win Bo Lee was less than two feet, she snapped her hand sharply upward and squeezed the right side of the ring with her pinkie.

With an airy spitting noise rendered inaudible by the joyous conversations in the hospitality suite, the tiny dart flew and stuck the back of Win Bo Lee's neck. The CGA's chairwoman jerked and cursed. She tried to reach around the back of her neck. But before she could, Teagan slapped her there, dislodging the dart, which fell to the floor. She crushed it with her shoe.

Win Bo Lee twisted around angrily and glared at Teagan, who looked deeply into her victim's eyes, savoring them, imprinting them in her memory, and then said, "I got it."

She crouched down before the Chinese woman could reply, and acted as if she were picking something up with her left hand. She stood and showed Win Bo Lee a dead bee.

"It's summer," Teagan said. "Somehow they get in here."

Win Bo Lee stared at the bee, and then up at Teagan, cooling her temper, and said, "You are quick, but not quicker than that bee. It stung me hard!"

"A thousand pardons," Teagan said. "Would you like some ice?"

The CGA chairwoman nodded as she reached around to massage her neck.

"I'll get you some," Teagan said.

She cleared the table in front of the CGA chairwoman, took one last look into Win Bo Lee's eyes, and then dropped the glasses at the bar. Heading toward the exit with no intention of returning, Teagan was already replaying every moment of her quiet attack as if it were a slow-motion video on a highlights reel.

CHAPTER 58

I AM SUPERIOR, Petra told herself as she moved parallel to the vault area along the railing and toward the Gurkha with the thin black mustache. *I am not like them. I am a weapon of vengeance, a weapon of cleansing.*

She carried a stack of towels that hid her right hand when she smiled at the Gurkha with the mustache and said, "For the vault station."

He nodded. It was the third time the fat woman had brought towels to the pit, so he didn't bother to go through them.

I am superior, Petra said over and over in her mind. And then, as it had when she was a young girl, during the rape and the killings, everything seemed to move in a strangely silent and slow-motion way for her. In this altered state, she spotted her quarry: a slight man in a red zip-up sweatshirt and white pants who was starting to pace as the first Chinese woman adjusted the springboard and prepared to vault.

Gao Ping was head coach of the Chinese women's gymnastics team and a known pacer in big competitions. Petra had seen that behavior in several films she'd studied of Ping, a demonstrative, high-energy man who liked to goad his athletes into delivering big performances. He was also a coach who had committed repeated crimes against the Olympic ideals, thereby sealing his fate.

The assistant coach, a woman named An Wu—no less a criminal herself—had taken a seat, her face as emotionless as Ping's was antic. An Wu was an easier target than the ever-moving head coach. But Cronus had ordered Petra to take Ping first, and the assistant coach only if the opportunity arose.

Petra slowed in order to time her movement to Ping's pacing. She handed the towels over the rail to another Games Master, and moved at an angle to the Chinese coach, who was bent over, exhorting his tiny athlete to greatness.

The first Chinese girl took off down the runway. Ping took two skipping steps after her, and then stopped right in front of Petra, no more than eight feet away.

She rested her hand on the rail, intent on the head coach's neck. When the Chinese girl hit the springboard, Petra fired.

I am a superior being, she thought as the dart hit Ping.

Superior in every way.

CHAPTER 59

THE CHINESE COACH slapped at the back of his neck just before his athlete nailed her landing and a roar went up from the crowd. Ping winced and looked around, bewildered by what had happened. Then he shook the sting off and ran, clapping, toward his vaulter, who beamed and shook her hands over her head.

"That little girl crushed that," Jack said.

"Did she?" Knight said, lowering his binoculars. "I was watching Ping."

"The Joe Cocker of gymnastics?" Jack remarked.

Knight laughed, but then saw the Chinese coach rubbing at his neck before starting his histrionic ritual all over again as his next athlete got set to vault.

"I think Joe Cocker got stung," Knight said, raising his binoculars again.

"By what, a bee? How can you see that from here?"

"I can't see any bee," Knight said. "But I saw his reaction."

Behind them, Knight heard Lancer talking in a strained voice into his radio, addressing the arena's interior and exterior security forces, fine-tuning how they were going to handle the medal ceremony.

Knight felt uneasy. He raised his binoculars and watched the Chinese coach cheer three more women through their vaults. As his last athlete took off down the runway, Ping jumped and hopped like a voodoo dancer. Even his taciturn assistant, An Wu, got caught up in the moment. She was on her feet, hand across her mouth, as the last girl twisted and somersaulted off the vaulting horse.

An Wu suddenly slapped at her neck as if she'd been stung.

Her athlete stuck her landing perfectly.

The audience erupted. The Chinese had won gold and the UK silver, the highest finish ever for a British Olympic gymnastics team. The coaches and athletes from both nations were celebrating. So were the Americans, who'd taken bronze.

Knight was aware of it all while using his binoculars to scan the raucous crowd cheering and aiming cameras above the vaulting area. With Ping doing a high-step dance and his girls celebrating with him, the attention of virtually everyone at that end of the arena was on the victorious Chinese team.

Except for a heavyset platinum-blond Games Master. She had her back turned to the celebration and was hurrying in an odd gait up the stairs, away from the arena floor. She disappeared into the walkway, heading for the outer halls.

Knight felt suddenly short of breath. He dropped his binoculars and said to Jack and Lancer, "There's something wrong."

"What?" Lancer demanded.

"The Chinese coaches. I saw them both slap at their necks, as if they'd been stung. Ping and then Wu. Right after the assistant coach slapped, I saw a chunky platinum-blond female Games Master hurrying out when everyone else was focused on the Chinese, cheering that last vault."

Jack closed one eye, as if aiming at some distant target.

Lancer pursed his lips. "Two slaps and an overweight usher moving to her post? Nothing more than that?"

"No. It just seemed out of sync with…out of sync, that's all."

Jack asked, "Where did the volunteer go?"

Knight pointed across the arena. "Out the upper exit between sections one fifteen and one sixteen. Fifteen seconds ago. She was moving kind of funny, too."

Lancer picked up his radio and barked into it. "Central, do you have a Games Master, female, platinum-blond hair, heavyset, on camera up there in the hallways off one fifteen?"

Several tense moments passed as Olympic workers moved the medals podium out onto the arena floor.

At last Lancer's radio squawked, "That's a negative."

Knight frowned. "No, she has to be there somewhere. She just left."

Lancer considered him again before calling into his radio: "Tell officers if they see a Games Master in that area, a chubby female with platinum-blond hair, she is to be detained for questioning."

"We might want to get a medic to look at the coaches," Knight said.

Lancer replied, "Athletes frown on being treated

by strangers, but I'll alert the Chinese medical teams at the very least. Does that cover it?"

Knight almost nodded before saying, "Where are those security cameras being monitored?"

Lancer gestured up toward a mirror-faced enclosed seating area in the balcony above them.

"I'm going up there," Knight said. "Get me in?"

CHAPTER 60

PETRA FOUGHT NOT to hyperventilate as she closed the door to the middle stall in the ladies' room just west of the high north entry to the arena. She took a deep breath and felt like screaming with the sense of power surging through her, a power she'd long forgotten.

See? I am a superior being. I have slain monsters. I have meted out vengeance. I am a Fury. And monsters don't catch Furies. Read the myths!

Shaking with adrenaline, Petra ripped off her platinum-blond wig, revealing her ginger hair pinned against her scalp. She dug the plastic barrettes out and let her short locks fall.

Petra reached up and grabbed hold of the outer metal edges of the seat-cover dispenser. She tugged and the entire unit came free of the wall. She set it on the seat, and then reached deep into the dark cavity she'd exposed and came up with a knapsack made of dark blue rubber, a dry bag that contained a change of clothes.

She set the bag on top of the dispenser, stripped out of her volunteer's uniform, and hung it on a peg on the stall door. Then she peeled off the rubber prostheses she'd glued to her hips, belly, and legs to render her chubby. She looked at the dry bag, thinking how much more heavy and cumbersome it would be given their anticipated escape route, and then dropped the rubber prostheses inside the hollow wall along with the wig.

Four minutes later, the seat-cover dispenser back in place and her uniform buried in the dry bag, Petra left the stall.

She washed her hands, assessing her outfit: low blue canvas sneakers, snug white pants, a sleeveless white cotton sweater, a simple gold necklace, and a blue linen blazer. She added a pair of designer eyeglasses with clear lenses and smiled. She could have been any old posh now.

The stall to Petra's immediate right opened.

"Ready?" Petra asked without looking.

"Waiting on you, sister," Teagan said, coming to the mirror beside Petra, her dark wig gone, revealing her sandy blond hair. She was dressed in casual attire and carried a similar knapsack-style dry bag. "Success?"

"Two," Petra said.

Teagan tilted her head in reappraisal. "They'll write myths about you."

"Yes, they will," said Petra with a grin, and together the Furies headed for the ladies'-room door.

Over loudspeakers out in the hall, they heard the arena announcer say, "*Mesdames et messieurs,* ladies and gentlemen, take your seats. The medal ceremonies are about to begin."

CHAPTER 61

KNIGHT'S ATTENTION ROAMED over various images on the split-screen security monitors in front of him, all showing views of the upper hallway off the O2's sections 115 and 116, where fans were hurrying back into the arena.

Two women, one slender with stylish sandy blond hair, and the other equally svelte with short ginger hair, exited the women's bathroom and merged with traffic returning to the inner arena. Knight considered them only briefly, still searching for a brassy, beefy platinum blonde in a Games Master uniform.

But something about the way the redhead had walked when she left the ladies' room nagged at Knight, and he looked back to the feed where he'd seen them. They were gone. Had she been limping? It had looked that way, but she was slender, not fat, and a redhead, not a blonde.

The medal ceremony began with the awarding of the bronze medals. Knight trained his binoculars north from the security station, looking for the redhead and her companion among the fans still hurrying back to their seats.

Knight's efforts were hampered by the announcement of the silver medal to Great Britain. That sent the host-country crowd up on its feet, clapping, whistling, and catcalling. Several men at the north end of the arena unfurled large Union Jacks and waved them about wildly, further obscuring Knight's view.

The flags were still waving when the Chinese team was called to the high spot on the podium. Knight temporarily abandoned the search and looked for the Chinese coaches.

Ping and Wu stood off to the side of the floor-exercise mat beside a short, stocky Chinese woman in her fifties.

"Who is she?" Knight asked one of the men manning the video station.

He looked and replied, "Win Bo Lee. Head of the Chinese Gymnastics Association. Bigwig."

Knight kept his binoculars on Ping and Wu as

the Chinese national anthem began and the country's flag started to rise. He was expecting an emotional outpouring from the Chinese head coach.

To his surprise, however, he thought Ping oddly somber for a man whose team had just won the Olympics. Ping was looking at the ground and rubbing the back of his neck, not gazing at the Chinese flag as it reached the arena rafters.

Knight was about to turn his binoculars north again to look for the two women when Win Bo Lee suddenly wobbled on her feet as if she were dizzy. The assistant coach, Wu, caught her by the elbow and steadied the CGA chairwoman.

The older woman wiped at her nose and looked at her finger. She appeared alarmed and said something to An Wu.

But then Knight's attention was caught by a jerky movement beside the older woman. As the last few bars of the Chinese national anthem played, Ping lurched up onto the floor-exercise mat. The victorious head coach staggered across the floor toward the podium, his left hand clutching his throat and his right reaching to his triumphant team as if they were a rope and he were drowning.

The anthem ended. The Chinese girls looked down from the flag, tears flowing down their cheeks, only to see their agonized coach trip and sprawl onto the mat in front of them.

Several girls started to scream.

Even from halfway across the arena, Knight could see the blood dribbling from Ping's mouth and nose.

CHAPTER 62

BEFORE PARAMEDICS COULD reach the fallen coach, Win Bo Lee complained hysterically of sudden blindness and then collapsed, blood seeping from her mouth, eyes, nose, and ears.

The fans began to grasp what was happening and shouts and cries of disbelief and fear pierced the arena. Many started grabbing their things and heading toward the exits.

Up in the arena's security pod, Knight knew that An Wu, the assistant coach, was in mortal danger, but forced his attention off the drama developing on the arena floor to watch the camera feeds showing the walkway where the two women had entered the arena. The men manning the security station were inundated with radio traffic.

One of them suddenly roared, "We've got an explosion immediately southeast of the venue on the riverbank! Marine unit responding!"

Thank God no one heard the bomb inside the arena, because more fans were moving toward the exits and the sound would have caused a stampede. An Wu suddenly dropped to the floor, bleeding, adding to the terror.

And then, right there on the screen nearest him on the security console, Knight spotted the sandy blonde and the redhead going through the north exit along with a steady flow of other jittery fans.

Though he could not make out their faces, the redhead was definitely limping. "It's her!" Knight shouted.

The men monitoring the security station barely glanced at him as they frantically tried to respond to questions flying at them over radios from all over the arena. Realizing they were being overcome by the rapid pace of developments, Knight bolted for the door, wrenched it open, and started pushing past shocked fans, hoping to intercept the women.

But which way had they gone? East or west?

Knight decided they'd head for the exit closest to transportation, and therefore ran down the west hallway, searching among the stream of people coming at him until he heard Jack shout, "Knight!"

He glanced to his right and saw Private's owner hustling out of the inner arena.

"I've got them!" Knight cried. "Two women, a sandy blonde and a redhead. She's limping! Call Lancer. Have him seal the perimeter."

Jack ran with him, trying to dial his phone while weaving through the crowd trying to leave.

"Damn it!" Jack exclaimed. "They're jamming cell service!"

"Then it's up to us," Knight grunted. He accelerated, determined that the two women would not get away.

In moments they reached the section of the north hallway he'd watched on camera. There was no way they had gotten by him, Knight thought, cursing himself for not taking the east hallway. But then, suddenly, he caught a glimpse of them several hundred feet ahead, two women going out through a fire-exit door.

"Got them!" Knight roared, throwing up his badge and yanking out his Beretta. He shot twice into the ceiling and bellowed, "Everyone down!"

It was as if Moses had parted the Red Sea. Olympic fans began diving to the cement floor and trying to shield themselves from Knight and Jack, who sprinted toward the fire exit. And that's when Knight understood.

"They're going for the river!" he cried. "They set off a bomb as a diversion to pull the marine unit off the arena!"

Then the lights flickered and died, throwing the entire gymnastics venue into pitch darkness.

CHAPTER 63

KNIGHT SKIDDED TO a halt in the blackness, feeling like he was teetering at the edge of a cliff and struck with vertigo. People were screaming everywhere around him as he dug out a penlight on the key chain he always carried. He snapped it on just as battery-powered red emergency lights started to glow.

He and Jack sprinted the last seventy feet to the fire exit and tried to shoulder the door open. Locked. Knight shot the lock, provoking new chaos among the terrified fans, but the door flew open when they kicked it.

They hurtled down the stairs and found themselves above the arena's loading dock, which was clogged with media production trucks and other support machinery for the venue. Red lights had gone on here as well, but Knight could not spot the pair of escaping women at first because there were so many people moving around below them, shouting, demanding to know what had happened.

Then he saw them, disappearing through an open door at the northeast end of the arena. Knight barreled down the staircase, dodged irate broadcasting personnel, and spotted a security guard standing at the exit.

Knight held up his badge and gasped, "Two women. Where did they go?"

The guard looked at him in confusion. "What women? I was—"

Knight pushed past him and ran outside. Every light at the north end of the peninsula was dead, but thunder boomed and lightning cracked all around, giving them flashes of glaring vision.

The unseasonable fog swirled. The rain was pelting. Knight had to throw up a forearm to shield his eyes. When the next flashes of lightning came, he peered along the nine-foot-high chain-link fence that separated the arena from a path along the Thames, which led east and south to the river bus pier.

The blond Fury was crouched on the ground

on the other side of the fence. The redhead had cleared the top and was climbing down.

Knight raised his gun, but it all went dark again and his penlight was no match for the night and the storm.

"I saw them," Jack grunted.

"I did, too," Knight said.

But rather than go straight after the two women, Knight ran to the fence where it was closest, pocketing the light and stuffing the gun into the back of his pants. He clambered up the fence and jumped off the top.

It had been five days since he'd been run over, but Knight's sore ribs still made him hiss with pain when he landed on the paved path. To his left, still well out on the water, he spotted the next river bus coming.

Jack landed beside Knight and together they raced toward the pier, which was lit by several soft red emergency lights. They slowed less than twenty yards from the ramp that led down onto the pier itself. Two Gurkhas lay dead on the ground, their throats slit from ear to ear.

Rain drummed on the surface of the dock. The river bus's engines growled louder as it approached. But then Knight swore he heard another engine start up.

Jack heard it, too. "They've got a boat!"

Knight vaulted the chain that was strung across the entrance to the ramp and ran down onto the dock, sweeping his gun and penlight from side to side, looking for movement.

A Metropolitan Police officer, the woman who'd been riding the Jet Ski, lay dead on the pier, eyes bulging, her neck at an unnatural angle. Knight ran past her to the edge of the dock, hearing an outboard motor starting to accelerate in the fog and rain.

He noticed the officer's Jet Ski tied to the pier, ran to it, saw the key in the ignition, jumped on, and started it while Jack grabbed the officer's radio and got on behind Knight, calling, "This is Jack Morgan with Private. Metropolitan Police Marine Policing Unit officer dead on Queen Elizabeth Two Pier. We are in pursuit of killers on the river. Repeat: we are in pursuit of killers on the river."

Knight twisted the throttle. The vehicle leaped away from the pier, making almost no noise, and in seconds they were deep into the fog.

The mist was thick, reducing visibility to less than thirty feet, and the water was choppy, with a strong current drawn east by the ebbing tide. Radio traffic crackled on Jack's radio in response to his call.

But he did not answer, and turned down the volume so they could better hear the outboard coughing somewhere ahead of them in the fog. Knight noticed a digital compass on the dashboard of the Jet Ski.

The outboard was heading north by northeast, toward the midchannel of the Thames, at a slow speed, probably because of the poor visibility. Feeling confident that he could catch them now, Knight hit the throttle hard and prayed they did not slam into anything. Were there buoys out here? There had to be. Halfway across the river, he spotted the blinking lighthouse at Trinity Buoy Wharf.

"They're heading toward the River Lea," Knight cried over his shoulder. "It goes back through Olympic Park."

"Killers heading toward mouth of River Lea," Jack barked into the radio.

They heard sirens wailing from both banks of the Thames now, and then the outboard motor went full throttle. The fog cleared a bit, and no more than one hundred yards ahead of them on the river Knight spotted the racing shadow of a bow rider with its lights extinguished. He heard its engine screaming.

Knight mashed his throttle to close the gap at the same moment he realized that the escape boat wasn't heading toward the mouth of the Lea at all; it was off by several degrees, speeding straight at the high cement retaining wall on the east side of the confluence.

"They're going to hit!" Jack yelled.

Knight let go of the throttle of the Jet Ski a split second before the speedboat smacked the wall dead-on and exploded in a series of blasts that mushroomed into fireballs and flares that licked and seared the rain and the fog.

Debris and shrapnel rained, forcing Knight and Jack to retreat, never hearing the light chop of three swimmers crawling eastward with the ebbing tide.

CHAPTER 64

THE STORM HAD passed and it was four in the morning by the time Knight climbed into a taxi and gave the driver his address in Chelsea.

Dazed, damp, and running on fumes, his mind nevertheless raced wildly with all that had happened since the Furies ran their boat into the river wall.

There were divers in the water within a half hour of the crash, searching for bodies, though the extreme tidal currents were hampering their efforts.

Elaine Pottersfield had been called off the search

of James Daring's office and apartment, and came to the O2 as part of a huge Scotland Yard team that arrived in the wake of the triple murder.

She'd debriefed Knight and Jack, and then spoke with Lancer, who'd been rushing to the arena floor when the lights went out and the venue erupted in chaos. The former decathlon champion had had the presence of mind to order the perimeter of the arena sealed after he'd heard Knight's shots in the hallway, but the order had not come in time to prevent the Furies' escape.

When Lancer ordered electricians to get the lights back on, they found that a simple timer-and-breaker system had been attached to the venue's main power line, and that the relay that triggered the backup generators had been disabled. Power was restored within thirty minutes, however, which enabled Knight and Pottersfield to closely study the security video while Lancer and Jack went to help screen the literally thousands of witnesses to the triple slayings.

To their dismay, the video of the two Furies showed little of their faces. The women seemed to know exactly when to turn one way or another, depending on the camera angles. Knight remembered spotting the two women leaving the ladies' room after the chubby Games Master disappeared and before the medal ceremony began, and said, "They had to have switched disguises in there."

He and Pottersfield went to search the bathroom. On the way, his sister-in-law said she'd found flute music on Daring's home computer as well as essays—tirades, really—that damned the commercial and corporate aspects of the modern Olympics. In at least two instances, the television star and museum curator had remarked that the kinds of corruption and cheating that went on in the modern Olympics would have been dealt with swiftly during the old games.

"He said the gods on Olympus would have struck them down one by one," Pottersfield said as they entered the ladies' room. "He said their deaths would have been a 'just sacrifice.'"

Just sacrifice? Knight thought bitterly. *Three people dead. For what?*

As he and Pottersfield searched the bathroom, he wondered why Pope had not called him. She must have gotten another letter by now.

Twenty minutes into the search, Knight found the loose seat-cover dispenser and tugged it out of the wall. A minute later, he fished out a platinum-blond wig from inside, handed it to Pottersfield, and said, "There's a big mistake. There has to be DNA evidence on that."

The chief inspector grudgingly slipped the wig into an evidence bag. "Well done, Peter, but I'd rather that no one else knows about this, at least until I can have it analyzed. And most certainly not your client, Karen Pope."

"Not a soul," he'd promised.

Indeed, around three that morning, shortly before Knight left the O2, he'd found Jack again and not mentioned the wig. Private's owner informed him, however, that a guard at the gate where all Games Master volunteers cleared security distinctly remembered the two chunky cousins who came through the scanners early, one with diabetes, both wearing identical rings.

The computer system identified them as Caroline and Anita Thorson, cousins who lived north of Liverpool Street. Police dispatched to the flat found Caroline and Anita Thorson, but both women were sleeping. They claimed not to have been anywhere near the O2, much less having been accredited Games Masters at the Olympics. They were being brought to New Scotland Yard for further questioning, though Knight did not hold much hope for a breakthrough there. The Thorson women had been used, their identities stolen.

The taxi pulled up in front of Knight's house just before dawn. Knight figured that Cronus or one of his Furies was a very sophisticated hacker and that they had to have had access at some point to the arena's electrical infrastructure.

Right?

He was so damn tired that he couldn't even answer his own question. He paid the driver and told him to wait. Knight trudged to his front door, went in, and turned on the hallway light. He heard a creaking noise and looked in the playroom. Marta yawned on the couch, dropping the blanket from her shoulders.

"I'm so sorry," Knight said softly. "I was at the gymnastics venue and they were jamming cell service. I couldn't get through."

Her hand went to her mouth. "I saw it on the television. You were there? Did they catch them?"

"No," he said in utter disgust. "We don't even know if they're alive or not. But they've made a big mistake. If they're alive, they'll be caught."

She yawned again, wider this time, and said, "What mistake?"

"I can't get into it," Knight replied. "There's a taxi out front waiting for you. I've already paid."

Marta smiled drowsily. "You're very kind, Mr. Knight."

"Call me Peter. When can you be back?"

"One?"

Knight nodded. Nine hours. He'd be lucky to get four hours of sleep before the twins awoke, but it was better than nothing.

As if she were reading his mind, Marta headed toward the door, saying, "Isabel and Luke were both very, very tired tonight. I think they'll sleep in for you."

CHAPTER 65

SHORTLY AFTER DAWN that morning, racked with a headache that feels like my skull is being axed in two, I thunder at Marta: "What mistake?"

Her eyes exude the same dead quality I'd first seen the night I rescued her in Bosnia. "I don't know, Cronus," she says. "He wouldn't tell me."

I look around wildly at the other two sisters. "What mistake?"

Teagan shakes her head. "There was no mistake. Everything went exactly according to plan. Petra even got off the second shot on Wu."

"I did," Petra says, looking at me with an expression that borders on delirium. "I was superior, Cronus. A champion. No one could have executed better. And on the river, we jumped off the boat

271

well before the wall and timed the tides on the money. We were a perfect ten in all aspects."

Marta nods. "I was back at Knight's home almost two hours before he came in. We've won, Cronus. They'll shut down the Olympics now for sure."

I shake my head. "Not even close. The corporate sponsors and the broadcasters won't let them stop until it's too late."

But what mistake could we have made?

I look at Teagan. "What about the factory?"

"I left it sealed tight."

"Go check," I say. "Make sure." Then I go to a chair by the window, wondering again what error we could have made. My mind rips through dozens of possibilities, but the truth is that my information is incomplete. I can't devise countermeasures if I do not know the nature of this supposed error.

Finally I glare at Marta. "Find out. I don't care what you have to do. Find out what the mistake is."

CHAPTER 66

AT TWENTY TO noon that same Wednesday, Knight pushed Isabel in the swing at the playground at the Royal Hospital. Luke had figured out the swing on his own, and was pumping wildly with his feet and hands, trying to get higher and higher. Knight kept gently slowing him down.

"Daddy!" Luke yelled in frustration. "Lukey goes up!"

"Not so up," Knight said. "You'll fall out and crack your head."

"No, Daddy," Luke grumbled.

Isabel laughed. "Lukey already has a cracked head!"

That did not go over well. Knight had to take them off the swings and separate them, Isabel in the sandbox and Luke on the jungle gym. When they'd finally become absorbed in their play, he yawned, checked his watch—another hour and a quarter until Marta was scheduled to return—and went to the bench, where he'd been using his iPad to track the news coverage.

The country, and indeed the entire world, was in an uproar over the slayings of Gao Ping, An Wu, and Win Bo Lee. Heads of state around the globe were condemning Cronus, the Furies, and their brutal tactics. So were athletes.

Knight clicked on a hyperlink that led him to a BBC news video. It began with reaction to the killings of the Chinese coaches, and featured parents of athletes from Spain, Russia, and Ukraine who fretted about security and wondered whether to dash their children's dreams and insist they leave. The Chinese had protested vigorously to the International Olympic Committee, and issued a press release stating their frustration that the host nation seemed unable to provide a safe venue for the games—which the Chinese had been able to do four years before in Beijing.

But the BBC story then tried to lay blame for the security breaches. There were plenty of targets, including F7, the corporate security firm hired to run the surveillance equipment at the venues. An

F7 spokesman vigorously defended their operation, calling it state of the art and run by "the most qualified people in the business." The BBC piece also noted that the computer security system had been designed by representatives of Scotland Yard and MI5, and had been touted as "impenetrable" and "unbeatable" prior to the start of the games. But neither law enforcement entity was responding to questions about what were obviously serious breaches.

That left the focus on "an embattled Mike Lancer," who'd faced the cameras after several members of Parliament called for him to step down or be fired.

"I'm not one to dodge blame when it's warranted," Lancer said, sounding alternately angry and grief-stricken. "These terrorists have managed to find cracks in our system that we could not see. Let me assure the public that we are doing everything in our power to plug these cracks, and I know Scotland Yard, MI5, F7, and Private are doing everything they can to find these murderers and stop them before any other tragedy can befall what should rightly be a global celebration of youth and renewal."

In response to the calls for Lancer's head, LOCOG chairman Marcus Morris was playing the stiff-upper-lip Brit, adamantly opposed to giving ground to Cronus, and positive that Lancer and the web of UK security forces in place would prevent further attacks, find the killers, and bring them to justice.

Despite the overall gloomy tone of the piece, the video closed on something of a positive note. The scene was the athletes' village, where shortly after dawn hundreds of athletes poured out onto the lawns and sidewalks. They burned candles in memory of the slain. American diver Hunter Pierce, Cameroonian sprinter Filatri Mundaho, and the girls of the Chinese gymnastics team had spoken, denouncing the murders as "insane, unwarranted, and a direct assault on the fabric of the games."

The piece closed with the reporter noting that police divers continued to probe the murky depths of the Thames near its confluence with the River Lea. They had found evidence that the speedboat that slammed the river wall contained explosives. No bodies had turned up.

"These facts do not bode well for an already shaken London Olympics," he'd intoned, ending the story.

"Knight?"

Sun reporter Karen Pope was coming through

the gate into the playground, looking anxious and depressed.

Knight frowned. "How did you find me here?"

"Hooligan told me you like to come here with your kids," she replied, and her unease deepened. "I tried your house first, then came here."

"What's wrong?" Knight asked. "Are you all right?"

"No, I'm not, actually," the reporter said in a shaky voice, taking a seat on the bench with him. Tears welled in her eyes. "I feel like I'm being used."

"Cronus?"

"And the Furies," she said, wiping at her tears angrily. "I didn't ask for it, but I have become part of their insanity, their terror. At first, you know, I admit it: I welcomed the story. Bloody brilliant for the career and all that, but now..."

Pope choked up and looked away.

"He's written you again?"

She nodded, and in a lost voice said, "I feel like I've sold my soul, Knight."

At that he saw the reporter in an entirely new light. Yes, she was abrasive and insensitive at times. But deep down she was human. She had a soul and principles, and this case tore at both. His estimation of Pope rose immeasurably.

"Don't think that way," Knight said. "You don't support Cronus, do you?"

"Of course not," she sniffed.

"Then you're just doing your job: a difficult thing, but necessary. Do you have the letter with you?"

Pope shook her head. "I dropped it off with Hooligan this morning." She paused. "A stoner messenger brought it to me last night at my flat. He said two fat women met him in front of King's College and gave him the letter to deliver. They were wearing official Olympic volunteer uniforms."

"It fits," Knight said. "What reason did Cronus give for killing the Chinese?"

"He claims that they were guilty of state-sponsored child enslavement."

Cronus claimed that China routinely ignored Olympic age rules, doctoring birth certificates in order to force children into what was effectively athletic servitude. Ping and Wu knew that 60 percent of the Chinese women's gymnastics team was underage. So did Win Bo Lee—who, Cronus claimed, was the architect of the entire scheme.

"There are plenty of supporting documents," Pope said. "Cronus makes the case quite well. The letter says the Chinese, quote, 'enslaved underage children for state glory,' unquote, and that the punishment was death."

She looked at Knight, crying again. "I could have published it all last night. I could have called my editor and made the deadline for today's paper. But I couldn't, Knight. I just... They know where I live."

"Lukey wants milk, Daddy," Luke said.

Knight turned from the distraught reporter to find his son staring at him expectantly. Then Isabel appeared. "I want milk, too!"

"Bollocks," Knight muttered, and then said apologetically, "I forgot the milk, but I'll go get some right now. This is Karen. She works for the newspaper. She's a friend of mine. She'll sit with you until I get back."

Pope frowned. "I don't think—"

"Ten minutes," Knight said. "Fifteen, tops."

The reporter looked at Luke and Isabel, and said reluctantly, "Okay."

"I'll be right back," Knight promised.

He ran across the meadow and out through the Royal Hospital grounds toward his home. The one-way trip took six minutes exactly, and he arrived sweating and breathing hard.

Knight went to put the key in the lock and was upset to find the door unlocked. Had he forgotten? It was completely unlike him, but he was operating on a limited amount of broken sleep, wasn't he?

He stepped inside the front hallway. A floorboard creaked somewhere above him. And then a door clicked shut.

CHAPTER 67

KNIGHT TOOK FOUR light steps to the front-hall closet and reached up high on a shelf for his spare Beretta.

Hearing a noise like furniture moving, he slid off his shoes, thinking: *My room or the kids'?*

Knight climbed the stairs like a cat, looking all around, and hearing a noise ahead of him. It was coming out of his room. He slid down the hallway, gun up, and peered at an angle into his room, seeing his desk, where his laptop lay shut.

He paused, listening intently. For several moments he heard nothing.

Then the toilet flushed. Thieves commonly relieve themselves in the homes of their victims.

Knight had known that for years and figured he was dealing with a burglar. Stepping over the threshold into his bedroom, he aimed the pistol at the closed door. The handle twisted. Knight flipped off the safety.

The door swung open.

Marta stepped out, spotted Knight and the gun.

Gasping, her hand flew to her chest, and she screamed, "Don't shoot!"

Knight's brows knitted, but he lowered his pistol several inches. "Marta?"

The nanny was gasping. "You scared me, Mr. Knight! My God, my heart feels like the fireworks."

"I'm sorry," he said, dropping the pistol to his side. "What are you doing here? I'm not supposed to see you for another hour."

"I came early so you can go to work early," she replied breathlessly. "You left me the key. I came in, saw the stroller gone, and thought you went to the park, so I started to clean the kitchen, and then came up to do the nursery."

"But you're up here in my bedroom," he said.

"I'm sorry," Marta replied plaintively, and then in an embarrassed tone added, "I had to go pee. Badly."

After a moment's pause in which he saw no guile

on the nanny's part, he pocketed the gun. "I apologize, Marta. I'm under stress. I overreacted."

"It's both our faults, then," Marta said, before Knight's phone rang.

He snatched it up and immediately heard Isabel and Luke crying hysterically.

"Pope?" he said.

"Where are you?" the reporter demanded in a harried voice. "You said you'd be right back, and your kids are throwing a world-class shit fit."

"Two minutes," he promised and hung up. He looked at Marta, who appeared worried. "My friend," he said. "She's not very good with kids."

Marta smiled. "Then it is a very good thing I came early, yes?"

"A very good thing," Knight said. "But we're going to have to run."

He sprang down the stairs and into the kitchen, where he saw that the breakfast dishes had been cleaned and put away. He got the milk and put it into a bag along with some cookies and two plastic cups.

He locked the apartment and together they hurried back to the park, where Luke was sitting off by himself in the grass, whacking the ground with his shovel, while Isabel knelt in the sandbox, crying and imitating an ostrich.

Pope was just standing there, out of her league, baffled about what to do.

Marta swooped in and gathered up Luke. She tickled his belly, which caused him to giggle and then to cry, "Marta!"

Isabel heard that, stopped crying, and pulled her hair out of the sand. She spotted Knight coming toward her and broke into a grin. "Daddy!"

Knight scooped his daughter up, brushed off the sand from her hair, and kissed her. "Daddy's here. So is Marta."

"I want milk!" Isabel said with a pout.

"Don't forget cookies," Knight said, handing his daughter and the sack containing the milk over to the concerned nanny, who brought the kids over to a picnic table and began to feed them.

"What caused the meltdown?" Knight asked Pope.

Flustered, the reporter said, "I don't know, actually. It was just like there was a time bomb ticking that I couldn't hear until it went off."

"That happens a lot," Knight remarked with a laugh.

Pope studied Marta. "The nanny been with you long?"

"Not a week yet," Knight replied. "But she's bloody fantastic. Best I've—"

Pope's cell phone rang. She answered and listened. After several moments she cried, "No fuggin' way! We'll be there in twenty minutes!"

The reporter clicked off her phone, and spoke with quiet urgency. "That was Hooligan. He pulled a fingerprint off the package Cronus sent me last night. He's run it and wants us at Private London ASAP."

CHAPTER 68

SURROUNDED BY A four-day growth of orange beard, the grin on Hooligan's face put Knight in mind of a mad leprechaun. It didn't hurt the image when Private London's chief scientist did a jig behind his lab desk and said, "We've got a third name—and, as Jack might say, it's a whopper that set off alarms. I've had two calls from The Hague in the past hour."

"The Hague?" Knight said, confused.

"Headquarters of the Balkan war crimes tribunal," Hooligan said as Jack rushed in, looking pale and drawn. "The print belongs to a woman wanted for genocide."

It was all coming at Knight so fast that his mind

was awhirl with disjointed thoughts. Daring and Farrell had both worked with NATO in some capacity at the end of the Balkan war, right? But war crimes? Genocide?

"Let's hear it," Jack said.

Hooligan went to a laptop computer and gave it several commands. On a large screen at one end of the lab, the grainy black-and-white photograph of a young teenage girl appeared. Her hair was chopped short in a bowl cut and she wore a white collared shirt. Knight could not say much more about her because the photograph was so blurry.

"Her name is Andjela Brazlic," Hooligan said. "This picture was taken approximately seventeen years ago, according to the war crimes prosecutor, which puts her in her late twenties now."

"What did she do?" Knight asked, trying to match the girl's blurry face with the charge of genocide.

Hooligan gave his computer another command and the screen jumped to an overexposed snapshot of three girls wearing white shirts and dark skirts. They were standing with a man and woman whose heads were out of the frame. Knight recognized the bowl-cut hairdo on one of them and realized he'd been looking at a blowup of this picture. Glaring sunlight obliterated the faces of the other two girls,

287

who had longer hair and were taller. He guessed them to be fourteen and fifteen.

Hooligan cleared his throat and said, "Andjela and her two sisters there, Senka, the oldest, and Nada, the middle girl, were indicted on charges that they participated in genocidal acts in and around the city of Srebrenica in late 1994 and early 1995, near the end of the civil war that exploded in the breakup of the former Yugoslavia. Allegedly the sisters were part of the kill squads Ratko Mladić oversaw that executed eight thousand Bosnian Muslim men and boys."

"Jesus," Pope said. "What makes three young girls join a kill squad?"

"Gang rape and murder," Hooligan replied. "According to the special prosecutor, not long after this photograph was taken in April of 1994, Andjela and her sisters were raped repeatedly over the course of three days by members of a Bosnian militia that also tortured and murdered their parents in front of them."

"That would do it," Jack said.

Hooligan nodded grimly. "The sisters are alleged to have executed more than one hundred Bosnian Muslims in retaliation. Some were shot. But most were struck through the skull, and postmortem through the genitals, with a pickax—the same sort

288

of weapon that was used to kill their mother and father.

"It gets worse." Private London's chief scientist pressed on. "The war crimes prosecutor told me that eyewitnesses testified that the sisters took sadistic delight in killing the Bosnian boys and desecrating their bodies—so much so that the terrified mothers of Srebrenica came up with an apt nickname for them."

"What was that?" Knight asked.

"The Furies."

"Jesus," Jack said. "It's them."

A moment of silence passed before Jack said to the reporter, "Karen, would you excuse us a moment? We have to discuss something that has nothing to do with this case."

Pope hesitated, and then nodded awkwardly, saying, "Oh, of course."

When she'd gone, Jack looked back at Knight and Hooligan. "I have something to tell you that's going to be tough to hear."

"We've been fired from the Olympic security team?" Knight asked.

Jack shook his head, paling. "Far from it. No, I just left a meeting with investigators with the Air Accidents Investigation Branch, the ones looking into the plane crash."

"And?" Hooligan said.

Jack swallowed hard. "They've found evidence of a bomb aboard the jet. There was no malfunction. Dan, Kirsty, Wendy, and Suzy were all murdered."

CHAPTER 69

"THIS BETTER BE good, Peter," Elaine Pottersfield grumbled. "I'm under insane pressure, and
not much in the mood for a fine dining experience."

"We're both under insane pressure," Knight shot
back. "But I have to talk to you. And I need to eat.
And you need to eat. I figured, why not meet here
and kill three birds with one stone?"

"Here" was a restaurant near Tottenham Court
Road called Hakkasan. It had been Kate's favorite
Chinese restaurant in London. It was also the chief
inspector's favorite Chinese restaurant in London.

"But this place is packed," Pottersfield said, taking a seat with some reluctance. "It will probably
take an hour to—"

"I've already ordered," Knight said. "The dish Kate liked best."

His sister-in-law looked down at the table. At that angle she looked every bit Kate's older sister. "Okay," she said at last. "Why am I here, Peter?"

Knight gave her the rundown on the Brazlic sisters—the Furies—and their alleged war crimes. As he was finishing his summary, their dinner, a double order of Szechuan-style Wagyu beef, arrived.

Pottersfield waited until the waiter left before asking, "And when were these sisters last heard of?"

"July 1995, not long after the NATO-supervised cease-fire expired," Knight replied. "They were supposedly apprehended by Bosnian police officers after the mother of two of their victims recognized the Furies when they tried to buy food in a local produce market. According to that same mother, the girls were taken at night to a police station in a small village southwest of Srebrenica, where they were to be turned over to NATO forces investigating the atrocities."

Pottersfield said, "And what? They escaped?"

Knight nodded. "Villagers heard automatic-weapons fire coming from inside the police station in the dead of night. They were too frightened to investigate until the following morning, when the bodies of seven Bosnians, including the two police

292

officers, were found massacred. The Brazlics have been hunted ever since, but none of them surfaced until today."

"How did they get out of the police station?" Pottersfield asked. "I'm assuming they'd been placed in restraints."

"You would think so," Knight agreed. "But here's the other strange thing. Mladić's kill squads used, for the most part, Soviet-era full-copper-jacket ammunition. So did the Bosnian police. It was Red Army surplus and found in all their un-fired weapons. But the seven Bosnian men in the station were killed by a 5.56-millimeter round throwing a very different kind of bullet—the kind given to NATO peacekeepers, in fact."

Pottersfield picked at her meal with chopsticks, thinking. After several bites, she said, "So maybe one of the men killed that night had a NATO weapon and the sisters got hold of it and fought their way out."

"That's one plausible scenario. Or a third party helped them, someone who was part of the NATO operation. I'm leaning toward that explanation."

"Evidence?" she asked.

"The bullets, primarily," Knight said. "But also because James Daring and Selena Farrell were in the Balkans in the midnineties, attached to that

NATO mission. Daring was assigned to protect antiquities from looters. But other than seeing Farrell in a photo holding an automatic weapon in front of a NATO field truck, I have no knowledge of her role in the operation."

"Not for long," Pottersfield said. "I'll petition NATO for her files."

"The war crimes prosecutor is already on it," Knight said.

The Scotland Yard inspector nodded, but her focus was far away. "So what's your theory, that this third entity in the escape—Daring or Farrell or both—could be Cronus?"

"Perhaps," Knight said. "It follows, anyway."

"In some manner," she allowed, while still managing to sound skeptical.

They ate in silence for several minutes before Pottersfield said, "There's only one thing that bothers me about this theory of yours, Peter."

"What's that?" Knight asked.

His sister-in-law squinted and shook her chopsticks at him. "Let's say you're right and Cronus was the person or persons who helped the sisters escape, and let's say that Cronus managed to turn these war criminals into anarchists, Olympics haters, whatever you want to call them.

"The evidence to date reveals people who are not

only brutal, but brutally effective. They managed to penetrate some of the heaviest security in the world, kill, and escape twice."

Knight saw where she was going. "You're saying they're detail-oriented, they've planned in the extreme, and yet they make mistakes with these letters."

Pottersfield nodded. "Hair, skin, and now a fingerprint?"

"Don't forget the wig," Knight said. "Anything on that?"

"Not yet, though this war-crimes angle should help us if DNA samples were ever taken from the sisters."

Knight ate a couple more bites, and then said, "There's also a question as to whether Farrell, Daring, or both had the wherewithal and the financial means to concoct a deadly assault on the Olympics. It has to cost money, and lots of it."

"I thought of that, too," Pottersfield replied. "This morning we took a look at Daring's bank accounts and credit card statements. That television show has made him wealthy. And his account shows several major cash withdrawals lately. Professor Farrell, on the other hand, lives more modestly. Except for hefty purchases at expensive fashion boutiques here and in Paris, and getting her hair done at trendy salons once a month, she leads a fairly austere life."

Knight remembered the vanity and the high-end clothes in the professor's bedroom and tried again to make it jibe with the dowdy woman he'd met at King's College. He couldn't. Was she dressing up to meet Daring? Was there something between them that no one else was aware of?

He glanced at his watch. "I'll pay and take my leave, then. The new nanny is working overtime."

Pottersfield looked away as he put his napkin on the table and raised his hand for the check. "How are they?" she asked. "The twins?"

"They're good," Knight said, and then gazed sincerely at his sister-in-law. "I know they would love to meet their Aunt Elaine. Don't you think they deserve to have a relationship with their mother's sister?"

It was as if invisible armor instantly wrapped around the Scotland Yard inspector. She went tight and said, "I'm simply not there yet. I don't know if I could bear it."

"They turn three a week from Saturday."

"Do you honestly think I could ever forget that day?" Pottersfield asked, getting up from the table.

"No, Elaine," Knight replied. "And neither will

I. Ever. But I have hope that at some point I'll be able to forgive that day. I hope you will, too."

Pottersfield said, "You'll take the check?"

Knight nodded. She turned to leave. He called after her. "Elaine, I'll probably be having a birthday party for them at some point. I'd like it if you came."

Pottersfield looked over her shoulder at him and replied, her voice raspy, "Like I said, Peter, I don't know if I'm there yet."

CHAPTER 70

IN THE TAXI on the way home, Knight wondered if his sister-in-law would ever forgive him. Did it matter? It did. It depressed him to think his kids might never get to know their mother's last living relative.

Rather than sink into a funk, however, he forced his mind to other thoughts.

Selena Farrell was a fashionista.

That fact bothered him so much that he called Pope. She answered, sounding in a snit. They'd had an argument in Hooligan's lab earlier in the day concerning when and how she should deal with the war-crimes information. She'd wanted to publish it immediately, but Knight and Jack had argued that she should wait to get independent corroboration from The Hague and from Scotland Yard. Neither man wanted the information attributed to Private.

Pope said, "So did your sister-in-law corroborate the fingerprint match?"

"I think that will probably be tomorrow, earliest," Knight said.

"Brilliant," the reporter complained. "And the prosecutor at The Hague is not returning my calls. So I've got nothing for tomorrow."

"There's something else you could be looking into," Knight offered as the taxi pulled up in front of his home. He paid the driver and stood out on the sidewalk explaining the vanity and clothes at Selena Farrell's home.

"High fashion?" she asked, incredulous. "Her?"

"Exactly my reaction," Knight said. "Which means a lot of things, it seems to me. She had to have had sources of money outside academia. Which means she had a secret life. Find it, and you just might find her."

"All well and good for you to say," Pope began.

God, she irritated him. "It's what I've got," he snapped. "Look, Pope, I have to tuck my kids in. I'll talk to you tomorrow."

He hung up feeling like the case had consumed him the way the mythical Cronus had consumed his own children. That thought left him supremely frustrated. If it wasn't for the Olympics he'd be working full-time to find out who had killed his four colleagues at Private and why. When this was over, he told himself, he would not stop until he solved that crime.

Knight went inside and climbed the stairs, hearing a door slide over carpet, followed by footsteps. Marta was leaving the nursery. She saw Knight and held her index finger to her lips.

"Can I say good night?" he whispered.

"They're already asleep," Marta said.

Knight glanced at his watch. It was just eight. "How do you do that? I can never get them down before ten."

"An old Estonian technique."

"You'll have to teach it to me sometime," Knight said. "Eight a.m.?"

She nodded. "I will be here." Then she hesitated before moving by him and climbing down the stairs. Knight followed her, thinking he'd have a beer and then get to sleep early.

Marta got on her jacket and started through the front door before looking back at him. "Have you caught the bad people?"

"No," Knight said. "But I feel like we're getting awfully close."

"That's good," she said. "Very, very good."

CHAPTER 71

SITTING AT HER desk in the *Sun*'s newsroom later that evening, half watching highlights of England's remarkable victory over Ghana in the final match of the preliminary round in men's soccer, Pope fumed yet again over the fact that she could not reveal the link between Cronus and the Furies and war crimes in the Balkans.

Even her editor, Finch, had told her that, as amazing a tale as it was, she did not have enough to publish—and might not for two, maybe even three days, at least until the prosecutor in The Hague agreed to talk to her on the record.

Three days! she moaned to herself. *That's Saturday. They'll never publish that kind of story on a*

Saturday. That means they'll wait for Sunday. Four days!

Every hard-news journalist in London was working the Cronus case now, all of them chasing Pope, trying to match or better her stories. Until today, she'd been way out ahead of the curve. Now, however, she feared that the war-crimes angle might leak before she could lay full claim to it in print.

And what was she to do in the meantime? Sit here? Wait for the war-crimes prosecutor to call? Wait for Scotland Yard to run the fingerprint against their database and confirm it to the world?

The situation was driving her batty. She should go home. Get some rest. But she was unnerved by the fact that Cronus knew where she lived, and she felt afraid to go home. Instead, she started poring over every angle of the story, trying to figure out where she could best push it forward.

At last her thoughts turned grudgingly to Knight's advice that she look more into Selena Farrell. But it had been four days since the professor's DNA had been matched to the hair found in the first letter from Cronus, and three days since MI5 and Scotland Yard launched the manhunt for her, and still there was nothing. She'd vanished.

Who am I to try if they can't find her? Pope thought before her pugnacious side asserted itself. *Well, why not me?*

The reporter chewed on her lip, thinking about Knight's revelation that Farrell was a fashion maven, and then remembered the full list of evidence taken from the professor's house and office that he had sent her the day before, at the aquatics center. She'd looked through the list, of course, searching for the evidence of anti-Olympic sentiment, the essays denouncing the games, and the recording of the flute music.

But she hadn't been looking for clothes, now, had she?

Pope called up the evidence list and began scrolling. It didn't take her long to find references to cocktail dresses from Liberty and skirts and blouses from Alice by Temperley. Big-money frocks. Hundreds of pounds, easy.

Knight said she'd had a secret life. Maybe he was right.

Excited now, Pope began scouring her notebook, looking for a phone number for the professor's research assistant, Nina Langor. Pope had talked to the assistant several times during the past four days, but Langor had consistently claimed that she was baffled by her boss's sudden disappearance, and had no idea why Farrell's DNA would have surfaced in the Cronus investigation.

The research assistant answered her phone guardedly, and sounded shocked when Pope told her about Farrell's haute-couture lifestyle.

"What?" Langor said. "No. That's impossible. She used to make fun of fashion and hairdos. Then again, she used to wear a lot of scarves."

"Did she have any boyfriends?" Pope asked. "Someone to dress up for?"

Langor got defensive. "The police asked the same thing. I'll tell you what I told them. I believe she was gay, but I don't know. She was a private person."

The assistant said she had to go, leaving Pope at eleven o'clock that Wednesday evening feeling as exhausted as if she'd run multiple marathons in the past six days. But she forced herself to return to the evidence list and continued on, finding nothing until the very end, when she saw a reference to a torn pink matchbook with the letters *CAN* on it.

She tried to imagine a pink matchbook with the letters *CAN*. Cancer institute? Breast cancer awareness? Isn't pink the color of that movement? Something else?

Stymied at her inability to make the evidence talk, Pope made a last-ditch effort around midnight, using a technique she'd discovered quite by accident a few years prior, when she had been presented with disparate facts that made no sense.

She started typing strings of words into Google to see what came up.

"Pink Can London" yielded nothing of interest. "Pink Can London Olympics" got her no further.

Then she typed "London Pink Can Gay Fashion Design Liberty Alice."

Google gnawed at that search query, and then spit out the results.

"Oh," Pope said, smiling. "So you were a lipstick lesbian, Professor."

CHAPTER 72

AT TEN THE following evening Pope turned onto Carlisle Street in Soho.

It had been an insanely aggravating and fruitless day. The reporter had called the war crimes prosecutor ten times and was assured each time by a saccharine, infuriatingly polite secretary that he would be returning her call soon.

Worse, she'd had to follow a story in the *Mirror* that described the intense global manhunt for Selena Farrell and James Daring. Worse still, she'd had to follow a story in the London *Times* regarding initial autopsy and toxicology reports on the dead Chinese gymnastics coaches. Holes the size of bee stingers had been found in both their necks. But they had not died of anaphylactic shock. They'd succumbed to a deadly neurotoxin called calciseptine, derived and synthesized from the venom of black mamba snakes.

Black mamba snakes? Pope thought for the hundredth time that day. Every paper in the world was going loony over that angle, and she'd missed it.

It only made her more determined when she went to the doors of the Candy Bar, submitted to a security search of her bag by a very large Maori woman, and then entered the ground floor. The club was surprisingly crowded for a Thursday night, and the reporter instantly felt uncomfortable as she sensed several glamorous women watching her, evaluating her.

But Pope walked right up to them, introduced herself, and showed them a photograph of Selena Farrell. They'd not seen her, nor had the next six women the reporter asked.

She went to the bar then, spotting a pink matchbook that fit the one described in the evidence list. One of the bartenders came over to her, and Pope asked what she'd recommend for a cocktail.

"Buttery Nipple?" the bartender said. "Butterscotch schnapps and Baileys?"

The reporter wrinkled her nose. "Too sweet."

"Jugs of Pimm's, then," said a woman on the bar stool next to Pope. Petite, blond, in her late thirties, and extremely attractive, she held up a highball glass with a mint sprig sticking out of the top. "Always refreshing on a hot summer's night."

"Perfect," Pope replied, smiling weakly at the woman.

Pope had meant to show the picture of Farrell to the bartender, but she'd already walked away to prepare her Pimm's. Pope set the photo on the bar and turned to the woman who'd recommended the drink. She was studying the reporter in mild amusement.

"First time at the Candy Bar?" the woman asked.

Pope flushed. "Is it that obvious?"

"To the trained eye," the woman said, a hint of lechery crossing her face as she held out a well-manicured hand. "I'm Nell."

"Karen Pope," she said. "I write for the *Sun*."

Nell's eyebrow rose. "I do so enjoy page three."

Pope laughed nervously. "Unfortunately, I don't."

"Pity," Nell said, her face falling. "Not even a wee bit?"

"A pity, but no," Pope replied, and then showed Nell the photograph.

Nell sighed and leaned closer to Pope to study

the picture of Farrell, who was wearing no makeup, a peasant skirt, and a matching scarf on her head.

"No," Nell said with a dismissive gesture. "I know I've never seen *her* here. She isn't exactly the type. But *you*, I must say, most definitely fit in here."

Pope laughed again before gesturing to the picture and saying, "Think of her in a tight cocktail dress from Liberty or Alice by Temperley, and her hair done by Hair by Fairy, and, well, you can't see it from this angle, but she has this tiny mole near her jaw."

"A mole?" Nell sniffed. "You mean with little hairs sticking out of it?"

"More like a beauty mark. Like Elizabeth Taylor used to have."

Nell looked confused, and then studied the photograph again.

A moment later, she gasped, "My God, it's Syren!"

CHAPTER 73

KNIGHT HEARD FEET padding around at seven thirty that next morning. He blinked open his eyes and saw Isabel holding her Pooh Bear blanket.

"Daddy," she said in high seriousness. "When am I three?"

"August eleventh," Knight grumbled, and glanced at that picture of Kate on the moor in Scotland. "A week from tomorrow, honey."

"What's today?"

"Friday."

Isabel thought about that. "So one more Saturday and one more Friday, and then the next one?"

Knight smiled. His daughter always fascinated

him with the out-of-the box way her mind worked. "Yes," he replied. "Give me a kiss."

Isabel kissed him. Then her eyes widened. "We get presents?"

"Of course, Bella," Knight replied. "It will be your birthday."

She got wildly excited, clapping her hands and dancing in a tight circle before stopping dead in her tracks. "What presents?"

"What presents?" Luke asked from the doorway. He was yawning as he came into the room.

"I can't tell you that," Knight said. "It won't be a surprise."

"Oh," Isabel said, disappointed.

"Lukey three?" his son asked.

"Next week," Knight assured him, and then heard the front door open. Marta. Early again. The world's first perfect nanny.

Knight got on sweatpants and a T-shirt, and carried the twins down the stairs. Marta smiled at them. "Hungry?"

"It's my birthday two Fridays and a Saturday from now," Isabel announced.

"And Lukey," her brother said. "I'm three."

"You will be three," Knight corrected.

"We'll have to plan a party, then," Marta said as Knight set the kids down.

"A party!" Isabel cried and clapped.

Luke hooted with delight, spun in circles, and cried, "Party! Party!"

The twins had never had a birthday party, or at least not on the exact date of their birth. That day had been so bittersweet that Knight had moved cake and ice cream celebrations a day or two later, and kept the festivities deliberately low-key. He was torn now over how he should reply to Marta's suggestion.

Luke stopped spinning and said, "Balloons?"

"Mr. Knight?" Marta said. "What do you think? Balloons?"

Before Knight could answer, the doorbell rang, and then rang again, and again, and again, followed by someone pounding the knocker so hard it sounded like a mason chipping stone.

"Who the hell is that?" Knight groaned, heading toward the door. "Can you get them breakfast, Marta?"

"Of course," she said.

The pounding on the door knocker started again before he looked through the security peephole, seeing an exasperated Karen Pope on his front stoop.

"Karen," he called out to her. "I don't have time to—"

"Make time," she barked. "I've made a break in the case."

Knight ran his fingers back through his sleep-ravaged hair, and then opened the door. Looking like she'd been up all night herself, Pope barged in while Marta went toward the kitchen with Luke and Isabel.

"Lukey want pancakes and bangers," Luke said.

"Pancakes and bangers it is," Marta replied as they disappeared.

"What's the break?" Knight asked Pope, heading into the living area and clearing enough toys off the couch so that they could sit.

"You were right," the reporter said. "Selena Farrell had a secret life."

She told Knight that the professor had an alter ego named Syren St. James, which she'd take on when she went to the Candy Bar to pick up women. As Syren, Farrell was everything the professor was not—flamboyant, funny, promiscuous, a party girl of the highest order.

"Selena Farrell?" Knight said, shaking his head.

"Think of that part of her as Syren St. James," Pope replied. "It helps."

"And you know all this how?" he asked, smelling sausages frying and hearing pots and bowls clanking in the kitchen.

313

"From a woman named Nell, who frequents the Candy Bar and has had several one-night stands with Syren over the past few years. She identified her by that mole near her right jawline."

Knight remembered how he'd thought that the professor would have been attractive under the right circumstances. He should have listened to his instincts.

"When was the last time she saw...uh, Syren?" he asked.

"Last Friday, late in the afternoon, before the games opened," Pope replied. "She came into the Candy Bar dressed to kill, but blew Nell off, saying she already had a date. Later, Nell saw Syren leave with a stranger, a woman wearing a pillbox hat with a black lace veil that covered the upper part of her face. I'm thinking that woman could be one of the Brazlic sisters, aren't you?"

In Knight's kitchen, something fragile crashed and shattered.

CHAPTER 74

THE ATHLETES' VILLAGE is well past stirring now. Swimmers from Australia are already heading to the aquatics center, where the men's fifteen-hundred-meter heats will take place. Cyclists from Spain are going to the velodrome for a light ride before the men's team pursuit competition later in the day. A Moldovan handball team just passed me. So did that American basketball player—that one with the name I always forget.

It's irrelevant. What matters is that we're at the end of week one and every athlete in the village is trying not to think of me and my sisters, trying not to ask themselves whether they'll be next. And yet they can't help but think of us, now, can they?

As I predicted, the media has gone berserk over

our story. For every weepy television tale of an athlete overcoming cancer or the death of a loved one to win a gold medal, there have been three more about the effect we are having on the games. Tumors, they've called us. Scourges. Black stains on the Olympics.

Ha! The only tumors and black stains are those generated by the games. I'm just revealing them for what they are.

Indeed, out walking among the Olympians like this—anonymous, earnest, and in disguise, another me—I'm feeling that except for a few minor glitches, everything has gone remarkably according to plan. Petra and Teagan took vengeance on the Chinese and executed their escape perfectly. Marta has ingratiated herself into Knight's life and monitors his virtual world, giving me an inside view of whatever investigations have been launched and why. And earlier this morning, I retrieved the second bag of magnesium shavings, the one I hid in the velodrome during its construction almost two years ago. Right where I left it.

The only thing that bothers me is...

My disposable cell phone rings. I grimace. Petra and Teagan were given precise orders before they left on their latest assignment midday yesterday: I forbade them to call me at all. Marta, then.

I answer and snap at her before she can speak. "No names, and toss that phone when we're finished talking. Do you know the mistake?"

"Not exactly," Marta says, with a note of alarm in her voice that is quite rare and therefore instantly troubling.

"What's wrong?" I demand.

"They know," she whispers. In the background I hear a little monster crying.

The crying and Marta's whisper hit me like stones and car bombs, setting off a raging storm in my skull that destroys my balance, and I go to one knee for fear I'll keel over. The light all around me seems ultraviolet, except for a diesel-green halo that pulses in time with the ripping sensations in my skull.

"You all right?" a man's voice asks.

I can hear the crying on the phone, which now hangs in my hand at my side. I look up through the green halo and see a groundskeeper standing a few feet from me.

"Fine," I manage, fighting for control against the rage building in me, making me want to cut the groundskeeper's head off for spite. "I'm just a little dizzy."

"You want me to call someone?"

"No," I say, struggling to my feet. Though the

green halo is still pulsing and the ripping goes on in my skull, the air around me is shimmering a bit less.

Walking away from the groundskeeper, I growl into the phone, "Shut that goddamn kid up."

"Believe me, if I could, I would," Marta retorts. "Here, I'll go outside."

I hear a door shut and the beeping of a car horn. "Better?"

Only a little. My stomach churns when I ask, "What do they know?"

In a halting voice, Marta tells me that they know about the Brazlic sisters, and it all starts again, the ripping, the diesel-green halo, and the ultraviolent rage that so completely permeates me now that I feel like a cornered animal, a monster myself, ready to rip out the throat of anyone who might approach me.

There's a bench ahead on the path and I sit on it. "How?"

"I don't know," Marta replies, and then explains how she overheard Pope mention the Brazlic sisters, which had so shocked her that she'd dropped a mixing bowl, which shattered on the kitchen floor.

Wanting to throttle her, I say, "Does Knight suspect?"

"Me? No," Marta says. "I acted embarrassed and apologetic when I told him the bowl was wet. He told me not to worry about it, and to make extra sure the floor was free of glass before letting his little brats walk around."

"Where are they now—Knight and Pope? What else do they know?"

"He left with her ten minutes ago, and said he would not be back until late," Marta replies. "I don't know any more than what I've told you. But if they know about the sisters, then they know what the sisters did in Bosnia, and the war crimes prosecutors know we are in London."

"They probably do," I agree at last. "But nothing more. If they had more, they'd be tracking you by one of your current names. They'd be at our doors."

After a moment's silence, Marta asks, "So what do I do?"

Feeling increasingly sure that the gap between who the Furies were and who they have become is wide enough to prevent a connection, I reply, "Stay close to those children. We may need them in the coming days."

CHAPTER 75

BY SEVEN P.M., the intensity inside the Olympic stadium was beyond electric. From his position in the stands on the west side of the venue, high above the track's finish line, Knight could sense the anticipation rippling through the eighty thousand souls lucky enough to have gotten a ticket to see who would be the fastest man on earth. The Private London investigator could also see and hear fear competing with anticipation. People were wondering whether Cronus would attack here.

The event was certainly high-profile enough. The sprint competition so far had gone down as expected. Both Shaw and Mundaho had been brilliant in the hundred-meter qualifying heats the day before, each of them dominating and winning easily. But while the Jamaican was able to rest between races, the Cameroonian had been forced to run in the classifications for the four-hundred-meter race.

Mundaho had performed almost superhumanly, turning in a time of 43:22 seconds, four one-hundredths of a second off Henry Ivey's world record performance of 43:18 at the 1999 world championships in Seville.

This evening, Mundaho and Shaw won their hundred-meter semifinal heats with the Cameroonian just two one-hundredths off Shaw's world record of 9:58 seconds. The men were getting ready to face each other in the hundred-meter dash final. After that, Shaw would rest and Mundaho would have to run in the four-hundred-meter semifinals.

Grueling, Knight thought as he scanned the crowd through his binoculars. Could Mundaho do it? Win the one hundred, two hundred, and four hundred at a single Olympic games?

In the end, did it matter? Would people really care, after all that had happened to London 2012? Aside from the joy Londoners expressed earlier in the day, when British runner Mary Duckworth won the women's marathon, the past forty-eight hours had seen a dramatic ratcheting up of the anxiety surrounding the games. On Saturday, the *Sun* finally published Pope's story describing the link between the killings and the Serbian Brazlic sisters, the wanted war crimes suspects. She had also detailed how both James Daring and Selena Farrell had served in the Balkans about the time the Brazlics were actively executing innocent men and boys in and around the city of Srebrenica.

Farrell, it turned out, was a volunteer UN observer assigned to NATO in the war-torn area. There were still not many details of the professor's exact duties on the mission, but Pope had discovered that Farrell was badly hurt in some kind of vehicular accident in the summer of 1995, and sent home. After a short convalescence, she'd resumed her doctoral studies and gone on with her life.

The story had caused an uproar that swelled when, late Saturday evening, the body of Emanuel Flores, a Brazilian judo referee, was discovered near a Dumpster in the Docklands, several miles from the ExCeL arena, where he'd been working, a venue that was not on Olympic grounds. An expert in hand-to-hand combat, Flores had nevertheless been garroted with a length of cable.

In a letter to Pope completely devoid of forensic

evidence, Cronus claimed that Flores had accepted bribes to favor certain athletes in the judo competition. The documentation supported the allegations in some ways and not others.

In reaction, broadcasters and journalists around the world demanded action from the British government, expressing uniform outrage that Cronus and his Furies seemed to be acting at will. This morning, Uruguay, North Korea, Tanzania, and New Zealand decided to pull their teams from the final week of competition. Members of Parliament and the Greater London Authority had reacted by stridently renewing calls for Mike Lancer to resign or be fired, and for the manhunt for Daring and Farrell to be intensified.

For his part, a visibly shaken Lancer had been in front of cameras all day, defending his efforts. Around noon, Lancer had announced that he was relieving F7 of its command over the entrances to Olympic Park and bringing in Jack Morgan of Private to oversee the effort. Together with Scotland Yard and MI5, they decided to institute draconian measures at the venues, including secondary screenings, more identification checks, and pat-downs.

It had not been enough to calm the games. Ten countries, including Russia, floated the idea that

James Patterson

the Olympics should be halted until security was assured.

But in an immediate and aggressive response, a staggering number of athletes had signed a digital petition drafted and distributed by American diver Hunter Pierce that not only condemned the murders but also defiantly and forcefully demanded that the IOC and LOCOG not give in to the idea of suspending the games.

To their credit, London's mayor, and the prime minister, and Marcus Morris were listening to the athletes and dismissing calls to halt the Olympics, saying that England had never bent to terrorism and wasn't about to start.

Despite the dramatic increase in security measures, some fans had stayed away from what was supposed to be the biggest event of the games. Knight could see scattered empty seats, something that would have been considered impossible prior to the start of the Olympics. But then again, almost everything that had happened so far would have been considered impossible prior to the games.

"Bloody bastards have ruined it, Knight," Lancer said bitterly. The security chief had come up alongside Knight as he was scanning the crowd. Like Knight, Lancer wore a radio earbud tuned to the

 324

stadium-security frequency. "No matter what happens from now on, 2012 will always be the tainted—"

The crowd around them leaped to its feet and started cheering wildly. The final competitors in the men's hundred-meter dash were coming out onto the track. Shaw, the reigning Olympic champion, entered first, taking little stutter sprints and loosening up his hands, knifing them in the air as though they were chopping tools.

Mundaho came out onto the track last and jogged in an almost sleepy lope before crouching and then hopping like a kangaroo down the track with such explosiveness that many in the crowd gasped, and Knight thought: *Is that possible? Has anyone ever done that before?*

"That man's a freak," Lancer remarked. "An absolute freak of nature."

CHAPTER 76

THE OLYMPIC FLAME atop the *Orbit* burned without disturbance or deflection and the flags around the stadium hung flat; the wind had died to nothing, perfect conditions for a sprint race.

Knight's earbud crackled with calls and responses among Jack, the security crew, and Lancer, who'd moved off to get a different view. Knight looked around. High atop the stadium, SAS snipers lay prone behind their rifles. A helicopter passed overhead. The war birds had been circling the park all day, and the number of armed guards around the track had been doubled.

Nothing bad is happening in here tonight, Knight told himself. An attack would be suicidal.

The sprinters went to starting blocks that relied

326

on a state-of-the-art, fully automated timing system, called FAT. Each block was built around ultrasensitive pressure plates linked to computers to catch any false starts. At the finish line, linked to those same computers, was an invisible matrix of crisscrossing laser beams calibrated to a thousandth of a second.

The crowd was on its feet now, straining for better views as the announcer called the sprinters to their marks. Shaw was running in lane three, and Mundaho in lane five. The Jamaican glanced at the Cameroonian pivoting in front of his blocks. Setting their cleats into the pressure sensors, the speedsters splayed their fingertips on the track, heads bowed.

Ten seconds, Knight thought. *These guys spend their whole lives preparing for ten seconds.* He couldn't imagine it: the pressure, the expectations, the will, and the suffering involved in becoming an Olympic champion.

"Set," the judge called, and the sprinters cocked their hips.

The gun cracked, the crowd roared, and Mundaho and Shaw were like twin panthers springing after prey. The Jamaican was stronger in the first twenty meters, uncoiling his long legs and arms sooner than the Cameroonian. But in the next

327

forty meters, the former boy soldier ran as if he had bullets chasing him.

Mundaho caught Shaw at eighty meters, but could not pass the Jamaican.

And Shaw could not lose the Cameroonian.

Together they streaked down the track, chasing history as if the other men in the race weren't even there, and appeared to lean and blow through the finish simultaneously with a time of 9:38, two-tenths of a second better than Shaw's incredible performance at Beijing.

New Olympic record!

New world record!

CHAPTER 77

THE STADIUM ROCKED with cheers for Mundaho and Shaw.

But who had won?

Up on the big screens, the unofficial results had Shaw in first and Mundaho second, and yet the times were identical. Through his binoculars, Knight could see both men gasping for air, hands on their hips, looking not at each other but up at the screens replaying the race in slow motion while judges examined data from the lasers at the finish line.

Knight heard the announcer say that although there had been ties in judged Olympic events like gymnastics in the past, and a tie between two American swimmers at the Sydney 2000 games, there had never been a tie in any track event at any modern Olympics. The announcer said that the referees would examine photos as well as take the time down to the thousandth of a second.

Knight watched referees huddling by the track, and saw the tallest of them shake his head. A moment later, the screens flashed OFFICIAL RESULTS and posted Shaw and Mundaho in a dead tie, with a time of 9:382.

"I decline to run another heat," the referee was heard saying. "I consider that the greatest footrace of all time and the time stands. Both men share the world record. Both men win gold."

The stadium rocked again with cheers, whistles, and yells.

Through his binoculars, Knight saw Shaw gazing up at the results and then over at the referee in skepticism and irritation. But then the Jamaican's expression melted into a grin that spread wide. He jogged to Mundaho, who was smiling back at him. They spoke. Then they clasped hands, raised them, and jogged toward cheering fans while holding out the flags of Jamaica and Cameroon.

The men took their long victory lap around the stadium together, and to Knight it was as if a pleasant summer rainstorm had come along to wash foul smoke from the air. Cronus and the

Furies seemed not as dominant a force at the London Olympics as they had been just a few minutes ago.

Running together in a grand display of sportsmanship was the sprinters' way of telling the world that the modern games were still a force to be reckoned with, still a force for good, a force that could demonstrate shared humanity in the face of Cronus's cruel assault.

Shaw said as much when he and Mundaho returned to the finish line and were interviewed by reporters. Knight saw it all up on the big screens.

"When I saw the tie, I could not believe it," the Jamaican admitted. "And to tell you the truth, my first response was that I felt angry. I had beaten my record, but I had not bested everyone, as I did in Beijing. But then, after all that has happened at these games, I saw that the tie was a beautiful thing, good for sprinting, good for athletics, and good for the Olympics."

Mundaho concurred, saying, "I am humbled to have run with the great Zeke Shaw. It is the honor of my life to have my name mentioned in the same breath as his."

The reporter then asked who would win the two-hundred-meter final Wednesday night. Both men tapped their chests and said, "Me."

Then they both laughed and slapped each other on the back.

Knight breathed a sigh of relief when both men left the stadium. At least Cronus had not targeted those two.

For the next hour, as the men's fifteen-hundred-meter semifinals and the three-thousand-meter steeplechase final were run, Knight's mind wandered to his mother. Amanda had promised she would not turn bitter and retreat into herself, as she had after his father's death.

But Knight's past two conversations with Gary Boss indicated that was exactly what she was doing. She would not take his calls. She would not take anyone's calls, even those who wanted to help arrange a memorial for Denton Marshall. According to her assistant, Amanda was spending every waking hour at her table, sketching designs—hundreds of them.

He'd wanted to go to see her yesterday and this morning, but Boss had urged him against coming. Boss felt this was something Amanda needed to go through alone, at least for a few more days.

Knight's heart ached for his mother. He knew at a gut level what she was going through. He'd thought his own grief for Kate would never end. And in a sense it never would. But he'd found a

332

way to keep going through his children. He prayed his mother would find her own way—a way other than through work.

Then he thought of the twins. He was about to call home to say good night when the announcer called for competitors in the men's four-hundred-meter semifinals.

People were on their feet again as Mundaho appeared in the tunnel from the warm-up track. The Cameroonian jogged out, as confident as he had been before the hundred-meter race, moving in that loose-jointed way he had about him.

But instead of taking those explosive kangaroo hops, the Cameroonian began to skip and then to bound, his feet coming way up off the track surface and swinging forward as if he were a deer or a gazelle.

What other man can do that? Knight thought in awe. *Where did the idea that he could do that even come from? The bullets flying at his back?*

The Cameroonian slowed near his blocks on lane one, at the inside and rear of the staggered start. Could Mundaho do it? Run a distance four times longer than what he'd just sprinted in world-record time?

Evidently Zeke Shaw wanted to know as well, because the Jamaican sprinter reappeared in the en-

333

try linking the practice track to the stadium and stood with three of the Gurkhas, all looking north toward the runners about to compete.

"Mark," the official called.

Mundaho set his race shoes with their tiny metal nubs against the blocks. He crouched and tensed when the official called, "Set."

The gun went off in the near-silent stadium.

The Cameroonian leaped off the blocks.

A thousandth of a second later, a blinding silver-white light blasted from the blocks as they exploded and disintegrated, throwing a low-angle wave of fire and hot jagged bits of metal that smashed into Mundaho's lower body from behind, hurling the Cameroonian off his feet and onto the track, where he lay crumpled and screaming.

BOOK FOUR

MARATHON

CHAPTER 78

KNIGHT WAS SO shocked he was unable to move for several seconds. Like many in the stadium, he watched and listened in gut-clenched horror as Mundaho writhed on the track, sobbing and groaning in agony as he reached for his charred and bleeding legs.

The other sprinters were stopped, looking back in shocked disbelief at the carnage in lane one. The intense metallic flame died, leaving the track scorched where the blocks had been and throwing off a burned chemical odor that reminded Knight of safety flares and burning tires.

Paramedics rushed to tend to the Cameroonian sprinter as well as to several race officials who'd also been hit by the burning shrapnel.

"I want everyone involved with those starting blocks held for questioning," Lancer bellowed over the radio, barely in control. "Find the timing judges, referees, everyone. Sequester them! All of them!"

Around Knight, fans were coming out of their initial shock, some crying, some damning Cronus. Many began to move toward the exits while volunteers and security personnel were trying to maintain calm.

"Can you get me on the field, Jack? Mike?" Knight asked.

"That's a negative," Jack said.

"Double that negative," Lancer said. "Scotland Yard has already ordered it sealed for their bomb forensics unit."

Knight was suddenly furious that this had happened to Mundaho and to the Olympics—that they had been caught up in the festering recesses of a twisted mind and made to suffer for it. He did not care what Cronus was going to claim the sprinter did.

Whatever he did or did not do, Mundaho did not deserve to be lying burned on the track. He should have been blowing the rest of the sprinters away in his quest for athletic immortality. Instead he was being lifted onto a gurney.

The people in the stadium around Knight began to clap as paramedics started to wheel the Cameroonian sprinter toward a waiting ambulance. They had IVs in his arm, and obviously had given him drugs, though Knight could see through his binoculars that the former boy soldier was still racked with hideous pain.

Knight heard people saying that London would have to end the games now, and he felt furious that Cronus might have won, that it all might be finished. But then he heard a cynic in the crowd say that there was no chance the games would be canceled. He'd read a story in the *Financial Times* that indicated that while London 2012's corporate sponsors and the official broadcasters were publicly aghast at Cronus's actions, they were privately astounded at the twenty-four-hour coverage the games were receiving and the public's seemingly inexhaustible appetite for the various facets of the story.

"The ratings for these Olympics are the highest in history," he said. "I predict: no chance they're canceled."

Knight had no time to think about any of it because Shaw suddenly came running out of the entryway to the stadium carrying the Cameroonian flag along with the dozen or so competitors still in the four-hundred-meter competition. They ran to the rear of the ambulance, exhorting the crowd to chant, "Mundaho! Mundaho!"

The people remaining in the stadium went crazy with it, weeping and cheering, as others were screaming denouncements of Cronus and the Furies.

Despite the medical personnel around him, despite the agony ripping through his body, and despite the drugs, Mundaho heard and saw what his fellow athletes and the fans were doing for him. Before the paramedics slid him into the ambulance, the Cameroonian sprinter raised his right arm and formed a fist.

Knight and everyone else in the stadium cheered the gesture. Mundaho was injured but not broken, burned but still a battle-hardened soldier. He might never run again, but his spirit and the Olympic spirit were still going strong.

CHAPTER 79

FEELING LIKE SHE wanted to puke, Karen Pope ate antacid pills and stared uncomprehendingly at the television in the *Sun* newsroom, watching as the medics loaded the defiant Cameroonian sprinter into the back of the ambulance. She and her editor, Finch, were waiting for Cronus's newest letter to arrive. So were the Metropolitan Police detectives who'd staked out the lobby, waiting for the messenger, hoping to rapidly trace where the letter was picked up.

Pope did not want to see what Cronus had to say about Mundaho. She did not care. She went to her editor and said, "I quit, Finchy."

"You can't quit," Finch shot back. "What are you talking about? This is the story of a lifetime you're on here. Ride it, Pope. You've been bloody brilliant."

She burst into tears. "I don't want to ride it. I don't want to be part of killing and maiming people. This isn't why I became a journalist."

"You aren't killing or maiming anyone," Finch said.

"But I'm helping to!" she shouted. "We're like the people who published the manifesto of the Unabomber over in the States when I was a kid! We're abetting murder, Finch! I'm abetting murder, and I just won't. I can't."

"You're not abetting murder," Finch said, softening his voice. "And neither am I. We are chronicling the murders, the same way Fleet Streeters before us chronicled Jack the Ripper. You're not helping, you're exposing. That's our obligation, Pope. That's your obligation."

She stared at him, feeling small and insignificant. "Why me, Finch?"

"I dunno. Maybe we'll find out someday. I dunno."

Pope could not argue anymore. She just turned, went to her desk, plopped in her seat, and put her head down. Then her BlackBerry beeped, alerting her to an incoming message.

Pope blew out air, picked up the phone, and

saw it was an e-mail with an attachment from "Cronus." She wanted to bash her phone into shards, but she kept hearing her editor telling her it was her obligation to expose these insane people for what they were.

"Here it is, Finch," she called tremulously across the room. "Somebody better tell the cops that there's no messenger coming."

Finch nodded and said, "I'll do it. You've got an hour to deadline."

Pope hesitated, then got angry and opened the attachment.

Cronus had expected Mundaho to die on the track.

His letter justified the "killing" as "just retribution for the crime of hubris," one of ancient Greece's greatest sins. Arrogant, vain, prideful, and a challenger to the gods—these were the accusations Cronus threw at Mundaho.

He attached copies of e-mails, text messages, and Facebook messages between Mundaho and his Los Angeles–based sports agent, Matthew Hitchens. According to Cronus, the discussions between the men were not about the struggle to attain greatness for its own sake or for the approval of the gods, as was the case during the ancient Olympics.

Instead, Cronus depicted the correspondence as

focused on money and material gain, with lengthy discussions over the probability that winning the sprint "trifecta" at the London Olympics could increase Mundaho's global value by several hundred million dollars over a twenty-year endorsement career.

"Mundaho put up for sale the gift the gods gave him," Cronus concluded. "He saw no glory in the simple idea of being the fastest man. He saw only gain, and therefore his arrogance toward the gods shone ever more brilliantly. In effect, Mundaho thought of himself as a god, entitled to great riches and to immortality. For the crime of hubris, retribution must always be swift and certain."

But Mundaho's not dead, Pope thought with overwhelming satisfaction.

She yelled to Finch: "Do we have a number for Mundaho's sports agent?"

Her editor thought a moment and then nodded. "It's here in a master list we compiled for the games."

He gave the number to Pope, who texted a message to the sports agent:

Know U R with Mundaho. Cronus makes claims against him and u. Call me.

Pope sent the text, put the phone down, and started framing the story on her computer, all the while telling herself she wasn't helping Cronus. She was fighting him by exposing him.

To her surprise, her phone rang within five minutes. It was an audibly distraught Matthew Hitchens en route to the hospital where they'd taken Mundaho. She expressed her condolences and then hit the sports agent with Cronus's charges.

"Cronus isn't giving you the whole story," Hitchens complained bitterly when she'd finished. "He doesn't say why Filatri wanted that kind of money."

"Tell me," Pope said.

"His plan was to use the money to help children who've lived in war zones and survived, especially those who've been kidnapped and forced to fight and die as soldiers in conflicts they don't understand or believe in. We've already set up the Mundaho Foundation for Orphaned Children of War, which was supposed to help Filatri achieve his dream beyond the Olympics. I can show you the formation documents. He signed them long before Berlin, long before there was any talk of him winning three gold medals."

Hearing that, Pope saw how she could fight

back. "So you're saying that, in addition to ruining the dreams and life of one former boy soldier, Cronus's acts may have destroyed the hopes and chances of war-scarred children all over the world?"

Hitchens got choked up, saying, "I think that about sums up this tragedy."

Pope thought of Mundaho, squeezed her free hand into a fist, and said, "Then that is what my story will say, Mr. Hitchens."

CHAPTER 80

MONDAY, AUGUST 6, 2012

A CATEGORY FIVE hurricane rampages through my brain, throwing daggers of lightning brighter than magnesium combusting, and everything around me seems saturated with electric blues and reds that don't shimmer or sparkle as much as sear and bleed.

That stupid bitch. She betrayed us. And Mundaho escaped a just vengeance. I feel like annihilating every monster in London.

But I'll settle for one of them.

I'm more than aware that this move could upset a careful balance I've struck for more than fifteen years. If I handle this wrong, it could come back to haunt me.

The storm in my skull, however, won't let me consider these ramifications very long. Instead, as though I were watching a flickering old movie, I see myself stick a knife in my mother's thigh, again and again; and I remember in a cascade of raw emotion how good, how right it felt to have been wronged and then avenged.

Petra is waiting for me when I reach my home around four in the morning. Her eyes are sunken, fearful, and red. We are alone. The other sisters have gone on to new tasks.

"Please, Cronus," she begins. "The fingerprint was a mistake."

The hurricane spins furiously again in my mind, and it's as though she's looking at me from the bottom of a whirling, thundering funnel.

"A mistake?" I say in a soft voice. "Do you realize what you've done? You've called the dogs in around us. They can smell you, Andjela. They can smell your sisters. They can smell me. They've got a cage and gallows waiting."

Petra's face twists up in an anger equal to my own. "I believe in you, Cronus. I've given you my life. I killed both Chinese coaches for you. But yes, I made a mistake. One mistake!"

"Not one," I reply in that same soft voice. "You left your wig in the wall of the ladies' room at the gymnastics venue. They've got your DNA now, too. It was impetuous. You did not follow the plan."

Petra begins to shake and to cry. "What do you want me to do, Cronus? What can I do to make it right?"

For several moments I don't reply, but then I sigh and walk toward her with open arms. "Nothing, sister," I say. "There's nothing you can do. We fight on."

Petra hesitates, but then comes into my arms and hugs me so fiercely that for a moment I'm unsure what to do.

But then my mind seizes on the image of an IV line stuck in my arm and connected to a plastic bag of liquids, and for a fleeting instant I consider what that image has meant to me, how it has consumed me, driven me, made me.

I am much taller than Petra. So when I return her hug, my arms fall naturally around the back of her neck and press her cheek tightly to my chest.

"Cronus," she begins, before she feels the pressure building.

She starts to choke.

"No!" she manages in a hoarse whisper, and then

thrashes violently in my arms, trying to punch and kick me.

But I know all too well how dangerous Petra is, how viciously she can fight if given ground; and my grip on her neck is relentless and grows tighter and stronger before I take a strong step back and then twist my hips sharply.

The action yanks Petra off her feet and swings her through the air with such force that when I whipsaw my weight back the other way, I hear the vertebrae in her neck crack and splinter as if struck by lightning.

CHAPTER 81

SHORTLY AFTER TEN in the morning, Marcus Morris shifted uncomfortably on the sidewalk outside Parliament, but then looked out forcefully at the cameras, microphones, and mob of reporters gathered around him. "Though he remains our respected colleague, someone who worked for more than ten years to see these games realized, Michael Lancer has been relieved of his duties for the duration of the Olympics."

"About bloody time!" someone shouted, and then the entire mob around *Sun* reporter Karen Pope exploded, roaring questions at the chairman

351

of the London Organising Committee like losing traders in a commodities pit.

Most of the questions were ones Pope wanted answered as well. Would the games go on? Or be suspended? If they went on, who would replace Lancer as the committee's chief of security? What about the growing number of countries withdrawing their teams from competition? Should they be listening to the athletes, who steadfastly argued against stopping or interrupting the games?

"We are listening to the athletes," Morris insisted in a strong voice. "The Olympics will go on. The Olympic ideals and spirit will survive. We will not buckle to this pressure. Four top specialists from Scotland Yard, MI5, SAS, and Private will oversee security for us in the final four days of the games. I am personally heartbroken that some countries have chosen to leave. It is a tragedy for the games and a tragedy for the athletes. For the rest, the games go on."

Morris then followed a phalanx of Metropolitan Police officers, who opened a hole in the mob for him and moved him toward a waiting car. The vast majority of the media surged as one after the LOCOG leader, bellowing all manner of questions.

Pope did not follow them. She leaned against the

wrought-iron fence that surrounds Parliament and reviewed her notes and reports from the morning and the evening before.

In a coup, she'd tracked down Elaine Pottersfield and learned that in addition to the radically intensified manhunt for Selena Farrell and James Daring, law enforcement efforts were focusing on the starting blocks that exploded, maiming Filatri Mundaho.

Mundaho remained in critical condition in London Bridge Hospital, but was said to be exhibiting a "tremendous fighting spirit" in the wake of two emergency surgeries to remove the shrapnel and treat his burns.

The starting blocks were another story. Made by Stackhouse Athletic Equipment, based on the company's famed Newton TI008 International "BEST" system, the starting blocks that exploded had been used ten times by ten different athletes in the previous days of qualifying.

The blocks were escorted to and from the track by IOC officials, and set up by a crew of timing specialists who claimed to have seen no issue with the blocks prior to the explosion. Several of those timing specialists were actually injured at the same time as Mundaho.

Between competitions, the blocks had been

locked away in a special underground room below the stadium. The Olympic athletics official who locked the blocks away the Saturday evening before the explosion was the same official who unlocked the storage room late Sunday afternoon. His name was Javier Cruz, a Panamanian, and he was the most grievously injured of the race officials, having lost an eye to the flying metal.

Scotland Yard bomb experts said the device was a block of metal machined to exactly replicate Stackhouse's standards. Except this machined block had been hollowed enough for shaved magnesium to be inserted along with a triggering device. Magnesium, an incredibly combustible material, explodes and burns with acetylene intensity.

Pottersfield had said, "The device would have killed a normal man. But Mundaho's superhuman reaction time saved his life, if not his limbs."

Pope flipped her notebook closed and felt like she had enough to write now. She thought to call Peter Knight to find out if he could add to what she knew, but then spotted a tall figure leaving the visitors gate at Parliament, shoulders rolled forward as he hurried south on St. Margaret Street, in the opposite direction of the dissipating mob of reporters.

She glanced back at them, realized none of them

had spotted Michael Lancer, and took off running after him. She caught up to Lancer as he entered Victoria Tower Gardens.

"Mr. Lancer?" she said, slowing beside him. "Karen Pope with the *Sun*."

The former Olympic security chief sighed and looked at her with such despair that she almost didn't have the heart to question him. But in her mind, she could hear Finch's voice shouting at her to continue on.

"Your firing," she said. "Do you think it's fair?"

Lancer hesitated, struggling inside, but then hung his head. "I do. I wanted the London games to be the greatest in history and the safest in history. I know that we tried to think of every possible scenario in our preparations over the years. But the truth is we simply did not foresee someone like Cronus, a fanatic with a small group of followers. In short, I failed. I'll be held responsible for what happened. It's my burden to bear and no one else's. And now, if you'll excuse me, I have to begin to live with that for the rest of my life."

CHAPTER 82

LAST TIME I'LL have to visit this hellhole, Teagan thought as she pushed a knapsack through a hole clipped in a chain-link fence that surrounded a condemned and contaminated factory building in the Docklands, several miles from Olympic Park.

She wriggled through after the knapsack, then picked it up and glanced at the inky sky. Somewhere a foghorn blasted. Dawn was not far off, and she had much to do before she could leave this wretched place for good.

The dew intensified the scent of the weeds as she hurried toward the dark shadow of the abandoned building, thinking how her sister Petra must be settling into her new life on Crete. Teagan had read the story about the fingerprint, and feared that Cronus would have been insanely angry with her sister. Instead, the reaction was practical rather than vengeful: her sister was sent to Greece early to prepare the house where they would live when all this was over.

Entering the building through a window she'd kicked out months before, Teagan imagined the house where Petra was, on a cliff above the Aegean, whitewashed against a cobalt sky, filled with all they could ever want or need.

She turned on a thin, red-lensed flashlight, clipped it to the cap she wore, and used the soft glow to navigate through what used to be the production floor of a textile mill. Wary of loose debris, she made her way to a staircase that descended into a musty basement.

A strong odor came to her soon enough, so eye-watering and foul that she stopped breathing through her nose and put the knapsack down on a three-legged bench. Bracing her weight against the bench to stop it from rocking, she removed eight IV bags from the knapsack.

Teagan arranged them in their proper order, and then used a hypodermic needle to draw liquid from a vial before shooting equal parts of the liquid into four of the bags. Finished, she got out the key that hung on a chain around her neck and picked up the eight IV bags, four in each hand.

When she reached the door where the stench was worst, she set the bags on the floor and slid the key into the padlock. The shackle freed with a click. She pocketed the lock and pushed the door open, knowing that if she were to breathe in through her nose she'd surely retch.

A moan became a groan echoing up out of the darkness.

"Dinnertime," Teagan said, and closed the door behind her.

Fifteen minutes later, she exited the storeroom feeling confident in the steps she had taken, the work she had done. Four days from now the...

She heard a crash from above her on the old production floor. Voices laughed and jeered before another crash echoed through the abandoned factory. She froze, thinking.

Teagan had been in the factory a dozen times in the last year, and she'd never once encountered another human and did not expect to. The building was contaminated with solvents, heavy metals, and other carcinogens, and the perimeter fence carried multiple hazardous-waste warning signs to that effect.

Her initial reaction was to go on the attack. But Cronus had been explicit. There were to be no confrontations if they could be avoided.

She shut off her flashlight, spun around, and groped for and shut the door to the storeroom. She struggled in her pocket for the padlock, got it finally, and set the shackle in the iron rings on the door and the jamb. A bottle bounced down the staircase behind her and shattered on the basement floor. She heard footsteps coming and drunken male voices.

Teagan reached up in the darkness to snap the lock shut, and felt the shackle catch before she ran a few steps and then paused, unsure. Did it lock?

A flashlight beam began to play back toward the staircase. She took off without hesitation this time, up on her toes, the way sprinters run. Having long ago committed the layout of the contaminated factory to memory, she dodged into a hall that would take her to a stone stairway and a bulkhead door.

Two minutes later, she was outside. Dawn threw the first rosy fingers of light across the London sky. She heard more crashing and hooting inside the factory, and decided it was probably a mob of drunken guys out for destruction. She told herself that once they got a whiff of that basement, they wouldn't be doing any further exploring. But as she crawled back through the hole in the fence, all Teagan could think about was the padlock, and whether it had clicked shut after all.

CHAPTER 83

MIDAFTERNOON THAT SECOND Friday of the games, the third-to-last day of competition, Peter Knight entered the lab at Private London and hurried gingerly to Hooligan as he held out a box wrapped in brown paper and packing tape.

"Is this a bomb?" Knight asked, dead serious.

Private London's chief scientist tore his attention away from the *Sun*'s sports page, which favorably assessed England's chances in the Olympic soccer finals against Brazil. He looked uneasily at the package. "What makes you think it's a bomb?"

Knight tapped on the return address.

Hooligan squinted. "Can't read that."

"Because it's ancient Greek," Knight said. "It says, 'Cronus.'"

"Fug."

"Exactly," Knight said, placing the box on the table beside the scientist. "Just picked it up at the front desk."

"Hear anything inside?" Hooligan asked.

"No ticking."

"Could be rigged digitally. Or remote-controlled."

Knight looked queasy. "Should we clear out? Call in the bomb squad?"

The scientist scratched at his scruffy red beard. "That's Jack's call."

Two minutes later, Jack was standing inside the lab, looking at the box. The American appeared exhausted. This was one of the few breaks he'd had from running security at Olympic Park since taking over on Monday. There had been no further attacks after the Mundaho incident; and that was, in Knight's estimation, largely due to Jack's Herculean efforts.

"Can you X-ray the box without blowing us up?" Jack asked.

"Can always try, right?" Hooligan said, picking up the box as if it had teeth.

The scientist took the box to a worktable at the far end of the lab. He started up a portable scanner similar to those being used at the Olympic venues, set the box outside the scanner, and waited for it to warm up.

Knight watched the box as if it could seal his fate, then tried to restrain his sudden urge to leave the lab. He had two children who would be three years old tomorrow. In some manner, he still had his mother. Could he risk being in a closed room with a potentially explosive device? To get his mind off the danger, he glanced at the television screen, which was showing news highlights and image after image of gold medal–winning athletes from all over the world taking their victory laps with the flags of their own nations and that of Cameroon.

It had all been spontaneous, the athletes showing their respect to Mundaho and defiance to Cronus. Scores of them had taken up the Cameroonian flag, including the English soccer team after it won its semifinal against Germany three evenings before. The media was eating it up, calling the gesture a universal protest against the lunatic stalking the games.

American Hunter Pierce remained at the forefront of the protest against Cronus. The diver had been interviewed almost every day since Mundaho's tragedy, and each time she had spoken resolutely of the athletes' solidarity in their refusal to allow the games to be halted or interrupted.

Mundaho's condition had been upgraded to serious. He had third-degree burns and wounds over much of his lower body, but he was said to be alert, well aware of the protests, and taking spirit from the global outpouring of support.

As heartening as that all was, Knight tore his attention off the screen in Private London's lab, believing that the assault would not stop because of the athletes' protests. Cronus would try to attack again before the end of the games.

Knight was sure of it. But where? And when? The relay races tomorrow afternoon? The soccer finals between England and Brazil at Wembley Stadium Saturday evening? The men's marathon on Sunday? Or the closing ceremonies that night?

"Here we go," Hooligan said, pushing the box from Cronus onto a small conveyor belt that carried it through the scanner. He twisted the scanner's screen so they all could see.

The box came into view and so did its contents.

Knight cringed.

"Jesus Christ," Jack said. "Are those real?"

CHAPTER 84

THE WOMAN'S DEATHLY pale hands had been severed at the wrists with a blade and a saw that left the flesh smooth and the bones ragged and chipped.

Hooligan asked, "Should I fingerprint her?"

"Let's leave that to Scotland Yard," Jack said.

"No matter," Knight said. "I'm betting those hands belong to a war criminal."

"Andjela Brazlic?" Jack asked.

Hooligan nodded. "The odds are definitely there, eh?"

"Why send them to you?" Jack asked Knight.

"I don't know."

The question continued to haunt Knight on his way home later that evening. Why him? He supposed that Cronus was sending a message with the hands. But about what? The fingerprint she'd left on the box? Was this Cronus's way of displaying his ruthlessness?

Knight called Elaine Pottersfield and told her that Hooligan was bringing the hands to Scotland Yard, and laid out his suspicions regarding their identity.

"If they are Andjela Brazlic's, it shows dissension in Cronus's ranks," the inspector speculated.

"Or Cronus is simply saying that it's fruitless to track this particular war criminal. She made a mistake. And now she's dead."

"That all?" she asked.

"We're going to Kate's forest in the morning," Knight said. "And the party is at five thirty."

The silence was brief. "I'm sorry, Peter," she said, and hung up.

Knight reached home around ten, wondering if his sister-in-law would ever be at peace with him or with Kate's death. It wasn't until he was standing at his front door that he allowed himself to realize that three years before, right about this time, his late wife had gone into labor.

He had a sudden memory of Kate's face after her water had broken—no fear, just sheer joy at the impending miracle. Then he recalled the ambulance taking her away. Knight opened the door and went inside, as deeply confused and heartbroken as he'd been thirty-six months before.

The house smelled of chocolate, and two brightly wrapped presents sat on the table in the hallway. He grimaced, realizing that he hadn't yet had a chance to go shopping for the kids. Work had been all-consuming. Or had he just let it be all-consuming so he would not have to think about their birthday and the anniversary of their mother's death?

With no good answer to any of it, Knight examined the presents and was surprised to see that they were from his mother. The gift tags were signed: "With love, Grandmother."

He smiled and tears brimmed in his eyes; if his mother had taken the time from her isolation, grief, and bitterness to buy her grandchildren presents, then maybe she was not allowing herself to retreat as completely as she had after his father's death.

"I'll go home then, Mr. Knight," Marta said, coming out of the kitchen. "They are asleep. Kitchen is clean. Fudge made. Luke made an unsuccessful attempt at the big-boy loo. I bought party favors, and ordered a cake, too. I can be here all day tomorrow through the party. But I will need Sunday off."

Sunday. The men's marathon. The closing ceremonies. Knight had to be available. Perhaps he could talk his mother or Boss into coming one more time.

"Sunday off, and you really don't need to be here before noon tomorrow," Knight said. "I usually take them to Epping Forest and the High Beach church the morning of their birthday."

"What's there?" she asked.

"My late wife and I were married at the church. Her ashes are scattered in the woods out there. She was from Waltham Abbey and the forest was one of her favorite places."

"Oh, I'm sorry," Marta said uncomfortably, and moved toward the door. "Noon, then."

"Noon sounds good," he said and shut the door behind her.

He turned off the lights, checked on the kids, and went to his bedroom.

Knight sat on the edge of his bed, gazing at Kate looking out from the photo at him and remembering in vivid detail the manner in which she'd died.

He broke down sobbing.

CHAPTER 85

"I'M THREE!" ISABEL yelled in her father's ear.

He jerked awake from a nightmare that featured Kate held hostage by Cronus—not the madman stalking the Olympics but the ancient Greek figure carrying a long scythe and hungering to swallow his children.

Dripping in sweat, his face contorted with dread, Knight looked in bewilderment at his daughter, who appeared upset and was stepping back from her father, holding her blanket tightly to her cheek.

His senses came to him, and he thought: *She's fine! Luke's fine! It was a horrible, horrible dream.*

Knight exhaled, smiled, and said, "Look at how big you are!"

"Three," Isabel said, her grin returning.

"Lukey three, too!" his son announced from the doorway.

"You don't say," Knight said as Luke bounced up onto the bed and into his arms. Isabel climbed up after him and cuddled into him.

Their smells surrounded him and calmed him and made him realize again what a lucky, lucky person he was to have them in his life, part of Kate that would live on and grow.

"Presents?" Luke asked.

"They're not here yet," Knight said, too quickly. "Not until the party."

"No, Daddy," Isabel protested. "That funny man bring presents yesterday. They're downstairs."

"Mr. Boss brought them?" he asked.

His son nodded grimly. "Boss no like Lukey."

"His loss," Knight said. "Go get the presents. You can open them up here."

That set off a stampede as they both scrambled off the bed. Twenty seconds later they were running back into the room, gasping and grinning like fools.

"Go ahead," Knight said.

Giggling, they tore into the wrapping and soon

had the presents from Amanda open. Isabel's gift was a beautiful silver locket on a chain. They opened the locket to find a picture of Kate.

"That Mommy?" Isabel asked.

Knight was genuinely touched at his mother's thoughtfulness. "Yes, so you can take her with you everywhere," he said in a hoarse voice.

"What this, Daddy?" Luke asked, eyeing his present suspiciously.

Knight took it, examined it, and said, "It's a very special watch, for a very big boy. You see, it has Harry Potter, the famous wizard, on the dial, and there's your name engraved on the back."

"Big-boy watch?" Luke asked.

"Yes," Knight said, and then teased: "We'll put it away until you're bigger."

Outraged, his son shoved out his wrist. "No! Lukey big boy! Lukey three!"

"I completely forgot," Knight said, and put the watch on his son's wrist, pleasantly surprised that the band was a near-perfect fit.

While Luke paraded around, admiring his watch, Knight hung the locket around Isabel's neck, closed the chain clasp, and oohed and aahed when she looked at herself in the mirror, the spitting image of Kate as a young girl.

He changed Luke, then bathed and fed them

both before getting Isabel into a dress and his son into blue shorts and a white collared shirt. With admonitions not to get their clothes dirty, Knight set a record time showering, shaving, and dressing. They left the house at nine, went to the garage a few blocks away, and retrieved a Range Rover they rarely used.

Knight drove north through the streets with Isabel and Luke in their car seats behind him, listening to the news on the radio. It was the last full day of Olympic competition, with many relay-race finals to be decided that evening.

The announcers talked of the heavy criticism being heaped on Scotland Yard and MI5 over their inability to make any kind of a major break in the Cronus investigation. No mention was made of the war criminal's hands, though. Pottersfield had asked that that be kept under wraps for the time being.

Many athletes who were finished with the competition were already leaving. Most others, like Hunter Pierce, had vowed to remain at Olympic Park until the end, no matter what Cronus and his Furies might try.

Knight drove to Enfield, then east and south of Waltham Abbey toward High Beach and Epping Forest.

"Lots of trees," Isabel said when they'd entered the forest proper.

"Your mommy liked lots of trees."

The dappled sunlight shone through the foliage that surrounded the High Beach church, which sat in a clearing not far into the woods. There were several cars parked, but Epping Forest was a popular place to walk and Knight did not expect anyone else to be here specifically for Kate. His mother was lost in her own grief, and Kate's parents had both died young.

They went into the empty church, where Knight had the children each light a candle in their mother's memory. He lighted one for Kate, and then lighted four more for his colleagues who died in the plane crash. Holding Isabel's and Luke's hands, he led them from the church and out along a path that led into the woods.

A light breeze rustled the leaves. Six or seven minutes later, the vegetation thinned and they passed through a tumbledown stone wall into a sparse grove of ancient oaks growing in long untamed grass that sighed in the summer wind.

Knight stood awhile looking at the scene, hugging his children to him, and struggling to control his emotions for their sake.

"Your mommy used to go to that church as a

little girl, but she liked to come out here," he told them softly. "She said the trees were so old that this was a blessed place where she could talk to God. That's why I spread her..."

He choked up.

"It was a perfect choice, Peter," a woman's emotion-drenched voice said behind them. "This was Kate's favorite place."

Knight turned, wiping tears with his sleeve.

Holding tightly to his pant leg, Isabel asked, "Who's that lady, Daddy?"

Knight smiled. "That's your aunt Elaine, honey. Mommy's older sister."

CHAPTER 86

"I KNEW I couldn't make the party," Knight's sister-in-law explained quietly on the ride back while the children slept in their car seats. "And anyway, I thought meeting them there would make me feel better."

They were nearing the garage where Knight kept the Range Rover.

"Did it?" Knight asked.

Pottersfield nodded and her eyes got glassy. "It seemed right, as if I could feel her there." She hesitated and then said, "I'm sorry. The way I treated you. I know it was all Kate's decision to have the twins at home. I just—"

"No more talk of that," Knight said, parking.

"We're beyond all of it. My children are lucky to have you in their lives. *I'm* lucky to have you in my life."

She sighed, and smiled sadly. "Okay. Need help?"

Knight looked over his shoulder at his sleeping children. "Yes; they're getting too big to carry that far by myself."

Pottersfield took Isabel and Knight hoisted Luke, and they walked the two blocks to his house. He heard the television playing inside.

"The new nanny," he said, fishing for his keys. "She always arrives early."

"You don't hear that much anymore."

"It's brilliant, actually," Knight admitted. "She's a miracle, the only one to ever tame them. She's got them helping to pick up their room and going to sleep at the snap of her fingers."

He opened the door and Marta appeared almost instantly. She frowned to see Luke sleeping on his father's shoulder. "Too much excitement, I think," she said, took him from Knight, and looked curiously at Pottersfield.

"Marta, this is Elaine," Knight said. "My sister-in-law."

"Oh, hello," Pottersfield said, studying Marta. "Peter speaks highly of you."

Marta laughed nervously and lowered her head, saying, "Mr. Knight is too kind." She paused and asked, "Did I see you on the television?"

"Maybe. I work at Scotland Yard."

Marta looked ready to reply when Isabel woke up grumpily, looked at her aunt, and whined, "I want my daddy."

Knight took her, saying, "Daddy has to go to work for a few hours, but he'll be back in time for the party."

Marta said, "We'll go get cake soon? And balloons?"

Isabel brightened and Luke roused. Pottersfield's cell phone rang.

The Scotland Yard inspector listened closely, began nodding, and then said, "Where are they taking her?"

She listened while Marta took Isabel from Knight and began carrying her and Luke down the hall toward the kitchen, saying, "Who wants apple juice?"

Pottersfield snapped shut her phone, looked at Knight, and said, "A constable just picked up Selena Farrell wandering incoherent, filthy, and covered in her own excrement somewhere inside the ruins of the old Beckton Gas Works. They're bringing her to London Bridge Hospital."

Knight glanced back over his shoulder at Marta, who held Isabel's and Luke's hands tightly.

"I'll be back by five to help you put up decorations," he promised.

"Everything will be under control by then," she replied confidently. "Leave everything to me, Mr. Knight."

CHAPTER 87

"ARE YOU SURE?" I demand, doing everything in my power not to scream into my cell phone.

"Positive," Marta hisses back to me. "She was found wandering the Beckton Gas Works, not far from the factory. Who was there last?"

First Petra and now you, Teagan, I think murderously as I glance at Marta's sister next to me behind the wheel of her car. My thoughts are boiling again. But I reply cryptically to Marta, "Does it matter?"

"I'd go clean that factory out if I were you," Marta says. "They're right behind us."

It's true. Over the homicidal buzz I've got going in my ears, I can almost hear the baying of dogs.

What a blunder! What a colossal blunder! Farrell

wasn't supposed to be freed until tomorrow morning, a diversion that would draw all police attention to her while I completed my revenge. I should have just killed Farrell when I had the chance. But no, I had to be clever. I had to pile deception upon deception upon deception. But this one has backfired on me.

My fingers go to that scar on the back of my head and the hatred ignites.

My hand has been forced. My only hope is ruthlessness.

"Take the children," I say. "Now. You know what to do."

"I do," Marta replies. "The little darlings are already fast asleep."

CHAPTER 88

THE SIGHTS, SOUNDS, and smells of London Bridge Hospital unnerved Knight in a way he did not expect. He hadn't been back in a medical facility of any sort since Kate's body was taken to one and it made him feel upended by the time he and Pottersfield reached the intensive care unit.

"This is what she looked like when they found her," the Metropolitan Police officer guarding the room said, showing them a picture.

Farrell was dressed as Syren St. James, filthy in the extreme, and looking as dazed as a lobotomy patient. An IV line hung out of one hand.

"She talking?" Pottersfield asked.

"Babbled about a body with no hands," the officer said.

"No hands?" Knight said, glancing at Pottersfield.

"Not much of what she said made sense. But you might have a better go now that they've given her an antinarcotic."

"She was on narcotics?" Pottersfield asked. "We know that for certain?"

"Powerful doses, crossed with sedatives," he replied.

They entered the intensive care unit. Professor Selena Farrell lay asleep in a bed surrounded by monitoring equipment, her skin a deathly gray. Pottersfield went to her side and said, "Professor Farrell?"

The professor's face screwed up in anger. "Go away. Head. Hurts. Bad." Her words were slurred and trailed off at the end.

"Professor Farrell," Pottersfield said firmly. "I'm Chief Inspector Elaine Pottersfield with the Metropolitan Police. I have to speak with you. Open your eyes, please."

Farrell's eyes blinked and she cringed. "Turn off lights. Migraine."

A nurse shut the drapes. Farrell opened her eyes again. She looked around the room, saw Knight, and turned back to Pottersfield, puzzled. "What happened to me?"

"We were hoping you could tell us, Professor," Knight said.

"I don't know."

Pottersfield said, "Can you explain why your DNA—your hair, to be exact—was found in one of the letters from Cronus to Karen Pope?"

The information was slow to penetrate Farrell's fogged brain. "Pope? The reporter?" she said to Knight. "My DNA? No, I don't remember."

"What do you remember?" Knight demanded.

Farrell blinked and groaned, and then said: "Dark room. I'm on a bed, alone. Tied down. Can't get up. My head is splitting open, and they won't give me anything to stop it."

"Who is 'they'?" Knight pressed.

"Women. Different women."

Pottersfield was beginning to look irritated. She said, "Selena, do you understand that your DNA links you to seven murders in the last two weeks?"

That shocked the professor and she became more alert. "What? Seven? I haven't killed anyone. I never...what, what day is it?"

"Saturday, August eleventh, 2012," Knight replied.

The professor moaned. "No. It felt like I was only there overnight."

"In the dark room with women?" Pottersfield asked.

"You don't believe me?"

"No," Pottersfield said.

Knight said, "Why did you fake getting sick and flee your office when Karen Pope played the flute music for you?"

Her eyes opened wider. "It made me sick because...I'd heard it before."

CHAPTER 89

I HANG UP the phone with Marta and look over at Teagan, feeling as if I'd like to rip her head off right now. But she's behind the wheel and an accident is out of the question at this late stage of the game.

"Turn around," I say, struggling for calm. "We've got to go to the factory."

"The factory?" Teagan replies nervously. "It's broad daylight."

"Farrell escaped. She was picked up inside the gasworks. Knight and the Scotland Yard inspector Pottersfield are with her at the hospital right now."

Teagan loses color.

"How could that have happened?" I demand softly. "She wasn't supposed to be freed until tomorrow morning. It was your responsibility to see to that, sister."

Panic-stricken, she says, "I should have told you, but I knew how much pressure you were under. There were drunken lads inside the factory when I was there yesterday morning. I figured the smell would keep them from the room. They must have broken the lock and let her go or something. I don't know."

"We've got to clean the place," I say. "Get us there. Now."

We don't talk on the drive, or during our entry into the toxic factory grounds, or as we sneak inside the basement. I have only been here once before, so Teagan leads. We both carry trash bags.

The smell coming from the open storeroom door is obscenely foul. But Teagan goes inside without hesitation. I glance at the iron rings on the door and the frame, unbroken, and then let my gaze travel across the floor.

The lock's in the corner, the shackle open but not broken.

I crouch, pick it up, and loop the shackle around my middle finger as though it were a brass knuckle, hiding the lock inside my palm. Inside, Teagan is already gloved and stuffing used IV equipment into the trash bag.

"Let's get this done," I say, and move toward her before squatting down to pick up a used syringe with my left hand.

Rising, feeling as vengeful as a spurned lover, I move the needle toward the trash bag as a feint before delivering an uppercut with my right hand, the shackle leading.

Teagan never has a chance. She never sees the blow coming.

The impact crushes her larynx.

She staggers backward, choking, purple-faced, her eyes bugging out of her head, staring at me in disbelief. The second blow breaks her nose, hurls her against the wall, and makes her understand that I am an infinitely superior being. My third strike connects with her temple and she crumples in the grime.

CHAPTER 90

"OF COURSE YOU'VE heard that music before," Pottersfield shot back. "It was all over your computer. So was a program used to take control of the Olympic stadium's electronic scoreboard the night of the opening ceremony."

"What?" the professor cried, struggling to sit upright and wincing in pain. "No, no! Someone began sending me that music about a year ago on my answering machine and in attachments to e-mails from anonymous accounts. It was like I was being stalked. After a while, anytime I heard it, I got sick."

"Convenient nonsense," Pottersfield snapped. "What about the program on your computer?"

"I don't know what program you're talking about. Someone must have put it on there, maybe whoever was sending me the music."

Knight was incredulous. "Did you report this cyberstalking to anyone?"

The classics professor nodded firmly. "Twice, as a matter of fact, at the Wapping police station. But the detectives said that flute music was not a crime, and I had no other proof that someone was stalking me. I said I had suspicions about who was behind the music, but they didn't want to hear any of it. They advised me to change my phone number and my e-mail address, which I did. It stopped. And the headaches stopped until you played the music again in my office."

Knight squinted, trying to make sense of this explanation. Was it possible that Farrell had been set up as a diversion of some sort? Why wasn't she just killed?

Pottersfield must have been thinking along the same lines because she asked, "Who did you think was behind the music?"

Farrell made a little shrugging motion. "Well, I've only known one person in my life who plays a panpipe."

Knight and Pottersfield said nothing.

"Jim Daring," the professor said. "You know, the

guy at the British Museum? The one who has the television show?"

That changes things, Knight thought, remembering how Daring had spoken highly of Farrell and repeatedly told him and Pope to go see her. Was it all part of a frame job?

Pottersfield still sounded sharply skeptical. "How do you know he played a panpipe, and whyever would he use the music to harass you?"

"He had a panpipe in the Balkans in the nineties. He used to play it for me."

"And?" Knight said.

Farrell looked uncomfortable. "He, Daring, was interested in me romantically. I told him I wasn't interested, and he got angry and then obsessed. He stalked me back then. I reported him, too. In the end it didn't matter. I was injured in a truck accident and airlifted out of Sarajevo. I haven't seen him since."

"Not once in how many years?" Knight asked.

"Sixteen? Seventeen?"

"And yet you suspected him?" Pottersfield said.

The professor turned stony. "I had no one else to suspect."

"I imagine not," the Scotland Yard inspector said. "Because he's missing, too. Daring, I mean."

The confusion returned to Farrell's face. "What?"

Knight said, "You claim you were held in a dark room and tended by women. How did you get out?"

Farrell considered the question for several moments before she said, "Boys, but I'm not...no, I definitely remember I heard boys' voices, and then I passed out again. When I woke up I could move my arms and legs. So I got up and found a door and..." She hesitated and looked off into the distance. "I think I was in some kind of old factory. There were brick walls."

Pottersfield said, "You told the officer about a dead body without hands."

There was fear on the professor's face as she looked back and forth from Knight to Pottersfield. "There were flies on her. Hundreds."

"Where?"

"I don't know," she said, grimacing and rubbing at her head. "Somewhere in that factory, I think. I was dizzy. I fell a lot. I couldn't think right at all."

After a long pause, Pottersfield seemed to come to some sort of conclusion. She pulled out her phone, got up, and took several steps away from Farrell's hospital bed. A moment later she said, "It's Pottersfield. You're looking for an abandoned factory of some sort near the Beckton Gas Works.

Brick walls. There could be a body in there with no hands. Maybe more."

In the meantime, Knight thought of the reporting that Karen Pope had done on Farrell, and asked, "How did you get into that room in the factory?"

The professor shook her head. "I don't remember."

"What's the last thing you do remember?" Pottersfield said, shutting her phone.

Farrell blinked, then tightened and replied, "I can't say."

Knight said, "Would Syren St. James know?"

The name clearly stunned the professor, who asked softly, "Who?"

"Your alter ego among the elite lesbians of London," Pottersfield said.

"I don't know what you're—"

"Everyone in London knows about Syren St. James," Knight said, cutting her off. "She's been in all the papers."

The professor looked crushed. "What? How?"

"Karen Pope," Knight replied. "She found out about your secret life and wrote about it."

Farrell cried weakly, "Why would she do that?"

"Because the DNA linked you to the killings," Pottersfield said. "It still does. The DNA says you're involved somehow with Cronus and his Furies."

Farrell went hysterical, shouting: "I am not Cronus! I am not a Fury! I've had another life, but that's no one's business but my own. I've never had anything to do with any killings!"

The attending nurse burst into the room and ordered them out.

"One more minute," Pottersfield insisted. "You were in the Candy Bar the last time you were seen, two weeks ago last night, Friday, July twenty-seventh."

That seemed to puzzle the professor.

"Your friend Nell said she saw you there," Knight said. "She told Pope you were with a woman wearing a pillbox hat with a veil that hid her face."

Farrell searched her memory, and then slowly nodded. "Yes. I went with her to her car. She had wine in the car and poured me some and..." She gazed at Pottersfield. "She drugged me."

"Who is *she?*" Pottersfield demanded.

Farrell, embarrassed, said, "Her real name? I couldn't tell you. I assume she was operating under a handle, as I was. But she told me to call her Marta. She said she was from Estonia."

CHAPTER 91

VIOLENT THUNDERSTORMS ripped through London late that Saturday afternoon.

Lightning brought rain that pelted off the windshield as Pottersfield's unmarked car sped toward Chelsea, siren wailing. The inspector kept glancing furiously at Knight, who looked as if he'd fought a ghost. He dialed Marta's cell phone yet again.

"Answer," he kept saying. "Answer, you bitch."

Pottersfield shouted, "How could you not have checked her out, Peter?"

"I did check her out, Elaine!" Knight shouted back. "You did, too! She was just so perfect for what I needed."

They screeched to a halt in front of Knight's house, where several other police cars were already parked, their lights flashing. Despite the rain, a crowd was gathering. Uniformed officers were already starting to put up barriers.

Knight leaped from Pottersfield's vehicle, feeling as if he were tottering on the edge of a dark and unfathomable abyss.

Bella? Little Lukey? It's their birthday.

Scotland Yard inspector Billy Casper met Knight at the door, his face somber. "I'm sorry, Peter. We got here too late."

"No," he cried, rushing inside. "No."

Everywhere Knight looked he saw the things that surrounded his children—the toys, baby powder, and packages of balloons, streamers, and candles. He walked numbly by it all into the kitchen. Luke's cereal bowl from breakfast still had milk in it. Isabel's blanket lay on the floor beside her high chair.

Knight picked it up, thinking, *Bella must be lost without it.* The enormity of his predicament suddenly threatened to crush him. But he refused to collapse, and fought back in the only way he knew how: he kept moving.

He found Pottersfield and said, "Check her apartment. Her address is on her résumé. And her prints have to be everywhere in here. Can you track her cell number?"

"If she's got it on," Pottersfield said. "In the meantime, call your friend Pope and I'll get to the media people I know. We'll get the twins' faces everywhere, Peter. Someone will have seen them."

Knight began to nod, but then said, "What if that's what they want?"

"What?" Pottersfield asked. "Why?"

"A sideshow," he said. "A diversion. Think about it. If you put their faces everywhere and tell the public that they've been kidnapped by a woman believed to be an associate of Cronus, law enforcement manpower and media attention go to Isabel and Luke, leaving the Olympics open to a final attack."

"We've got to do something, Peter."

Knight couldn't believe he was saying it, but he replied, "We can wait them out a few hours at least, Elaine. See if they get nervous. See if they call. If they don't call by, say, eight, then put their faces everywhere."

Before she could reply, he tugged out his cell phone and dialed Hooligan's number.

Knight heard cheering and Hooligan crowed, "Did you catch that, Peter? It's one-one. We're tied!"

"Come to my house," Knight said. "Now."

"Now?" Hooligan cried, sounding a little drunk.

"Have you gone bonkers? This is for the bloody gold medal and I've got midfield seats."

"Cronus has my kids," Knight said.

Silence, then: "No! Fug. I'll be right there, Peter. Right there."

Knight hung up. Elaine held out her hand for his cell phone. "I'll need it for a few minutes while we put on a trace."

He handed her the phone and went upstairs. He got Kate's picture and brought it with him into the nursery as thunder shook the house. He sat on the daybed, looked at the empty cribs and the wallpaper Kate had picked out, and wondered if he had been destined for tragedy and loss.

Then he noticed the bottle of liquid children's antihistamine on the changing table. He set Kate's picture down and went over, seeing that the bottle was almost empty. At that, he felt duped and enraged. She'd been drugging his kids right under his nose.

Pottersfield knocked and came in. She glanced at the photograph of Kate on the daybed, and then handed him his phone. "You're now linked to our system. Any call coming in to your number we should be able to trace. And I just got an alert. We found two bodies in a condemned factory contaminated with hazardous waste not far from the gasworks. Both women in their thirties. One was beaten to death within the last few hours, no ID. The other died earlier this week and was handless. We're assuming it's Andjela Brazlic and her older sister, Nada."

"Two Furies gone. It's just Marta and Cronus now," Knight said dully. "Do you think Daring could be Cronus? After what Farrell told us? The stalking in the Balkans...the flute?"

"I don't know."

Knight suddenly felt surrounded by doubt, strong and claustrophobic. "Does it matter where I am when a call comes in?"

"It shouldn't," Pottersfield replied.

He looked at Kate's photograph and said, "I can't just sit here, Elaine. I feel like I have to move. I'm going to take a walk. Is that okay?"

"Just keep your cell phone on."

"Tell Hooligan to call me when he gets here. And Jack Morgan should be notified. They're at the stadium for the relays."

She nodded and said, "We'll find them."

"I know," he said, even though his conviction was wavering.

Knight put on his slicker and left by the rear door in case the media were already camped outside. He walked down the alley, trying to decide whether to wander aimlessly, or to get the car and drive back to the High Beach church to pray. But then he understood that he really had just one place to go, only one person he wanted to see.

Knight altered his direction and trudged through the rainy city, passing pubs and hearing cheering inside. It sounded like England was winning soccer gold while he was losing everything that ever mattered to him.

His hair and his pant legs were soaking wet when he reached the door on Milner Street and rang the bell and pounded the knocker while looking up at the security camera.

The door opened, revealing Boss. "She can't be seen," he said snippily.

"Get out of my way, little man," Knight said in a tone so threatening that his mother's assistant stood aside without protest.

Knight opened the door to his mother's studio without knocking. Amanda was hunched over her design table, cutting fabric. A dozen or more new original creations hung on mannequins around the room.

His mother looked up icily. "Haven't I made it abundantly clear that I wish to be left alone, Peter?"

Walking toward her, Knight said, "Mother—"

But she cut him off: "Leave me alone, Peter. What in God's name are you doing here? It's your children's birthday. You should be with them."

It was the final straw. Knight felt dizzy and then blacked out.

CHAPTER 92

KAREN POPE HURRIED through the drizzling rain and the dwindling light toward Knight's house in Chelsea. She'd been tipped by the *Sun*'s police-beat reporter that something big was going on at the Private operative's home, and she'd gone there immediately, dialing Knight's number constantly on the way.

But Pope kept getting an odd beeping noise and then a voice saying that his number was "experiencing network difficulties." She could see the police barrier ahead and...

"Hey—Peter call you in, too, then?" Hooligan asked, trotting up beside her. His eyes were red and his breath smelled of cigarettes, garlic, and beer. "I came from the bloody gold-medal game. I missed the game-winning goal!"

"Missed it for what?" she demanded. "Why is Scotland Yard here?"

He told her and Pope felt like crying. "Why? Why his kids?"

It was the same thing she asked Pottersfield when they got inside.

"Peter believes it's a diversionary tactic," the inspector said.

Hooligan could not hide the slight slur in his voice as he said, "Maybe. I mean, this Marta was here the past fortnight, right?"

"Give or take, I think," Pope said.

"Right. So I'm asking myself why," Hooligan replied. "And I'm thinking Cronus sends her in as a spy. He can't get someone inside Scotland Yard, but he can get this Marta inside Private, right?"

"Okay," Pottersfield said, squinting.

"Where are Peter's computers? His phones?"

"He's got his cell with him," Pottersfield said. "House phone is in the kitchen. I saw the computer upstairs in his room."

Twenty minutes later, Hooligan found Pottersfield and Pope talking with Billy Casper. "Thought you'd want to see this, Inspector," he said, holding up two small evidence bags. "Picked up the bug on the phone and the keystroke recorders on the DSL cable. I'm betting his cell's bugged as well. Maybe more."

"Call him," Pottersfield said.

"I tried," he said. "And texted him. I'm getting no answer, other than something about network difficulties."

CHAPTER 93

DARKNESS WAS FALLING outside Amanda's studio. Knight's cell phone lay on the coffee table. He sat on the couch, looking at the phone, his brain feeling scalded and his stomach emptier than it had ever been.

Why hadn't they called?

His mother sat beside him, saying, "It's more than anyone as good as you should have to bear, but you can't give up hope, Peter."

"Absolutely not," Boss said emphatically. "Those two barbarians of yours are fighters. You have to be as well."

But Knight felt as beaten as he had when he held his newborns and watched his wife's body rushed to the ambulance. "It's their birthday," he said softly. "They were expecting what any three-year-old expects. Cake and ice cream and..."

Amanda reached out and stroked her son's hair. It was such a rare and unexpected gesture that Knight looked over at her with a feeble smile. "I know how horrid life's been for you lately, Mother, but I wanted to thank you for caring about them. The only presents they got to open were from you."

She looked surprised. "Is that so? I didn't think they'd get there so soon."

"I brought them over," Boss said. "I thought they should be there."

Knight said, "Thank you, Boss. They loved them. And I must say, Mother, that putting the picture of Kate in the locket was one of the kindest and most thoughtful things you've ever done."

His mother, normally stoic, got tears in her eyes. "Boss and I worried because they weren't toys."

"No, no, they loved them," Knight insisted. "Luke was wearing that watch as if it were a gold medal. And the necklace fits Isabel perfectly. I don't think she'll ever take it off."

Amanda blinked several times, and then glanced at Boss before asking, "You think they're wearing them now, Peter? The watch and the necklace?"

"I would assume so," Knight replied. "I didn't see them in the house."

Amanda looked to Boss, who was grinning. "Did you activate them?"

Boss replied, "Even before I registered the warranties!"

"What are you two talking about?" Knight said.

"Didn't you look at the boxes they came in, Peter?" Amanda cried. "The necklace and watch were manufactured by Trace Angels, a company I've invested in. There are tiny GPS transmitters embedded in the jewelry so parents can track their children!"

CHAPTER 94

KNIGHT BOLTED OUT the door to his mother's house, watching two tiny, heart-shaped icons pulsing and moving slowly on a map on the screen of his iPhone.

According to the map, Luke and Isabel were less than two miles away! That realization had caused Knight to run from his mother's without a moment's hesitation. He went out into the street to find a cab and to see why his phone was having trouble connecting indoors.

Knight punched in Elaine Pottersfield's number again, and got nothing but a message about network problems. He was about to turn and rush back into Amanda's home when he saw a taxi coming.

He hailed it and jumped inside. "Lancaster Gate tube station," he said.

"Yah, mon," the driver said. "Hey, it's you!"

Knight did a double take, realizing it was the same driver who'd chased the taxi that had tried to run him and Lancer down.

"Cronus has my kids."

"De crazy guy blew up Mundaho?" the Jamaican cried.

"Go like hell, man," Knight said.

They roared northwest toward Brompton Road while Knight again tried Pottersfield's number. It did not go through, but he'd no sooner ended the attempt than the iPhone buzzed, alerting him to a text.

It was from Hooligan and read:

At your house. Your computer and phone bugged. Assume your cell bugged 2. Maybe traceable. Call.

Traceable? Knight thought. *They've been tracking me?*

"Pull over," he yelled.

"But your kids, mon!" the taxi driver said.

"Pull over," Knight said, forcing himself to calm down. He glanced at the beating hearts on his screen. They'd gone into an address on Porchester Terrace.

"Do you have a cell phone?"

"My old lady's phone died this morning," the driver said, stopping at the curb. "I gave her mine to use while hers be fixed."

"Son of a…" Knight said. He looked at the screen one last time and memorized the address where the twins were being held.

Then he handed the phone to the driver along with two fifty-pound notes. "Listen carefully, mate. I'm going to leave this phone with you, and you're going to drive it out to Heathrow."

"What?"

"Don't argue," Knight said, now scribbling on a business card. "Drive it to Heathrow and then circle back to this address in Chelsea. You'll see police there. Ask for Inspector Pottersfield or Hooligan Crawford with Private. Give them the phone. There'll be a reward in it for you."

"What about your kids, mon?"

But Knight was already gone, running across Brompton Road toward Montpelier Street, heading north toward Hyde Park, thinking that the last thing he wanted was to have police arrive en masse, surround the place, and force Marta's hand—or Cronus's hand, for that matter. It could cost Luke and Isabel their lives, and Knight could not survive that. He'd scout the place out, and then find a phone so he could alert Elaine, Jack, Hooligan, Pope, and everyone else in London.

Knight was gasping for air by the time he reached the trail that parallels the west shore of the Serpentine. His lungs were on fire when he left the park ten minutes later and crossed Bayswater Road across from the Lancaster Gate tube station.

He went west on Bayswater, passed a crowd of revelers at the Swan pub, still celebrating England's come-from-behind victory over Brazil, and finally took a right onto Porchester Terrace. The address he sought was on the west side of the street near Fulton Mews.

Knight stayed on the eastern sidewalk, moving methodically north until he'd gotten as close to the address as he dared. He desperately wished he had his binoculars with him, but he could see that the white apartment building had balconies on every floor and iron bars on the first-floor windows.

There were identical apartment buildings to either side of the building Knight was targeting. Every window in the building was dark, save for a light that glowed from French doors leading to the balcony of a flat on the northeast corner of the third floor. Was this where Marta had his children?

Rain began to fall again, hard enough that Knight decided he would not look out of place if he put the hood on his slicker up and walked past the building on the east side of the street.

Were Isabel and Luke inside? Cronus? Was this their hideout? Knight walked by, taking nonchalant glances at the doorway, wondering if he should risk crossing to the other side for a closer look before he went to one of the hotels over on Inverness Terrace to call Elaine.

Then he noticed how close that balcony was to the balcony immediately to the north, which was attached to a wholly separate building. It appeared to Knight that one would almost certainly be able to see from that balcony on the adjacent building into the apartment where he believed Luke and Isabel were being held.

Hell, you could probably jump from one balcony to the other.

Knight slowed and studied the facades of the apartment buildings, trying to figure out how to climb up there. But then lights went on behind the French doors of the adjacent balcony. Someone was home there.

Instantly a plan hatched in Knight's mind. He'd ring the doorbell of the adjacent apartment, explain what was going on, and ask to use their

411

phone to call Pottersfield and to access the balcony for surveillance purposes. But then he thought to go to the rear of the two buildings to see if any other lights were on. It took him three minutes. No other lights. He returned to Porchester Terrace just as a woman came out the front door of the apartment building he wished to enter.

Knight bolted by her, smiled at her as if they were old friends, bounded up the steps, and caught the security door before it could shut. Even better. He'd go straight up and knock at the door of the apartment on the southeast corner of the third floor. When they saw his Private badge, they were sure to let him in.

He ran up the two flights of stairs and came up into a center hallway that smelled of frying sausages. The third floor was divided into four separate flats. Knight went to the southeast-facing apartment, 3B, heard a television inside, and knocked sharply before holding up his Private badge and ID to the peephole.

He heard footsteps approach and then a pause before locks were thrown and the apartment door opened to reveal a puzzled Michael Lancer, who said, "Knight? What are you doing here?"

CHAPTER 95

LANCER WORE A sweat suit and looked like he had not shaved in days. And his eyes were sunken and hollow, as if he'd slept little since being fired from his position with the London Organising Committee.

"*You* live here, Mike?" Knight asked, incredulously.

"Past ten years," Lancer replied. "What's going on?"

Puzzled now, Knight said, "Can I come in?"

"Uh, sure," Lancer said, standing aside. "Place is a mess, but... why are you here?"

Knight walked down a hallway into a well-appointed living area. Beer bottles and old Chinese food containers littered the coffee table. The southern wall was exposed brick. Pressed against it was an open armoire that held a television tuned to the BBC's wrap-up of the last full day of Olympic competition. Beside it was a desk and on top of it a glowing laptop computer. A blue cable came out of the side of the computer and was plugged into a wall socket.

Seeing that cable, Knight suddenly realized that it all made sense.

"What do you know about your neighbors on the other side of that wall?" he asked, spotting the French doors that led out onto the balcony.

"You mean in the other building?" Lancer asked, puzzled.

"Exactly," Knight said.

The LOCOG member shook his head. "Nothing. It's been empty for almost a year, I believe. I mean, I haven't seen anyone on the balcony in almost a year."

"Someone's in there now," Knight said, and then gestured to the blue cable. "Is that a CAT5E line linked to the Internet?"

Lancer seemed to be struggling to understand where Knight was going with all these questions. "Yes, of course."

"No Wi-Fi?" Knight asked.

"The CAT has much higher security. Why are

you so interested in the flat in the building next door?"

"Because I believe Cronus or one of his Furies has rented it so they could tap into your computer line."

Lancer's jaw dropped. "What?"

"That's how they were able to crack the Olympic security system," Knight went on. "They tapped into your line, stole your passwords, and in they went."

The former decathlete looked at his computer, blinking. "How do you know all this? How do you know they're next door?"

"Because my children are in there."

"Your children?" Lancer said, shocked.

Knight nodded, his hands balled into fists. "A woman named Marta Brezenova, a nanny I hired recently, kidnapped them on Cronus's behalf. She doesn't know that the twins are wearing pieces of jewelry fitted with a GPS transmitter. Their signals are coming from that flat."

"Jesus," Lancer said, dumbstruck. "They were right next to me the whole...we've got to call Scotland Yard, MI5. Get a special weapons unit in here."

"You do that," Knight said. "I'm going to see if I can look into that apartment from your balcony. And tell them to come in quietly. No sirens. I don't want my kids getting killed on a knee-jerk reaction."

Lancer nodded emphatically, pulled out his cell phone, and began punching in numbers as Knight slipped out through the French doors onto the rain-soaked balcony. He moved by wet patio furniture and tried to see into the other flat.

The other balcony was less than six feet away and featured an iron balustrade. The French doors had gauzy white curtains hanging over them that let light out but gave Knight no clear idea of the interior layout. To his right, Knight could hear Lancer talking on his phone, explaining what was going on.

A wind came up. The French doors on the far balcony blew open several inches, revealing stark white carpet and a white country-style table on which several computers stood glowing, all connected to blue CAT5E lines.

Knight was about to go back into Lancer's apartment to tell him what he'd seen when he heard his son whine from somewhere in the adjacent flat, "No, Marta! Lukey want to go home for birthday party!"

"Shut up, you spoiled little bastard," Marta hissed before Knight heard a loud slap, and Luke went hysterical. "And learn to use the loo!"

CHAPTER 96

THE PRIMAL INSTINCT of a father wanting to protect his child seized Knight so completely that without considering the consequences he climbed up on Lancer's railing, thirty feet above the ground, crouched, and dove forward.

As Knight pushed off the wet rail, his shoes slipped ever so slightly, and he knew in an instant that he wasn't going to make it onto the balcony next door. He wasn't even going to reach the railing, and he thought for sure he was going to plunge and break every bone in his body.

But somehow his fingers snagged the feet of the iron balusters where they met the balcony, and he held on for dear life, dangling and wondering how long he could go on this way.

"Shut up!" Marta snapped, and slapped Luke again.

Luke's sobs turned bitter, and that was enough to trigger a massive surge of adrenaline in Knight. He swung his body left and right as though he were a pendulum, feeling the iron biting into his hands but not caring because on the third swing he was able to catch the edge of the balcony with the toe of his right shoe.

Seconds later he was over the railing and onto the balcony itself, his muscles trembling, tasting a chemical tang in his mouth. Luke's crying had become muffled and nasal, as if Marta had gagged him.

Ignoring the sting in his hands, Knight gripped his Beretta and eased up to the open French doors. He peeked inside and saw that the living area was similar in layout to Lancer's place. The furnishings were wildly different, however, with a much colder touch. Everything in the room, except a gold-and-red tapestry that hung on the north wall, was the same stark white as the carpet. Luke's muffled cries were coming from a hallway by the kitchen.

Knight pushed the doors fully open and stepped inside. He kicked off his shoes and padded quickly to the hallway. He had no illusions about what he was doing now. Marta was instrumental in the death of Denton Marshall. She'd helped destroy his mother's happiness. She tried to destroy the Olympics, and she'd taken his children. He would not hesitate to kill her to save them.

Luke's cries softened enough to allow Knight to hear Isabel weeping, too, and then a deeper groaning. All of it was coming out of a room on the left. The door was open and the lights were on. Knight hugged the wall and reached the doorway. He looked farther down the hallway and saw two more doors; both were open and the lights in the rooms were off.

It was all going down in the room right next to him. He thumbed the safety.

Gun leading, Knight stepped into the doorway, sweeping the room, spotting Isabel lying on her side on a bare mattress on the floor to his right, tied up, tape across her mouth, looking toward Marta.

The nanny was about fifteen feet from Knight, her back turned to the door, and was changing Luke's diaper on a table against the wall. She had no idea Knight was standing in the doorway behind her, searching for a clear shot.

But James Daring did.

The museum curator and television star was staring at Knight, who understood much of the situation in a heartbeat. He stepped forward, aiming the pistol, and said, "Get away from my son, you war-criminal bitch, or I will head-shoot you and enjoy it."

The nanny pivoted in disbelief toward Knight, her attention darting to a black assault rifle standing in the corner several feet away.

"Don't even think about it," Knight said, taking a step. "Get down on your belly, hands up behind your head, or I will kill you. Right now."

Marta's eyes went dead and vacant, but she started to slowly comply, lowering her center, watching him the way a cornered lioness might.

Knight took another step toward her, gripping the Beretta two-handed, seeing her framed in his pistol sight. "I said get down!" he yelled.

Marta went flat and put her hands up behind her head.

Glancing at Daring, Knight said, "Cronus?"

The television personality's eyes went lazy before Knight heard a close thudding noise, and something viciously hard hit his head.

It was like storms he'd seen come up over dry flats in Portugal: thunder boomed so loudly that it deafened Knight even as heat lightning crackled, sending electric tentacles through his brain, so brilliant that they blinded him into darkness.

CHAPTER 97

THE SOUNDS OF hydraulic doors opening and shoes slapping on tile stirred Karen Pope from her edge-of-consciousness sleep.

The *Sun* reporter lay on a couch in Private London's lab, feeling wrecked by fatigue compounded with worry. No one had heard from Knight since he walked out the rear door to his house. Not Pottersfield, not Hooligan, not Pope, not Morgan, not anyone else at Scotland Yard or Private.

They'd waited for him at his home until shortly after dawn, when Pottersfield had left to examine the bodies of the two dead women found in the abandoned factory. Pope and Hooligan returned to Private to run the fingerprints he'd taken from Knight's house through the Balkan war crimes database.

They'd gotten a hit almost immediately: Senka, the oldest of the Brazlic sisters, had been all over the place. When Hooligan informed Pottersfield, the inspector told them that preliminary fingerprint work on the more recently slain woman positively identified her as Nada, the middle Brazlic sister.

At that point, around eight that Sunday morning, Pope had hit a wall of exhaustion and lain down on the couch, using one of Hooligan's lab coats for a blanket. How long had she slept?

"Hooligan, wake up," she heard Jack say. "There's a beat-up Rasta at the front desk looking for you. He says he's got something he was supposed to hand-deliver to you for Knight. And he refuses to give it to me."

At that Pope cracked an eye, seeing the American standing at Hooligan's desk trying to rouse Private London's chief scientist from a nap. Above him, the clock read 10:20.

Two hours and twenty minutes? She sat up groggily, then got to her feet and stumbled after

Hooligan and Jack to the reception area, where a Jamaican sat gingerly in a chair by the elevator. A large bandage covered his grossly swollen cheek. One arm was covered in a cast and rested in a sling.

"I'm Hooligan," the scientist said.

The Rasta struggled up and shook with his good hand, saying, "Ketu Oladuwa. I drive de cab."

Hooligan gestured at the cast and bandage. "Crash?"

Oladuwa nodded. "Big-time, mon. On my way to Heathrow. Broadsided by a panel van. I been in hospital all night."

Pope said, "What about Knight?"

"Ya, mon," the Rasta said, digging in his pocket and coming up with a smashed iPhone. "He gimme dis one here last night and tell me to drive it to Heathrow and then back to his home to find you or some inspector with da police. I went to Knight's home when I got out of hospital dis morning, and police told me you gone, so I came here."

"To give us a smashed phone?" Jack asked.

"Wasn't smashed before da accident," the Rasta said indignantly. "He said something on dat phone help you find his kids."

"Fug," Hooligan grunted. He snatched the relics

of Knight's phone from Oladuwa, spun around, and took off for the lab with Pope and Jack close on his heels.

"Hey!" Oladuwa yelled after them. "Him say I get reward!"

CHAPTER 98

KNIGHT SURFACED FROM oblivion slowly, starting deep in the reptilian part of his brain, awakening to the smell of frying meat. At first he had no sense of who he was, or where he was—just that odor of frying meat.

Then he understood he was lying prone on something hard. His hearing returned next, like pounding surf that cleared to static and then to voices, television voices. Knight knew who he was then, and dimly recalled being in the bedroom with his children, Marta, and Daring before it all went blank. He tried to move. He couldn't. His wrists and hands were bound.

The flute began, airy and trilling, and Knight forced his eyes open, seeing blurrily that he was not in that bedroom in the white apartment anymore. The floor below him was hardwood, not carpeted. And the walls around him were dark, paneled, and heaved to and fro like a churning sea.

Knight felt nauseated and shut his eyes, still hearing the flute music. He heard the broadcast announcers arguing before he moved his head and felt a terrible throbbing at the back of his skull. After several seconds, he opened his eyes a second time, finding that his focus was better. He spotted Isabel and Luke unconscious on the floor not far away, still bound and gagged.

Then he twisted his head, trying to locate the source of the music, seeing a four-poster at the center of the room. On it lay James Daring.

Dazed as he was, Knight understood Daring's predicament at a glance. It was the same predicament he'd seen the museum curator in before it had all gone to blackness: the television star lay spread-eagle on the mattress, lashed to the bedposts, and wearing a hospital gown. His mouth was taped shut. An IV line ran into his wrist from a bag hanging on a rack by the bed.

The flute music stopped and Knight saw someone backlit by brilliant sunlight coming toward him across the room.

Mike Lancer carried a black combat shotgun

loosely in his left hand and a glass of orange juice in his right. He set the juice on a table and squatted down near Knight. He gazed at him in amusement and said, "Awake at last. Feel like things got rearranged upstairs, did you?" He laughed and displayed the weapon. "Brilliant, these old riot guns. Even air-driven, the beanbags really pack a wallop, especially if delivered to the head at close range."

"Cronus?" Knight said, still hazy, and smelling alcohol on Lancer's breath.

Lancer said, "You know, I had a feeling about you right from the beginning, Knight, or at least since Dan Carter's untimely death—a premonition that you would come closest to figuring me out. But I took the necessary precautions, and here we are."

Deeply confused, Knight said, "The Olympics were your life. Why?"

Lancer rested the riot gun against the inside of his knee and reached back to scratch at the side of his head. As he did, Knight saw his face flush with anger. Lancer stood up, grabbed the juice glass, and drank from it before saying, "The modern games have been corrupt since the beginning. Bribed judges. Genetic freaks. Drug-fueled monsters. It needed to be cleaned up, and I was the one to—"

Even in Knight's blurry state, it didn't sound right, and he said, "Bullshit. I don't believe you."

Lancer glared at him before whipping the glass at Knight. It missed and shattered against the wall behind him. "Who are you to question my motives?" Lancer roared.

Concussion or not, threat or not, things were becoming clearer to Knight, who said, "You didn't do this just to expose. You sacrificed them in front of a world audience. There has to be a warped sense of rage behind that."

Lancer got angrier. "I am an emanation of the Lord of Time." He looked over at the twins. "Cronus. Devourer of children."

The implied threat ripped through Knight. How far gone was the man?

"No," Knight said, following his foggy instincts. "Something happened to you. Something that filled you with hatred and made you want to do all this."

Lancer's voice rose. "The Olympics are supposed to be a religious festival, one where honorable men and women compete before the eyes of heaven. The modern games are its exact opposite. The gods were offended by the arrogance of men, the hubris of mankind."

Knight's vision blurred slightly, and he felt sickened again, but his brain was working better with each passing second. He shook his head. "The gods weren't offended. You were offended. Who were they? The arrogant men?"

"The ones that have died in the last two weeks," he retorted hotly. Then he smiled. "Including Dan Carter and your other dear colleagues."

Knight stared at him, unable to comprehend the depths of the man's depravity. "You bombed that plane?"

"Carter was getting a little too close," Lancer replied. "The others were collateral damage."

"Collateral damage!" Knight shouted, feeling like he wanted to kill the man standing before him, ripping him limb from limb. But then his head began to clang and he lay there looking at Lancer.

After several moments he said, "Who offended you?"

Lancer's expression went hard as he stared off into the past.

"Who?" Knight demanded.

The former decathlete glared at Knight in utter fury and said, "Doctors."

CHAPTER 99

IN BROAD, BITTER strokes, I tell Knight a story that no one except the Brazlic sisters has ever heard in its entirety, starting with the hatred I was born with, right through stabbing my mother and killing the monsters who stoned me after I went to live with Minister Bob in Brixton, the roughest neighborhood in all of London.

I tell Knight that after the stoning, in the spring of my fifteenth year, Minister Bob had me enter a track meet because he thought I was stronger and faster than most boys. He had no idea what I was capable of. Neither did I.

During that first meet I won six events—the one hundred, the two hundred, the javelin, the triple jump, long jump, and discus. I did it again in a regional competition, and a third time at a junior national meet in Sheffield.

"A man named Lionel Higgins approached me after Sheffield," I tell Knight. "Higgins was a private decathlon coach. He told me I had the talent to be the greatest all-around athlete in the world and to win the Olympic gold medal. He offered to help me figure out a way to train full-time, and filled my head with false dreams of glory and a life lived according to the Olympic ideals of competing fairly, may the best man win, and all that nonsense."

Snorting scornfully, I say: "The monster slayer in me bought the phony spiel hook, line, and sinker."

I go on to tell Knight how I lived the Olympic ideals for the next fifteen years of my life. Despite the headaches that would lay me low at least once a month, Higgins arranged for me to join the Coldstream Regiment, where, in return for a decade of service, I'd be allowed to train. I did so, furiously, single-mindedly—some say maniacally—for a shot at athletic immortality that finally came for me at the Barcelona games in 1992.

"We expected the oppressive heat and humidity," I tell Knight. "Higgins sent me to India to train for it, figuring that Bombay would be worse than Spain. He was right. I *was* the best prepared, and I was mentally ready to suffer more than any-one else."

Wrapped in the darkest of my memories, I shake my head like a terrier breaking a rat's spine and say, "None of it mattered."

I describe how I led the Barcelona decathlon after the first day, through the 110-meter hurdles, high jump, discus, pole vault, and the four hun-dred. Temperatures were in the upper nineties and the oppressive, saturated air took its toll on me: I cramped up and collapsed after placing second in the four hundred.

"They rushed me to a medical tent," I tell Knight. "But I wasn't concerned. Higgins and I figured I would need a legal electrolytic boost after day one. I kept calling for my coach, but the med-ical personnel wouldn't let him in. I could see they were going to put me on an IV. I told them I wanted my own coach to replenish the fluids and minerals I lost with a mixture we'd fine-tuned to my metabolism. But I was in no condition to fight them when they put the needle in my arm and con-nected it to a bag of God only knows what."

Looking at Knight, feeling livid, I'm reliving the experience all over again. "I was a ghost of myself the next day. The javelin and the long jump were my best events, and I cratered in both. I didn't finish in the top ten and I was the reigning world champion."

The anger in me is almost overwhelming when I say, "No dream realized, Knight. No Olympic glory. No proof of my superiority. Sabotaged by what the modern games have become."

Knight stares at me with the same distrustful and fearful expression Marta gave me when I offered to save her and her sisters in that police station in Bosnia.

"But you were world champion," Knight says. "Twice."

"The immortals win Olympic gold. The superior wins gold. I was robbed of my chance by monsters. It was premeditated sabotage."

Knight gazes at me in disbelief now. "And so you started plotting your revenge right then, twenty years ago?"

"The scope of my revenge grew over time," I admit. "It began with the Spanish doctors who doped me. They died of natural causes in September of 1993. The referees who oversaw the event were in separate car crashes in ninety-four and early ninety-five."

"And the Furies?" Knight asks.

I sit on a stool a few feet from him. "Hardly anyone knows that in the summer of 1995, after my regiment ended its service in the Queen's Guard, we were sent into Sarajevo for a rotation with the NATO peacekeeping mission. I lasted less than five weeks due to a roadside bomb that cracked my head for the second time in my life."

Knight's words were less slurred now, and his eyes less glassy when he said, "Was that before or after you helped the Brazlic sisters escape from that police station near Srebrenica?"

I smile bitterly. "After. With new passports and new identities, I brought the Furies to London and set them up in a flat next door. We even cut a secret door behind my armoire and their tapestry so we could appear to live separate lives."

"Dedicated to destroying the Olympics?" Knight asks acidly.

"Yes, that's right. As I said, the gods were behind this, behind me. It was fate. How else do you explain that very early on in the process I was asked to be a member of the organizing committee and, lo and behold, London won the bid? Fate allowed me to be on the inside from the start, hiding things where I needed them, altering them if they suited my purpose, given full access to every inch of every venue. And now with everyone hunting you and your children, fate will allow me to finish what I've begun."

Knight contorts his face. "You're insane."

"No, Knight," I reply. "Just superior in ways you can't understand."

I stand up and start to walk away. He calls after me, "So are you going to wipe out all the Furies before your big finale? Kill Marta and then escape?"

"Not at all," I chuckle. "Marta's out putting your daughter's necklace and your son's watch on trains to Scotland and France. When she's done, she'll return here, release Mr. Daring, and kill your children, then you."

CHAPTER 100

KNIGHT'S HEAD FELT rocked and pounding, as if it had been struck again. His attention staggered to his sleeping children. The necklace and wristwatch *were* gone. There was no way to trace them now. And what about the taxi driver? Why hadn't he given the phone to Hooligan or Pottersfield? Why hadn't they come for him? Were they tracking Marta to the trains?

Knight looked back to Lancer, who was gathering a bag and some papers.

"My kids have done nothing," Knight said. "They're just three years old. Innocent."

"Little monsters," Lancer said flatly, turning for the door. "Good-bye, Knight. It was nice competing with you, but the better man has won."

"No, you haven't!" Knight shouted after him. "Mundaho proved it. You haven't won. The Olympic spirit lives on whatever you do."

That hit a nerve, because Lancer turned and marched back toward Knight only to flinch and stop at a gunshot.

It came from the television, and caused Lancer to relax into a smirk.

"The men's marathon has started," he said. "The final game has begun. And you know what, Knight? Because I'm the superior man, I'm going to let you live to see the ending. Before Marta kills you, she's going to let you witness exactly how I snuff out that Olympic spirit once and for all."

CHAPTER 101

A HALF HOUR later, at exactly noon, Pope glanced nervously from coverage of the men's marathon to Hooligan, who was still hunched over the shards of the iPhone, trying to coax Knight's whereabouts from them.

"Anything?" the reporter asked, feeling completely stymied.

"SIM card's pretty fuggin' hammered, eh?" Private London's chief scientist replied without looking up. "But I think I'm getting close."

Jack had left to oversee security at the finish line of the men's marathon. Elaine Pottersfield was in the lab, however. The Scotland Yard inspector had arrived only a few moments before, agitated and exhausted by the events of the past twenty-four hours.

"Where did this cabbie say he picked up Peter?" she asked impatiently.

Pope said, "Somewhere in Knightsbridge, I think. If Oladuwa had a cell phone we could call him, but he said his wife's got it."

Pottersfield thought a moment. "Milner Street, perhaps?"

"That was it," Hooligan grunted.

"Knight was at his mother's, then," the inspector said. "Amanda must know something." She yanked out her phone and started scrolling for the number.

"Here we are," Hooligan said, picking his head up from two sensors clipped to a surviving piece of Knight's SIM card to look at the screen, which was covered with the gibberish of code.

He leaned over to a keyboard and began typing even as Pope heard Pottersfield say hello, identify herself as both a police detective and the sister of Knight's dead wife, and ask to speak with Amanda Knight. Then she left the lab.

Two minutes later, the image on Hooligan's screen morphed from a display of electronic hieroglyphics to a blurry screenshot of a website. Pope said, "What is that?"

"Looks like a map of some sort," Hooligan replied as the inspector burst back into the lab. "Can't read the URL, though."

"Trace Angels!" Pottersfield shouted. "It says Trace Angels!"

CHAPTER 102

THE CROWD ALONG the south side of Bird-cage Walk, facing St. James's Park, is bigger and deeper than I had anticipated. But then again, the men's marathon is one of the final competitions of the games.

It's beastly hot, half past eleven, and the leaders are coming around to start the second of four laps that constitute the racecourse. I hear the roar, and spot them running west toward the Victoria Memorial and Buckingham Palace.

Carrying a small shoulder bag, I push to the front of the crowd, holding up my Olympic security pass, which was never taken from me. It's critical that I be seen now, here, at this moment. I'd planned to find any constable I could. But when

I look down the side of the course, I see someone familiar. I duck under the barrier tape and walk toward him, holding up the pass.

"Inspector Casper?" I say. "Mike Lancer."

The Scotland Yard captain nods. "Seems to me you got a raw deal."

"Thank you," I say, then add, "I'm no longer official, of course, but I was wondering if I could cut across the street when there's a gap in the runners. I wanted to watch from the north side if I could."

Casper considers the request, then shrugs and says, "Sure, why not?"

Thirty seconds later, I'm across the street and pushing back through the crowd and into the park. Inside, I move east, glancing at my watch and thinking that Marta will release Daring in ninety minutes or so, right around the end of the marathon, a move that should attract heavy police attention and give me enough of an edge to ensure that I can't possibly be beaten.

I won't be defeated today, I think. *Not today. And never again.*

CHAPTER 103

IN LANCER'S SPARE bedroom, with his mouth taped shut and his head pounding and woozy, Knight had spent the last thirty minutes alternating between trying to break free of his bonds, gasping in frustration, and looking longingly at his unconscious children, dully aware of the marathon coverage blaring from the television.

It was 11:55. In mile eleven, in kilometer seventeen, just shy of an hour into the race, runners from the UK, Ethiopia, Kenya, and Mexico had broken away from the main pack along Victoria Embankment. They were using each other to chew up ground as they headed past the London Eye toward Parliament at Olympic-record pace, despite the blistering heat.

Knight wondered grimly what atrocity Lancer had waiting somewhere along the marathon route, but refused to contemplate what Marta might have in store for him and the twins in the aftermath of the last race of the games.

He closed his eyes and began to pray to God and to Kate, pleading with them to help him save their children. He told them he'd be fine dying if only to be with Kate again. But the children, they deserved to . . .

Marta walked into the room carrying the black riot gun Knight had seen the night before as well as a plastic bag containing three two-liter Coke bottles. Her dark hair had been chopped and dyed, rendering it a violent blond tipped with silver highlights that somehow matched the black leather skirt, tank top, and calf-high boots she wore. With her bleached hair and heavy makeup, Knight might never have recognized her as the dour nanny who'd first approached him at the playground if he hadn't spent so much time around her in the last two weeks.

Marta paid Knight no mind, as if he and everyone else in the room were an afterthought. She set the Coke bottles on a dresser, then cradled the gun and went to Daring's side. She set the gun down, picked up a hypodermic needle, and shot it into the IV line leading into the museum curator's arm.

"Time to wake up," she said, and gathered up the gun again.

She fished an apple from her pocket. She bit into it, her attention lazily on the marathon coverage.

Luke stirred and opened his eyes, looking right at his father. His eyes went wide. Then his brows knitted, his face got beet-red, and he began making whining noises, not of fear, but as if he desperately wanted to tell his father something. Knight recognized that red-faced expression and understood the meaning behind the stifled cries immediately.

At the noise, Marta looked over with such a cold expression that Knight's pounding brain screamed at him to make her look at him and not his son.

Knight began to moan behind his tape. Marta glanced over, chewing a bite of apple, and said, "Shut up. I don't want to hear you cry like your little boy."

Instead of complying, Knight got louder and smashed his feet against the floor, trying to not only alert someone below but to bother Marta. He wanted to get her talking. He knew enough about hostage negotiations to understand how crucial it was to get a captor talking.

Isabel woke up and started to cry.

Marta took up the gun, stomped over to Knight, and laughed. "We own the flat below, too. So go ahead, make noise. No one hears you."

With that she kicked him in the stomach. Knight doubled up and rolled over on his back, moaning and feeling glass from the shattered juice tumbler crunch and cut beneath him. Luke began to wail. Marta glared at the children. Knight was sure she was going to kick them. But then she squatted and ripped the tape off Knight's mouth. "Tell them to shut up or you're all dead right now."

"Luke wants to use the loo," Knight said. "Take the tape off. Ask him."

Marta shot him a foul look, then scuttled to his son and peeled off the tape. "What?"

Knight's son shrank from Marta, but looked at his father and said, "Lukey need go poop. Big-boy loo."

"Crap in your pants for all I care."

"Big-boy loo, Marta," the boy insisted. "Lukey go big-boy. No nappy."

"Give him a chance," Knight said. "He's just three."

Marta's expression turned into a disgusted sneer. But she got out a knife and cut free Luke's ankles. Gun in one hand, she hauled Knight's son to his feet and snarled, "If this is another false alarm, I'll kill you first."

They moved past Daring and disappeared out the door into the hallway. Knight glanced all around, rolled back slightly, and heard glass crunch again, felt tiny shards of it pricking his arms and back.

The pain jolted his brain into realizing his opportunity, and he began frantically arching his back and moving around, fingers groping desperately beneath him. *Please, Kate. Please.*

The index finger of his right hand felt the keen edge of a larger shard, perhaps two inches long, and he tried to coax it into his hand. But he fumbled and dropped it. Cursing under his breath, Knight groped again. But he hadn't found it when he heard Luke cry, "See, Marta! Big boy!"

A second later, he heard a flush and moved his fingers about in a frenzy. Nothing. He heard footsteps, arched his hips one more time, and pushed himself back closer to where the glass had shattered. Then Luke walked in, wrists still taped in front of him, beaming at his father.

"Lukey big boy now, Daddy," he said. "Lukey three. No nappies."

CHAPTER 104

"GOOD JOB, LAD," Knight said, lying back, smiling at his son, and glancing at Marta, who still cradled the gun. He felt a thick chunk of the bottom of the juice glass lying on the floor just below the small of his back.

The fingers of his right hand closed around it even as Marta said to Luke, "Go sit down next to your sister and don't move." She turned to inspect Daring, whose body was now shifting on the bed.

"Wake up," she said again. "We have to go soon."

Daring moaned as Knight twisted the chunk of glass into the duct tape around his wrists and began to saw at it. Luke came dutifully toward his father, smiling and saying, "Lukey big boy."

His attention jumping back to Marta, Knight said, "Brilliant. Now sit down, like Marta told you to."

But his son didn't budge. "We go home, Daddy?" Luke said, and Bella began to whine in agreement behind her gag. "We go have party?"

"Soon," Knight said, feeling the tape begin to cut and part. "Very soon."

But then Marta snatched up the gun and a roll of duct tape and started toward Luke. His son took one look at the tape and cried, "No, Marta!"

Luke started to duck and run. Marta became infuriated. Pointing the gun at Knight's son, she barked, "Sit down. Now. Or you die."

But Knight's son was too young to fully understand the implications of having a loaded weapon aimed at you. "No!" Luke said impudently, and jumped onto the mattress by Isabel, his eyes darting around, looking for escape.

"I'll teach you, then," Marta said, stalking toward Luke, her eyes fully on the boy and not Knight, who felt his wrists come free.

As she passed him, looking to corner his son, Knight lashed out with his bound feet.

They connected hard with Marta's Achilles tendons and she gave off a cry as her legs buckled and she fell sideways to the floor. The gun clattered away.

Knight twisted around, clutching that chunk of glass, and tried to slash her with it. But her reaction time was stunningly fast. She threw up her forearm, taking the cut there before kneeing Knight in the chest.

The wind knocked out of him, Knight let go of the glass chunk.

Insane with fury, Marta jumped to her feet and snatched up the gun. She marched to one of the Coke bottles, opened it, and stuffed the muzzle inside into the liquid before saying, "I don't care what Cronus wants. I have had enough of you and your bastard children."

Marta deftly wrapped duct tape around her bleeding arm, and then around the gun barrel and the mouth of the bottle before swinging around the crudely silenced weapon. Her eyes had gone dark and dead, and Knight had a glimpse of what all those Bosnian boys must have seen when the Brazlic sisters had come calling. With grim intent, Marta marched toward Luke, who still stood by his sister, saying to Knight, "The boy goes first. I want you to see how it's done."

"Lancer is going to kill you!" Knight shouted after her. "Just like he killed your sisters!"

That stopped her progress. She turned to him and said, "My sisters are very much alive. They have already escaped London."

"No," Knight said. "Lancer killed them both. He broke Andjela's neck, and then cut off her hands and sent them to me. Nada's throat was cut from ear to ear."

"That's a lie!" she snarled and came at him, raising the gun.

"They were found in the same abandoned factory near the gasworks where you kept Selena Farrell."

That information made Marta pause briefly. "How come it hasn't been on the news?"

"The police probably haven't alerted the press," Knight said, fumbling for an answer. "They do that, you know—hide things."

"You're lying," she said, and then shrugged. "And even if it is true, so much the better for me. I am sick of them. I think of killing them myself from time to time."

Marta pushed off the safety.

CHAPTER 105

SIRENS SUDDENLY WAILED nearby, coming closer, and Knight's heart surged with renewed hope.

"They're coming for you now," he said, grinning insanely at Marta and the bottom of the Coke bottle. "You're going to the gallows now, no matter what you do to me and my children."

"No," she laughed caustically. "If they go anywhere, they go next door, not here. In the meantime, I'll kill you and then use the tunnel to escape."

She tried to press the Coke bottle to Knight's head, but he batted at it with his hand and jerked around as the sirens came closer and louder, and he thought: *Buy time. At least the twins will be saved.*

But then Marta stepped on the side of Knight's neck with her boot, choking him as she lowered the silenced rifle.

He looked up at her, walleyed, and grabbed at her ankles, trying to upset her balance. But she just ground her boot deeper and harder into his neck until his strength was gone.

Marta peered down at him dreamily. "Good-bye, Mr. Knight. Too bad I don't have a pickax."

CHAPTER 106

KNIGHT THOUGHT OF Kate in the instant before Marta's eyes snapped wide open. She screamed in agony, yanked the Coke bottle off his head and her boot off his neck, firing the rifle. With a weird wet thud, the silenced gun blew a hole in the wall just above Knight's head. Coke and plastic shreds showered down on him as Marta screamed in agony once more. Frenzied, she spun away from Knight, groping wildly behind her.

Luke had bitten into Marta's hamstring and was holding on like a snapping turtle while his nanny furiously pounded against the boy, screaming again and again. Knight kicked her hard in the shin and she dropped the gun before elbowing Luke in the side.

The boy slammed against the wall and went still.

Knight crawled after the gun while Marta glared at Luke and felt down her leg for the gaping wound he'd left, not noticing Knight until he was inches from the gun.

She cursed and lunged toward Knight as his finger found the trigger and he tried to swing the gun at her. She swept her free arm and struck the side of the barrel, deflecting his aim even as the gun went off a second time, followed by a deafening boom that disoriented Knight for a second. He looked around, dizzy, praying he'd shot Marta somehow.

But then the oldest Fury kicked him in the ribs and ripped the gun from his hands. Gasping and grinning in triumph, she aimed the muzzle at Knight's unconscious son.

"Watch him die," she snarled.

The shot sounded distant and otherworldly to Knight, but aimed perfectly at his breaking heart; and he fully expected Luke's body to jump at the bullet's impact.

Instead, Marta's throat exploded in a slurry of blood before the war-criminal nanny crumpled and sprawled dead between Knight and his son.

Dumbfounded and slack-jawed, Knight twisted his head around and spotted Kate's older sister rising from a shooting crouch.

BOOK FIVE

THE FINISH LINE

CHAPTER 107

TWENTY-FIVE MINUTES after Pottersfield shot and killed wanted war criminal Senka Brazlic, the Scotland Yard inspector and Knight were in her car, sirens and lights on, racing through the streets of Chelsea, heading toward the Mall, where the top runners were well into their fourth and final lap of the marathon route.

Ordinarily, the men's marathon ends in the host city's Olympic stadium. But the London organizers—largely at Lancer's urging, it turned out—decided that taking the runners through the scruffy East End was not the best way to sell the city's stunning attributes to the world.

Instead, organizers opted to have the marathoners run four laps, each featuring London's most notable landmarks as telegenic backdrops for the race—from Tower Hill to Parliament along the Thames past the London Eye and Cleopatra's Needle, and starting and finishing on the Mall, well in sight of Buckingham Palace.

"I want his picture in everyone's handheld," Pottersfield shouted into her radio. "Find him! Having the marathon here was his idea!"

Knight was thinking about how bloody brilliant she was at her job. She'd called up the Trace Angels site, seen that the kids had been put on trains, but then thought to look at their whereabouts earlier and saw the address on Porchester Terrace.

After contacting the trains and getting word from conductors that there were no children matching the Knight kids' description on board, she'd led the Scotland Yard contingent to the building near Lancaster Gate. They were in the Furies' flat when the crudely silenced gun went off next door, and they heard it. They'd discovered the entrance to Lancer's place behind that tapestry on the wall, and then they threw a stun grenade a moment after Knight shot the weapon.

Setting down her radio, Pottersfield said shakily, "We'll get him. Everybody's hunting him now."

Knight grunted, staring out the window into the glaring light, still feeling dizzy and achy from the blows he'd taken. "You okay, Elaine? Having to shoot?"

"Me? You shouldn't even be here, Peter," Pottersfield scolded. "You should be back there in that ambulance with your kids going to the hospital. You need to be looked at yourself."

"Amanda and Boss are on their way to meet Luke and Bella. I'll get examined when Lancer's stopped."

Pottersfield downshifted and shot onto Buckingham Palace Road. "You're sure Lancer said the attack was on the marathon?"

Knight struggled to remember before replying. "Before he left, I told him that no matter what he might do, the Olympic spirit would never die. I told him Mundaho had proved it. That got him insanely angry, and I felt certain he would kill me. But then the starting gun for the marathon went off. And he said something like: 'The men's marathon. The final game has begun. And because I'm the superior man, I'm going to let you live to see the ending. Before Marta kills you, she's going to let you witness exactly how I snuff out that Olympic spirit once and for all.'"

Pottersfield skidded the car to a stop in front of the police barrier opposite St. James's Park and got out, holding up her badge to the officers guarding it. "He's with Private and with me. Where's Inspector Casper?"

The bobby, who looked miserable in the beastly heat, pointed north toward the roundabout in front of Buckingham Palace and said, "You want I should call him?"

Knight's sister-in-law shook her head before vaulting the barrier and bullying her way through the crowd onto Birdcage Walk, with Knight following somewhat woozily behind her. Runners well back from the leaders were heading toward the Victoria Memorial at the center of the roundabout.

Stout Billy Casper was already hustling toward Knight and Pottersfield. "Sweet Jesus, Inspector," he said. "I had the bastard right in front of me not an hour ago. He went into St. James's Park."

"Did you get Lancer's picture?"

"Everyone in the force got it ten seconds ago," Casper replied, and then looked grim. "The route is more than twelve kilometers long. There's a half million people, maybe more, lining the route. How the hell are we going to find him?"

"At the finish, or somewhere near it," Knight said. "It fits his flair for the dramatic. Have you seen Jack Morgan?"

"He's way ahead of you, Peter," the police inspector replied. "As soon as he heard that Cronus was Lancer and that he was still on the loose, he went straight to the finish line. Smart guy, for a Yank."

But twenty-six minutes later, as roars went up from back along the marathon route south of St. James's Park, Lancer had not been sighted, and every aspect of the timing system had been reexamined for booby traps.

Standing high atop stands erected along the Mall, Knight and Jack were using binoculars to look up into the trees to see if Lancer had climbed one and set himself up as a sniper. Casper and Pottersfield were doing much the same thing on the other side of the street. But their views were hampered by scores of large Union Jacks and Olympic flags fluttering on poles that extended westward toward Buckingham Palace.

"I checked him out myself," Jack said somberly, lowering his binoculars. "Lancer, I mean. When he did some work for us a few years back in Hong Kong. He was squeaky clean, nothing but raves from everyone who'd ever known him. And I don't remember ever seeing that he'd served in the Balkans. I'm sure I would have remembered that."

"He was there less than five weeks," Knight said.

"Long enough to recruit bloodthirsty bitches as mad as he is," Jack said.

"Probably why he left the deployment off his résumé," Knight said.

Before Jack could reply, the roar came closer and people in the stands around the Victoria Memorial leaped to their feet as two policemen on motorcycles appeared about a hundred yards in front of the same four runners who'd broken free of the main pack back at mile twelve.

"The motorcyclists," Knight said, and raised his binoculars, trying to see the faces of the officers. But quickly he could tell that neither man was Lancer.

Behind the motorcycles, the top four runners appeared—the Kenyan, the Ethiopian, the barefoot Mexican, and that lad from Brighton—each of them carrying Olympic and Cameroonian hand flags.

After twenty-six miles and one hundred eighty-five yards; after forty-two thousand and twelve meters, the Kenyan and the Brit were leading, sprinting side by side. But two hundred yards from the finish, and hard by the leaders, the Ethiopian and the Mexican split and sprinted to the leaders' flanks.

The crowd went wild as the whippet-thin runners churned down the straightaway toward gold and glory, four abreast and none giving ground.

464

Twenty yards from the finish, the lad from Brighton surged, and it looked as if the UK was going to have its first men's marathon gold to go with the historic win by Mary Duckworth in the women's race the previous Sunday.

Astonishingly, however, mere feet from the finish, the British lad slowed, the four marathoners raised their flags, and the foursome went through the tape together.

For a second, the crowd was stunned and Knight could hear broadcasters braying about the unprecedented act and what it was supposed to mean. And then everyone on the Mall saw it for what it was and started lustily cheering the gesture, Peter Knight included.

He thought: *You see that, Lancer? Cronus? You can't snuff out the Olympic spirit, because it doesn't exist in any one place; it's carried in the hearts of every athlete who's ever striven for greatness, and always will be.*

"No attack," Jack said when the cheering died down. "Maybe the show of force along the route scared Lancer off."

"Maybe," Knight allowed. "Or maybe he wasn't talking about the end of the marathon at all."

CHAPTER 108

THE NAUSEATING ENDING to the men's marathon keeps replaying on the screens around the security stations as I wait patiently in the sweltering heat in the line at the north entrance to Olympic Park off Ruckholt Road.

My head is shaved and, along with every bit of exposed skin, stained with henna to a deep russet tone ten times as dark as my normal color. The white turban is perfect. So is the black beard, the metal bracelet on my right wrist, and the Indian passport—as well as the sepia contact lenses, the eyeglasses, and the loose white kurta pajamas that, together with a dab of patchouli oil, complete my disguise as Jat Singh Rajpal, a tall Sikh textile

466

trader from Punjab lucky enough to hold a ticket to the closing ceremonies.

I'm two feet from the screeners when my face, my normal face, appears on one of the television screens that had been showing the finish of the marathon.

At first, I feel panicked, but then quickly compose myself and take several discreet glances at the screen, hoping it's just some kind of recap of the events of the Olympics, including my dismissal from the organizing committee. But then I see the banner scrolling beneath my image and the news that I'm wanted in connection with the Cronus murders.

How is it possible?! Many voices thunder in my head, triggering one of those insanely blinding headaches. It's everything I can do to stay composed when I step toward an F7 guard, a burly woman, and a young Scotland Yard constable, inspecting tickets and identification.

"You're a long way from home, Mr. Rajpal," the constable says, looking at me without expression.

"One is willing to make the journey for an event as wonderful as this," I say in a practiced accent that comes through flawlessly despite the pounding in my skull. I have to fight not to reach up under my turban to touch that scar throbbing at the back of my head.

The guard glances at a laptop computer screen. "Have you been to any other events during the games, Mr. Rajpal?" she asks.

"Two," I say. "Athletics this past Thursday evening, and field hockey earlier in the week. Monday afternoon. The India-Australia game. We lost."

She scans the screen and nods. "We'll need to put your bag and any metal objects through the screener."

"Without hesitation," I say, putting the bag on the conveyor belt and depositing coins, my bracelet, and my cell phone in a plastic tray that follows it.

"No *kirpan?*" the constable asks.

I smile. Clever lad. "No. I left the ceremonial dagger at home."

The constable nods. "Appreciate that. We've had a few of your blokes try to come in with them. You can go on through now."

Moments later, my headache recedes. I've retrieved my bag, which contains only a camera and a large tube of what appears to be sunscreen. Moving quickly by Eton Manor, I cross an elevated pedestrian bridge that leads me onto the northeast concourse. Skirting the velodrome, the basketball arena, and the athletes' village, I make my way south past the sponsors' hospitality area. I pause to look at them, realizing that I've overlooked many possible violators of the Olympic ideals.

No matter, I decide. My final act will more than compensate for the oversight. At that thought, my breath quickens. So does my heart, which is hammering when I smile at the guards at the bottom of the loose spiral staircase that climbs between the legs of the *Orbit*. "The restaurant?" I say. "Still open?"

"Until half past three, sir," one of them replies. "You've got two hours."

"And if I wish food after that?" I ask.

"The other vendors down here will all be open," he says. "Just the restaurant is closing."

I nod and start the long climb, barely giving notice to the nameless monsters descending the staircase, all of them oblivious to the threat I represent. Twelve minutes later, I reach the level of the slowly revolving restaurant, and go to the maître d'.

"Rajpal," I say. "Table for one."

She frowns. "Would you be willing to share?"

"It would be a great pleasure," I reply.

She nods. "It will still be ten or fifteen minutes."

"Might I use the gents' while I wait?" I ask.

"Of course," she says, and stands aside.

Other prospective patrons press in behind me, leaving the woman so busy that I'm sure she's already begun to forget about me. When she calls my name, she'll figure I got tired of waiting and left. Even if she has someone check the men's room, they won't find me. Rajpal is already gone.

I go to the men's room and take the stall I need, which is, luckily, vacant. Five minutes go by before the rest of the facility empties. Then, as quickly as I can, I pull myself up to a sitting position on the stall dividers and push up one of the ceiling tiles to reveal a reinforced crawl space built so maintenance workers could easily get at the electrical and cooling systems.

A few moments of struggle and I'm lying up there in the crawl space, the ceiling tile back in place. Now all I have to do is calm myself, prepare myself, and trust in fate.

CHAPTER 109

KNIGHT AND JACK were inside Olympic Park by four that afternoon. The sunlight was still glaring and the heat shimmered off the pathways. According to Scotland Yard and MI5, which had collectively seized control of security under orders from the prime minister, Mike Lancer had made no effort to get inside the park using his security pass, which someone immediately flagged after the warning about him was issued.

Around four thirty, Knight's head still ached as he followed Jack into the empty stadium, where teams with bomb-sniffing dogs were patrolling. At the moment, his thoughts were less about finding Lancer than they were about his children. Were they all right in the hospital? Was Amanda by their side?

Knight was getting ready to call his mother when Jack said, "Maybe he did get spooked at the marathon. Maybe that was his last chance; he saw it wasn't going to work, and he's making his escape."

"No," Knight said. "He's going to try something here. Something big."

"He'll have to be Houdini," Jack observed. "You heard them—they've gone to war-zone security levels. They're putting double teams of SAS snipers up high and every available member of Scotland Yard in the halls and stairways."

"I'm hearing you, Jack," Knight said. "But given what the insane bastard has done so far, we can't be sure any security level is going to work. Think about it. Lancer oversaw one and a half billion in security spending for the Olympics. He knows every contingency Scotland Yard and MI5 provided for in their plans. And for much of the past seven years that lunatic has had access to every inch of every venue as it was built. Every goddamn inch."

CHAPTER 110

AT THREE THIRTY that afternoon, echoing through the fourteen-inch gap between the men's-room ceiling and the roof of the *Orbit,* I hear hydraulic gears braking and halting, and feel the slow rotation of the observation deck stop. Closing my eyes and calming my breathing, I prepare for what lies ahead. My fate. My destiny. My just and final due.

At ten minutes to four, I squeeze the tube of special skin cream onto the turban cloth and use it to turn my skin nearly black. A maintenance crew enters and cleans the room below me. I can hear their mops slapping the walls for several minutes, followed by a half hour of silence that is interrupted only by the soft sounds of the movements I make as I stain my head, neck, and hands.

At twelve past four, the first bomb-sniffing dog team enters the men's room, and I have the sudden terrible thought that the monsters might have been clever enough to bring an article of my clothing to prime their beasts. But the patrol is in and out in under a minute, fooled, no doubt, by the patchouli oil.

They return at five and again at six. When they leave after the third time, I know my hour is at hand. Cautiously, I grope around under a strip of insulation, finding a loaded ammunition clip put there seven months ago. Pocketing the clip, I lower myself into the stall, and then strip off my remaining clothes, leaving me two-tone, black and white—a terror to behold in the mirror.

Naked now except for my wristwatch, I rip a length of the turban fabric and wrap the two ends around my hands, leaving an eighteen-inch section dangling slack. Taking a position tight to the wall next to the door, I settle in to wait.

At six forty-five, I hear footsteps and men's voices. The door opens, comes right up against my face, before it swings back the other way, revealing the back of a tall, athletic black monster in a tracksuit, carrying a large duffel bag.

He is big. I assume he's skilled. But he is no match for a superior being.

The slack turban fabric flicks over his head and settles below his chin. Before he can even react, I've got my knee in his back and I'm throttling the life out of him. Seconds later, still feeling the quivering and soft nasal whining of his death, I drag the monster's body to the farthest stall, then move to his duffel bag with a glance at my watch. Thirty minutes until showtime.

It takes me less than half that to don the parade uniform of the Queen's Guard and set the black bearskin hat on my head, feeling its familiar weight settle above my eyebrows and tight to my ears. After a minor adjustment, I've got the leather chin strap taut and snug to my jaw. Last, I pick up his automatic rifle, knowing full well, and not caring, that it's empty. The ammunition clip is full.

Then I return to the middle stall and wait. At a quarter past seven, I hear the door open and a voice growl, "Supple, we're up."

"On it in two," I reply with a cough. "Go to the hatch."

"See you topside," he says.

It makes me think *I hope not* before I hear the door close behind him.

Out of the stall now, I go to the door, tracking

the sweeping second hand of my watch. When exactly ninety seconds have passed, I take a deep breath and step out the door into the hallway, carrying the duffel.

At a quick pace, eyes gazing evenly ahead, face expressionless, I walk through the restaurant to the glass doors on the right side of the dining room. Two SAS men are already unlocking the doors. As they swing them open, exposing me to the heat, I set my bag next to another duffel, identical to mine, and charge by them onto the observation deck and through a narrow doorway that is open and guarded by yet another SAS operator.

I've timed it perfectly. The guard hisses, "Cutting it damn close, mate."

"Shaving it close is what the Queen's Guard does, mate," I say, ducking by him into a tight stairwell with a narrow steel staircase that leads up through a retractable bulkhead door to the roof of the observation deck and open air.

I can see the early evening sky and clouds racing above me. Hearing distant trumpets calling, I climb toward my fate, so close now I can feel it like a burning in my muscles and taste it like sweet sweat on my lips.

CHAPTER 111

THE TRUMPETERS STOOD to either side of the stage down on the floor of the Olympic stadium, blowing a plaintive melody that Knight did not recognize.

He stood high in the stands at the north end of the venue, using binoculars to scan the crowd, tired, his head aching, and feeling overly irritated by the lingering heat and the horns launching the closing ceremonies. As the trumpeting stopped, the screens around the stadium jumped to a feed showing a medium-range view of the Olympic cauldron high atop the *Orbit,* flanked, as it had been since the opening ceremonies, by ramrod-straight members of the Queen's Guard.

The guardsmen on the raised platform on the

roof of the *Orbit*'s observation deck shouldered their guns, pivoted forty-five degrees, and marched stiff-legged, arms pumping, in opposite directions toward two new guardsmen, who climbed up onto the roof from bulkhead doors on either side of the observation deck and moved toward the platform and cauldron. The entering and exiting guards passed each other exactly halfway between the cauldron and the stairwells, with the guards relieved of duty disappearing from the roof and the new pair climbing the platform from either side and standing at attention by the Olympic flame.

Knight roamed the crowd for the next hour and a half. As the summer sky began to darken and winds began to stir, he was buoyed by the fact that despite the threat Lancer still posed, an incredible number of athletes, coaches, judges, referees, and fans had decided to attend the closing ceremonies when they just as easily could have gone home to more certain safety.

The affair had originally been planned as a celebration as joyous as the opening ceremonies had been before the death of the American shot-putter. But organizers had tweaked the ceremony in light of the murders, and made it more somber and meaningful by enlisting the London Symphony Orchestra to back Eric Clapton, who delivered a heart-wrenching version of his song "Tears in Heaven."

In that same vein, as Knight moved south inside the stadium, Marcus Morris was giving a speech that was part elegy to the dead and part celebration of all the great and wonderful things that had happened at the London games in spite of Cronus and his Furies.

Knight glanced at the program and thought: *We've got a few more speeches, a spectacle or two, the turning over of the Olympic flag to Brazil; and then a few words by the mayor of Rio and...*

"Anything, Peter?" Jack asked over the radio earbud. They'd changed security frequencies in case Lancer was trying to monitor their broadcasts.

"Nothing," he replied. "But it still doesn't feel right."

That thought was paramount in Knight's mind until organizers broke from the scheduled program to introduce some "special guests."

Dr. Hunter Pierce appeared on the stage along with Zeke Shaw and the four runners who'd won marathon gold. They pushed Filatri Mundaho in a wheelchair before them, a sheet over his legs and medical personnel following.

Mundaho had suffered third-degree burns over much of his lower body, and had endured several excruciating medical procedures in the past week. The coholder of the world record in the hundred-meter dash should have been in agony, unable to rise from his hospital bed. But you'd never have known it.

The former boy soldier's head was up, proud, and erect. He was waving to the crowd, which leaped to its feet and began cheering for him. Knight's eyes watered. Mundaho was showing incredible, incredible courage as well as an iron will and a depth of humanity that Lancer could not even begin to fathom.

They gave the sprinter his gold medal, and during the playing of the Cameroonian national anthem Knight was hard-pressed to find someone in the stadium who wasn't teary-eyed.

Then Hunter Pierce began to talk about the legacy of the London games, arguing that it ultimately would signify a rekindling of and rededication to Pierre de Coubertin's original Olympic dreams and ideals. At first Knight was held rapt by the American diver's speech.

But then he forced himself to tune her out, to try to think like Lancer, and like his alter ego, Cronus. He thought about the last few things the madman had said to him. He tried to see Lancer's words as if they were printed on blocks that he could pick up and examine in detail: *At the end, just before you die, Knight, I'm going to make sure that you and your children witness how I ingeniously manage to snuff out the Olympic spirit forever.*

Knight considered each and every word, exploring their meaning in every sense. And that's when it hit him—the sixth-to-last word in the sentence.

He triggered his radio microphone and said, "You don't snuff out a spirit, Jack."

"Come back with that, Peter?" Jack said.

Knight was already running toward the exit, saying, "Lancer told me he was going to 'snuff out the Olympic spirit forever.'"

"Okay . . ."

"You don't snuff out a spirit, Jack. You snuff out a flame."

CHAPTER 112

LOOK AT ME NOW, hiding in plain sight of a hundred thousand people and cameras linked to billions more.

Fated. Chosen. Gifted by the gods. I am clearly a being superior in every way, certainly to pathetic Mundaho and Shaw and that conniving bitch Hunter Pierce, and the other athletes down there on the stage inside the stadium, all of them condemning me as a . . .

The wind is picking up. I shift my attention to the wind, to the northwest, far beyond the stadium, far beyond London. Out there on the horizon, dark clouds are boiling up into thunderheads. What could be more fitting as a backdrop?

Fated, I think before hearing a roar go up in the stadium.

What's this? Sir Elton John and Sir Paul McCartney are coming onto the stage and taking seats, face-to-face, at identical white pianos? Who's that with them? Marianne Faithfull? Oh, for pity's sake, they're singing "Let It Be" to Mundaho.

At their monstrous screeching, you can't begin to understand how much I want to stand at ease, rub my scar, and end this hypocritical pabulum right now. But, eyes locked dead ahead into the approaching storm, I tell myself to calm down and follow the plan to its natural and fated ending.

To keep the infernal singing from getting to me, I focus on the fact that just a few minutes from now, I *will* reveal myself. And when I do I'll be able to rejoice in their shared horror—McCartney, John, and Faithfull, too. I'll watch them all trampling over Mundaho as they run for the exits and I joyously make one final sacrifice in the name of every true Olympian who ever lived.

CHAPTER 113

HEARING THE CROWD in the stadium singing "Let It Be," Knight raced toward the base of the *Orbit,* seeing Jack already there ahead of him, interrogating the Gurkhas who were guarding the staircase that wound its way up the tower's DNA-like superstructure toward the circular observation deck.

When Knight arrived, legs cramping and head splitting, he gasped, "Was Lancer up there?"

"They say the only people who went up after three thirty were SAS snipers, a dog team, and the two Queen's Guardsmen protecting the—"

"Can we alert them, the men on the roof?" Knight said, cutting Jack off.

"I don't know," Jack said. "I mean, I don't think so."

"I think Lancer plans to blow the cauldron, maybe this entire structure. Where's the propane tank and line that feeds the flame?"

"It's over this way," called the strained voice of a man hurrying to them.

Stuart Meeks was head of facilities at Olympic Park. A short man in his fifties who sported a pencil-thin mustache and slick black hair, he carried an iPad and sweated profusely as he used an electronic code to open a door set flush in the concrete that led down into a massive utility basement that ran beneath the western legs of the *Orbit* and out under the river and the plaza toward the stadium.

"How big is the tank down there?" Knight asked as Meeks lifted the door.

"Huge—five hundred thousand liters," Meeks said, holding out the iPad, which showed a schematic diagram of the gas system. "But as you see here, it serves all the propane needs in the park, not just the cauldron. The gas is drawn from the main reservoir here into smaller holding tanks at each of the venues, and in the athletes' village, of course. It was designed, like the electrical station, to be self-sufficient."

Knight gaped at him. "Are you saying if it blows, everything blows?"

"No, I don't..." Meeks stopped, losing color. "I honestly don't know."

Jack said, "Peter and I were with Lancer about two weeks ago up on the observation deck shortly after he'd finished inspecting security on the cauldron. Did Lancer go down into this basement during that inspection, Stu?"

Meeks nodded. "Mike insisted on looking at everything one last time. From the tank up the line all the way to the coupling that connects the piping to the cauldron. It took us more than an hour."

"We don't have an hour," Knight said.

Jack was already on the ladder, preparing to climb down to inspect the giant propane tank. "Call in the dogs again, Stu. Send them down as soon as they get here. Peter, trace the gas line up to the roof."

Knight nodded before asking Meeks if he had any tools with him. The facilities director unsnapped a Leatherman from a holster on his hip and told Knight he'd send the schematic diagram of the gas line system to his phone. No more than twenty yards up the spiral staircase that climbed the *Orbit,* Knight felt his phone buzz, alerting him to the arrival of the diagram.

He was about to open the link when he thought of something that made the diagram seem irrelevant. He keyed his microphone and said, "Stuart, how is the gas line to the cauldron controlled? Is there a manual valve up there that will have to be closed for the cauldron to go out, or will it be done electronically?"

"Electronically," Meeks replied. "Before it connects to the cauldron the line runs through a crawl space that's part of the ductwork in the ceiling above the restaurant and below the roof."

Despite the pounding in his skull and his general sense of irritability, Knight was picking up the pace as he climbed. The wind was strong now. In the distance he thought he heard a rumble of thunder.

"Any way to get on the roof?" he asked.

"There are two retractable bulkhead doors and staircases on opposite sides of the roof," Meeks said. "That's how the guardsmen have been climbing up and down for their shifts. There's also an exhaust grate in the ductwork several feet from that valve you asked about."

Before Knight could think about that, he heard Jack say, "Main tank appears clear. Stuart, we know the max volume and what it's holding?"

There was long pause before Olympic Park's facilities supervisor said in a hoarse voice, "It was filled again at dawn, day before yesterday, Jack."

Two hundred feet above Olympic Park, Knight

now understood that underground, between the *Orbit* and the stadium, was a mega-explosive device capable of toppling the tower, certainly, but also capable of causing tremendous damage to the south end of the stadium and everyone seated there, not to mention what might happen if a central eruption set off other detonations around the venue.

"Evacuate, Jack," Knight said. "Tell security to stop the ceremonies and get everyone out of the stadium and out of the park."

"But what if he's watching?" Jack said. "What if he can remotely trigger it?"

"I don't know," Knight said, feeling torn. His personal inclination was to turn around and get the hell out of there. He was a father. He'd almost died once already today. Did he dare test fate twice?

Still climbing, Knight examined the schematic diagram on his phone, looking for the digitally controlled valve beneath the cauldron, between the roof and the restaurant ceiling. At a glance, he was almost positive that that control valve was the most likely place for Lancer to attach a triggering device to the main gas line.

If he could reach it, he could defuse it. If he couldn't...

CHAPTER 114

LIGHTNING FLASHED IN the distance and the wind began to gust as Knight reached the entrance to the observation deck of the *Orbit*. Samba music blared from inside the Olympic stadium as part of Brazil's celebration of the 2016 games.

Though they'd been warned he was coming, the Gurkhas at the entry insisted on checking Knight's ID before allowing him to enter. Inside, he was met by the SAS supervisor, a man named Creston, who said he and his team and a skeleton television crew had been on the deck since roughly five o'clock, when the restaurant was closed to everyone but members of the Queen's Guard, who were using the restrooms inside to change in and out of uniform.

Queen's Guard, Knight thought. *Lancer's regiment served in the Guard. Hadn't he said that?*

"Get me in that restaurant," Knight said. "There might be a triggering device tied into the gas line above the kitchen."

In seconds, Knight was running through the restaurant toward the kitchen with the SAS supervisor in tow. Knight looked over his shoulder at him. "Are the doors to the roof open?"

"No," the sniper said. "Not until the end of the ceremony. They're timed."

"No way to talk to the guardsmen up there?"

He shook his head. "They aren't even armed. It's a ceremonial bit."

Knight pressed his microphone. "Stuart, where do I go up through the ceiling?"

"In the kitchen, left of the stove hood," Meeks replied. "The kitchen is past the restrooms and through the double doors."

As Knight went into the hallway toward the kitchen, he saw the restrooms, remembered that's where the guardsmen got changed, and had a sudden strange intuition. "When did the relieved guards leave?" he asked the sniper.

He shrugged. "Right after their shift. They had seats inside the stadium."

"They changed and left?"

He nodded.

Still, rather than barge into the kitchen, Knight stopped and pushed on the door to the ladies' room.

"What are you doing?" the sniper asked.

"Not sure," Knight said, seeing it empty and then squatting to peer under the stalls. All empty.

He quickly crossed to the men's room and did the same, finding a black man's naked body stuffed into the farthest stall.

"We have a dead guardsman in the men's room up here," Knight barked into his radio as he headed toward the kitchen. "I believe Lancer has taken his uniform and is now on the roof."

He looked at the sniper. "Figure out how to get those roof doors open."

The sniper nodded and took off with Knight going the opposite direction, bursting into the kitchen and quickly spotting the trapdoor in the ceiling to the left of the restaurant's stove hood. Dragging a stainless steel prep table over beneath the trapdoor, he triggered his mike and said, "Can we get a visual on the guards to confirm one of them is Lancer?"

Listening to Jack relay the request to the snipers high atop the stadium, Knight noticed the padlock on the trapdoor for the first time. "I need a combination, Stu," he said to his radio.

Meeks gave it to him, and, with shaky hands, Knight spun the dial and felt the lock give. He used a broom to push the trapdoor open, then looked around the kitchen one last time to see if there was anything he might be able to use or would need to shut down a gas line. The kind of kitchen torch chefs use to caramelize sugar caught his eye. He snagged it and tossed it up into the crawl space.

Then Knight swung his arms twice to loosen them before jumping up and grabbing the sides of the trapdoor frame. He hung there a second, took a deep breath, and raised his legs in front of him before driving them backward with such force that he was able to muscle his way up into the cavity between the restaurant ceiling and the roof of the *Orbit.*

Knight tugged out a thin flashlight, flipped it on, and, pushing the torch before him, wiggled toward a piece of copper pipe that bisected the ductwork about six feet away. Knight didn't have to get much closer to see the bumpy black electrical tape wrapped around it, attaching a cell phone and something else to the gas line.

"I've got the trigger, a small magnesium bomb taped to the gas line," he said. "It's not on a timer. He's going to blow it remotely. Shut down the entire gas system. Put out the Olympic flame. Now."

CHAPTER 115

BLOW, WINDS, BLOW.

Lightning cracks and thunder blasts northwest toward Crouch End and Stroud Green, not far at all from where my drug-addled parents gave birth to me. It is fitting. It is fated.

Indeed, as the jackass who runs the International Olympic Committee prepares to have the flags lowered, declare the games over, and order the flame extinguished, I fully embrace my destiny. Breaking from rigid attention, I gaze into the black wall of the oncoming storm, thinking how remarkable it is that my life has been like an oval track, starting and finishing in much the same place.

Pulling out a cell phone from my pocket, I hit a number on speed dial and hear it connect. Pocketing the phone, I take up my rifle, take two strides forward, and pivot to my right, toward the cauldron.

CHAPTER 116

A FEW MINUTES earlier, Karen Pope trudged out into stands on the west side of the Olympic stadium just as IOC president Jacques Rogge, looking haggard and grave, walked to the lectern on the stage. The reporter had just filed her latest update to the *Sun*'s website, describing the escape of Knight and his children, the death of Marta and her sisters, and the global manhunt for Mike Lancer.

As Rogge spoke over a quickening wind and against the intensifying rumble of thunder, Pope was thinking that these cursed games were finally almost over. Good-bye and good riddance, as far as she was concerned. She never wanted to write about the Olympics ever again, though she knew that was an impossible dream. She felt depressed and lethargic, and wondered if what she was feeling was as much battle fatigue as the desperate need to sleep. And Knight wasn't answering his phone. Neither was Jack Morgan, or Inspector Pottersfield. What was going on that she didn't know about?

As Rogge droned on, preparing to declare the games at an end, Pope happened to look up at the cauldron atop the *Orbit,* seeing the flame billow in the wind. She admitted that she looked forward to seeing it extinguished, while feeling somewhat guilty about the...

The Queen's Guardsman to the cauldron's left suddenly lifted his gun, threw off his bearskin hat, walked out in front of the Olympic flame, pivoted, and opened fire. The other guard jerked, staggered, and fell off the platform on his side. His body hit the roof, slid, and slipped off the *Orbit,* plunging to the ground.

Pope's gasp of horror was obliterated by the screams of the multitude in the stadium rising into one trembling cry before a booming voice came over the public-address system: "You sorry, inferior creatures. You didn't think an instrument of the gods would let you off that easy, did you?"

CHAPTER 117

I CLUTCH THE cell phone in my left hand, speaking into it, and hearing the power in my voice echo back to me. "All you SAS snipers out there in the park, be stupid. I'm holding a triggering device. If you shoot me, this entire tower, much of the stadium, and tens of thousands of people will be blown up."

Below me, the crowd erupts and turns as frenzied as rats fleeing a sinking ship. Seeing them scurry and claw, I smile with utter satisfaction.

"Tonight marks the end of the modern Olympics," I thunder. "Tonight we snuff out the flame that has burned so corruptly since that traitor Coubertin came up with this mockery of the true games more than a century ago!"

CHAPTER 118

KNIGHT HEARD THE gunshots and Lancer's booming threat through an exhaust grate in the roof of the ductwork several feet beyond the gas line and the triggering device.

He didn't have the time to try to defuse the trigger, and for all he knew Lancer had booby-trapped it to go off if it was tampered with.

"How about cutting off the tanks?" he asked over his radio.

"It's a disaster, Peter," Jack shot back. "He's welded the valves open."

Above him, Lancer launched into a longer tirade, beginning with the doctors in Barcelona who drugged him to keep him from winning gold in the decathlon, preventing him from being named the greatest all-around athlete in the world. And in the background, Knight could hear the petrified crowd trying to escape the stadium and understood that he only had one chance.

He pushed the kitchen torch forward, and shimmied after it past the gas line and the triggering device until he lay beneath the exhaust grate.

Through the slats he saw flashes of approaching lightning and the billowing glow of the Olympic flame, still burning.

Four bolts held the grate in place. All of them looked sealed with some kind of chemical resin. Maybe he could melt it.

Knight grabbed the torch, turned it on, and aimed the flame at each bolt in turn. As fast as he could, he melted the resin until it ran gooey, and then grabbed the nearest bolt head with the pliers on the Leatherman tool Meeks had given him. He wrenched at it, thrilled that it gave.

CHAPTER 119

LIGHTNING INSCRIBES THE sky and thunder booms like cannon fire as I bellow at the crazed crowd trying to escape the stadium, "For these reasons and a thousand others, the modern games must end. Surely you understand!"

But instead of screams of terror, or even cheers of agreement, I'm hearing something I did not expect in return. The monsters are booing me. They're catcalling, and casting filthy slurs at my genius, my superiority.

These are the final indignities suffered by a martyr for a just cause—stabbing, hurtful, but nothing like a roadside bomb, or even a rock; nothing that can stop me from seeing my fate fulfilled.

Still, this rejection is enough to raise a wave of

hatred in me like no other, a tsunami of loathing for all the monsters in the stadium before me.

Looking up into the thundering, dark sky, which is hurling lightning and spitting rain, I cry, "For you, gods of Olympus. I do this all for you!"

CHAPTER 120

KNIGHT WAS ALREADY well beyond the exhaust vent, up on the raised platform surrounding the cauldron, and running in full stride through the pouring rain.

Before the madman's thumb could hit the send button, Knight hit Lancer low, hard, and from the side, a stunning blow that caused the crazed murderer to lurch and fall to the floor of the platform. His automatic weapon skittered away.

Knight landed on top of Lancer, who still clutched the cell phone. The former decathlon champion was some ten years older than Knight. But he quickly proved bigger, stronger, and a more skilled fighter.

Lancer backhanded Knight so hard the Private

London agent was thrown to the side, almost into the scalding wall of the cauldron. The infernal heat and the drenching rain revived him almost instantly.

He twisted, seeing that Lancer was trying to regain his feet. But Knight kicked viciously at his ankle and connected. The madman howled, stumbled to one knee, and was rising again when Knight got his right forearm around Lancer's bull-thick neck from behind, trying to get a choke hold on him and seize the cell phone before the gas bomb could be triggered.

He squeezed Lancer's throat and grabbed at his thumb, trying to pry his grip loose from the phone. But then Lancer jammed his chin down on Knight's forearm, twisted his torso, and threw elbows that struck Knight hard in his ribs, still bruised from the Fury's attempt to run him down.

The Private London agent grunted in dire pain, but held on, calling forth a vision of Luke and Isabel before taking a cue from his son. He bit brutally at the back of the insane man's head, feeling a chunk of thick scar tissue tear away from Lancer's scalp. Lancer screamed in agony and rage.

Knight released and bit again, lower this time, sinking his teeth into neck muscles the way a lion might try to cripple a buffalo.

Lancer went berserk.

He swung and bucked, bellowing in blind, primal fury and throwing meaty fists over his shoulder, hitting Knight in the head before pummeling his torso with his elbows again, blows so hard that several of the Private agent's ribs cracked and broke.

It was too much.

All Knight's air flew out of him, and the pain in his side was so fiery that he released the bite and the choke hold he'd had on Lancer's neck. He fell to the platform in the rain, groaning and fighting for air and relief from the agony that consumed him.

Blood dripping from the bite wounds, Lancer turned and glared down at Knight in triumph and in loathing.

"You had no chance, Knight," he gloated, backing away and raising the cell phone toward the sky again. "You were up against an infinitely superior being. You had no—"

Knight whipped the Leatherman at Lancer.

It flew end over end before the narrow prongs of the pliers struck and pierced Lancer's right eye, deep into the soft tissue.

Staggering backward, still clutching the cell phone, reaching in futility for the tool that had sealed his fate, Lancer let out a series of bloodcurdling screams worthy of some mythical creature of doom, like Cronus after Zeus threw him deep into the darkest and most abysmal pit in Tartarus.

For a second, Knight feared that Lancer would find his balance and manage to trigger the bomb.

But then lightning exploded directly over the *Orbit,* throwing a single white-hot, jagged bolt that bypassed the lightning rods fixed high above the observation deck and struck the butt end of the Leatherman tool sticking from Lancer's eye, electrocuting the self-described instrument of the gods and hurling him back and over into the cauldron, where he was engulfed and consumed by the roaring Olympic flame.

EPILOGUE

CHAPTER 121

ON THE THIRD floor of London Bridge Hospital, sitting in a wheelchair, Knight stiffly smiled at the people gathered around the beds that held Luke and Bella. While the effects of what turned out to be a concussion had mellowed to a dull thumping in his head, his broken and bruised ribs were killing him, making each breath feel like saws were working in his chest.

But he was alive. His kids were alive. The Olympics had been saved and avenged by forces far beyond Knight's understanding. And Scotland Yard chief inspector Elaine Pottersfield had just entered the room carrying two small chocolate cakes, each adorned with three burning birthday candles.

Never one to miss the chance to sing, Hooligan broke into "Happy Birthday" and was joined by the twins' nurses and doctors, as well as Jack Morgan, Karen Pope, Knight's mother, and even Gary Boss, who'd arrived early to decorate the hospital room with bright balloons and bunting.

"Close your eyes and make a wish," the twins' aunt said.

"Dream big!" their grandmother cried.

Isabel and Luke closed their eyes for a second, and then opened them, took deep breaths, and blew out every one of the candles. Everyone cheered and clapped. Pottersfield cut the cake.

Ever the journalist, Pope asked, "What did you wish for?"

Knight's son got annoyed. "Lukey not telling you. It's secret."

But Isabel looked at Pope matter-of-factly and said, "I wished we could have a new mommy."

Her brother's face clouded. "No fair. That's what Lukey wished for."

There were soothing moans of sympathy all around and Knight felt his heart break once again.

His daughter was staring at him. "No more nannies, Daddy."

"No more nannies," he promised, glancing at his mother. "Right, Mother?"

"Only if they are under my direct and constant supervision," she said.

"Or mine," Boss said.

Cake and ice cream were served. After several bites, Pope said, "You know what threw me about Lancer, kept me from ever considering him as a suspect?"

"What's that?" Hooligan asked.

"He had one of his Furies try to run him down on day one," she said. "Right?"

"Definitely," Knight said. "I'll bet he had that planned from the beginning. I just happened to be there."

"There was another clue if you think about it," Hooligan said. "Cronus never sent you a letter detailing the reasons Lancer should have died."

"I never thought of that," Knight said.

"Neither did I," Jack said, getting up from his chair and dumping his paper plate into the trash can.

After they had gorged themselves on cake and unwrapped the presents everyone had brought, Knight's children were soon drowsy. When Isabel's eyes closed, and when Luke started to rock and suck his thumb, Amanda and Boss left with whispered promises to return in the morning to help see Knight and the twins home.

His sister-in-law was next to depart, saying, "Hiring a war criminal as your nanny was not your finest hour, Peter, but ultimately you were brilliant. Absolutely brilliant. Kate would have been so proud of how hard you fought for your children, for the Olympics, for London, for everyone."

Knight's heart broke yet again. "I'd hug you, Elaine, but..."

She blew him a kiss, said she was going to check up on Selena Farrell and James Daring, and walked out the door.

"I've got a present for you before I leave, Peter," Jack said. "I want you to have an obscene raise, and I want you to take your kids somewhere tropical for a few weeks. It's on Private. We'll work out the details after I get back to L.A. Speaking of which, I've got a jet to catch."

After Private's owner had gone, Pope and Hooligan got up to leave as well. "We are off to the pub, then," Hooligan said. "Highlights of the entire Olympic football tournament to watch."

"We?" Knight said, arching his eyebrow at Pope.

The reporter slipped her arm through Hooligan's and smiled. "Turns out we share a lot in common,

Knight. My brothers are all football-mad lads as well."

Knight smiled. "There's a certain symmetry there."

Hooligan grinned and threw his arm around Pope's shoulder. "Think you're fuggin' right about that, Peter."

"Fuggin' damn right," Pope said, and they departed, laughing.

The nurses followed and Knight was left alone in the hospital room with his children. He looked up at the television a moment and saw a shot of the Olympic flame still burning over London. After Lancer's death, Jacques Rogge had asked that flame burn on a while longer, and the government had immediately agreed.

It was, Knight decided, a good thing.

Then he let his attention dwell on Luke and Isabel, thinking how beautiful they were, and thanking the gods for saving them from a cruel ending.

He sighed, thinking of how his heart fell apart when Isabel and Luke both wished for a new mother, and again when Elaine told him how proud Kate would have been of him.

Kate. He missed her still and thought morosely that maybe she had been his singular mate, the one and only love that fate had in store for him. Maybe it was his destiny to go on alone. To raise the children and...

A knock came at the door frame and a cheery American woman's voice called softly from out in the hall, "Mr. Knight? Are you in there?"

Knight looked toward the door. "Yes?"

A very beautiful and athletic woman slipped in. He knew her immediately and tried to get to his feet, whispering, "You're Hunter Pierce."

"I am," the diver said, smiling brightly now and studying him closely. "Don't get up. I heard you were injured."

"Only a bit," he said. "I was lucky. We were all lucky."

Pierce nodded, and Knight could not help but think she was dazzling up close and in person.

He said, "I was there at the aquatics center. When you won gold."

"Were you?" she said, pressing her fingers to her throat.

Knight's eyes were watering and he did not know why. "It was the finest example of grace under pressure that I've ever had the honor of witnessing. And the way you spoke out against Cronus, forcefully, consistently. It was...well, simply remarkable, and I hope people have told you that."

The diving champion smiled. "Thank you. But all of us—Shaw, Mundaho, all the athletes—they sent me here to tell you that we thought *your* performance last night outshined us all."

"No, I—"

"No, really," she said emphatically. "I was there in the stadium. So were my children. We saw you fight him. You risked your life to save ours, and the Olympics, and we, I...I wanted to thank you in person from the bottom of my heart."

Knight felt emotion forming a ball in his throat. "I...don't know what to say."

The American diver looked over at his children. "And these are the brave twins we read about in the *Sun* this morning?"

"Luke and Isabel," Knight said. "The lights of my life."

"They're beautiful. I'd say you're a blessed man, Mr. Knight."

"Peter," he said. "And honestly, you can't know how grateful I am to be here and to have them here. What a blessing it all is. And, well, to have you here, too."

There was a long moment when they were both looking at each other as if they'd just recognized something familiar and long-forgotten.

Pierce cocked her head and said, "I'd only meant

to pop in for a bit, Peter, but I just had a better thought."

"What's that?" he asked.

The American diver smiled again, and affected a corny British accent, saying: "Would you fancy me wheeling you out of here down to the café? We can have a spot of tea and catch up while your little lovelies are off sailing in the Land of Nod."

Knight felt flooded with happiness.

"Yes," he said. "Yes, I believe I'd like that very much."

ACKNOWLEDGMENTS

We would like to thank Jackie Brock-Doyle, Neil Walker, and Jason Keen at the London Organising Committee of the Olympic Games for their willingness to be helpful, candid, and yet understandably circumspect regarding a project like this one. The tour of the Olympic Park construction site was incredibly instructive. We would have gotten nowhere without Alan Abrahamson, Olympic expert and operator of 3WireSports.com, the world's best source of information about the games and the culture that surrounds them. A special thanks goes out as well to Vikki Orvice, Olympic reporter at the *Sun* and a wealth of knowledge, humor, and gossip. We are also grateful to the staff at the British Museum, One Aldwych, and 41 for their invaluable aid in suggesting settings for scenes outside the Olympic venues. Ultimately, this is a fictional story of hope and an affirmation of Olympic ideals, so please grant us a degree of license regarding the various events, venues, and characters likely to dominate the stage during the London 2012 summer games.

ABOUT THE AUTHORS

JAMES PATTERSON has had more *New York Times* bestsellers than any other writer, ever, according to *Guinness World Records*. Since his first novel won the Edgar Award in 1977, James Patterson's books have sold more than 240 million copies. He is the author of the Alex Cross novels, the most popular detective series of the past twenty-five years, including *Kiss the Girls* and *Along Came a Spider*. Mr. Patterson also writes the best-selling Women's Murder Club novels, set in San Francisco, and the top-selling New York detective series of all time, featuring Detective Michael Bennett.

James Patterson also writes books for young readers, including the Maximum Ride, Daniel X, Witch & Wizard, and Middle School series. In total, these books have spent more than 230 weeks on national bestseller lists.

About the Authors

His lifelong passion for books and reading led James Patterson to launch the website ReadKiddoRead.com to give adults an easy way to locate the very best books for kids. He writes full-time and lives in Florida with his family.

MARK SULLIVAN is the author of eight mystery and suspense novels, including *Rogue,* forthcoming in October 2012. He lives in Montana with his wife and sons.

BOOKS BY JAMES PATTERSON

FEATURING ALEX CROSS

Kill Alex Cross • *Cross Fire* • *I, Alex Cross* • *Alex Cross's* Trial (with Richard DiLallo) • *Cross Country* • *Double Cross* • *Cross* • *Mary, Mary* • *London Bridges* • *The Big Bad Wolf* • *Four Blind Mice* • *Violets Are Blue* • *Roses Are Red* • *Pop Goes the Weasel* • *Cat & Mouse* • *Jack & Jill* • *Kiss the Girls* • *Along Came a Spider*

THE WOMEN'S MURDER CLUB

10th Anniversary (with Maxine Paetro) • *The 9th Judgment* (with Maxine Paetro) • *The 8th Confession* (with Maxine Paetro) • *7th Heaven* (with Maxine Paetro) • *The 6th Target* (with Maxine Paetro) • *The 5th Horseman* (with Maxine Paetro) • *4th of July* (with Maxine Paetro) • *3rd Degree* (with Andrew Gross) • *2nd Chance* (with Andrew Gross) • *1st to Die*

FEATURING MICHAEL BENNETT

Tick Tock (with Michael Ledwidge) • *Worst Case* (with Michael Ledwidge) • *Run for Your Life* (with Michael Ledwidge) • *Step on a Crack* (with Michael Ledwidge)

THE PRIVATE NOVELS

Private Games (with Mark Sullivan) • *Private: #1 Suspect* (with Maxine Paetro) • *Private* (with Maxine Paetro)

OTHER BOOKS

The Christmas Wedding (with Richard DiLallo) • *Kill Me If You Can* (with Marshall Karp) • *Now You See Her* (with Michael Ledwidge) • *Toys* (with Neil McMahon) • *Don't Blink* (with Howard Roughan) • *The Postcard Killers* (with Liza Marklund) • *The Murder of King Tut* (with Martin Dugard) • *Swimsuit* (with Maxine Paetro) • *Against Medical Advice* (with Hal Friedman) • *Sail* (with Howard Roughan) • *Sundays at*

Tiffany's (with Gabrielle Charbonnet) • *You've Been Warned* (with Howard Roughan) • *The Quickie* (with Michael Ledwidge) • *Judge & Jury* (with Andrew Gross) • *Beach Road* (with Peter de Jonge) • *Lifeguard* (with Andrew Gross) • *Honeymoon* (with Howard Roughan) • *Sam's Letters to Jennifer* • *The Lake House* • *The Jester* (with Andrew Gross) • *The Beach House* (with Peter de Jonge) • *Suzanne's Diary for Nicholas* • *Cradle and All* • *When the Wind Blows* • *Miracle on the 17th Green* (with Peter de Jonge) • *Hide & Seek* • *The Midnight Club* • *Black Friday* (originally published as *Black Market*) • *See How They Run* (originally published as *The Jericho Commandment*) • *Season of the Machete* • *The Thomas Berryman Number*

FOR READERS OF ALL AGES

Maximum Ride: The Manga, Vol. 5 (with NaRae Lee) • *Witch & Wizard: The Fire* (with Jill Dembowski) • *Witch & Wizard: The Manga, Vol. 1* (with Svetlana Chmakova) • *Daniel X: Game Over* (with Ned Rust) • *Daniel X: The Manga, Vol. 2* (with SeungHui Kye) • *Middle School: The Worst Years of My Life* (with Chris Tebbetts, illustrated by Laura Park) • *Maximum Ride: The Manga, Vol. 4* (with NaRae Lee) • *ANGEL: A Maximum Ride Novel* • *Witch & Wizard: The Gift* (with Ned Rust) • *Daniel X: The Manga, Vol. 1* (with SeungHui Kye) • *Maximum Ride: The Manga, Vol. 3* (with NaRae Lee) • *Daniel X: Demons and Druids* (with Adam Sadler) • *Med Head [Against Medical Advice teen edition]* (with Hal Friedman) • *FANG: A Maximum Ride Novel* • *Witch & Wizard* (with Gabrielle Charbonnet) • *Maximum Ride: The Manga, Vol. 2* (with NaRae Lee) • *Daniel X: Watch the Skies* (with Ned Rust) • *MAX: A Maximum Ride Novel* • *Maximum Ride: The Manga, Vol. 1* (with NaRae Lee) • *Daniel X: Alien Hunter* (graphic novel; with Leopoldo Gout) • *The Dangerous Days of Daniel X* (with Michael Ledwidge) • *Maximum Ride: The Final Warning* • *Maximum Ride: Saving the World and Other Extreme Sports* • *Maximum Ride: School's Out—Forever* • *Maximum Ride: The Angel Experiment* • *santaKid*

For previews and information about the author, visit JamesPatterson.com or find him on Facebook or at your app store.